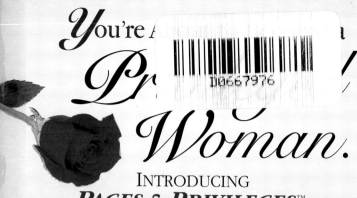

You're A Privileged Woman.

INTRODUCING
PAGES & PRIVILEGES™.

It's our way of thanking you for buying
our books at your favorite retail store.

GET ALL THIS FREE
WITH JUST ONE PROOF OF PURCHASE:

◆ **Hotel Discounts** up
to 60% at home and
abroad ◆ **Travel Service**
- Guaranteed lowest
published airfares
plus 5% cash back

$50 VALUE

on tickets ◆ **$25 Travel Voucher**

◆ **Sensuous Petite Parfumerie** collection

◆ **Insider Tips Letter**
with sneak previews
of upcoming books

*You'll get a FREE personal card, too.
It's your passport to all these benefits– and to
even more great gifts & benefits to come!*

There's no club to join. No purchase commitment. No obligation.

Enrollment Form

☐ *Yes!* I WANT TO BE A *Privileged Woman.*

Enclosed is one *PAGES & PRIVILEGES*™ Proof of Purchase from any Harlequin or Silhouette book currently for sale in stores (Proofs of Purchase are found on the back pages of books) and the store cash register receipt. Please enroll me in *PAGES & PRIVILEGES*™. Send my Welcome Kit and FREE Gifts -- and activate my FREE benefits -- immediately.

More great gifts and benefits to come like these luxurious Truly Lace and L'Effleur gift baskets.

▼ DETACH HERE AND MAIL TODAY! ▼

NAME (please print)
_____

ADDRESS _____ APT. NO _____

CITY _____ STATE _____ ZIP/POSTAL CODE _____

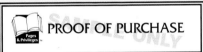

PROOF OF PURCHASE

SAMPLE ONLY

Please allow 6-8 weeks for delivery. Quantities are limited. We reserve the right to substitute items. Enroll before October 31, 1995 and receive one full year of benefits.

NO CLUB!
NO COMMITMENT!
Just one purchase brings you great **Free Gifts and Benefits!**
(More details in back of this book.)

Name of store where this book was purchased_____

Date of purchase_____

Type of store:

☐ Bookstore ☐ Supermarket ☐ Drugstore

☐ Dept. or discount store (e.g. K-Mart or Walmart)

☐ Other (specify)_____

Which Harlequin or Silhouette series do you usually read?
_____

Complete and mail with one Proof of Purchase and store receipt to:

U.S.: *PAGES & PRIVILEGES*™, P.O. Box 1960, Danbury, CT 06813-1960

Canada: *PAGES & PRIVILEGES*™, 49-6A The Donway West, P.O. 813, North York, ON M3C 2E8

PRINTED IN U.S.A

"...AN INTENSELY EMOTIONAL, SPELLBINDING TALE OF A LOVE THAT TRANSCENDS HATRED AND BETRAYAL." —*ROMANTIC TIMES*

"...WELL RESEARCHED AND BRILLIANTLY LAID BEFORE THE READER...A BANQUET FOR THE HEART...." —*THE PAPERBACK FORUM*

"POWERFUL!"
—AUTHOR KATHERINE DEAUXVILLE

"FIRE AND SWORD HAS CLASSIC WRITTEN ALL OVER IT." —*BOOKLOVERS*

**PRAISE FOR NEWCOMER
MERLINE LOVELACE'S PREVIOUS TITLES**

"...SENSUOUS AND EXCITING. A MUST FOR ALL HISTORICAL STORY LOVERS...."
—*RENDEZVOUS* ON **SWEET SONG OF LOVE**

"...A UNIQUE AND COMPELLING TALE... MS. LOVELACE IS AN AUTHOR TO WATCH..."
—*ROMANTIC TIMES* ON **SIREN'S CALL**

"...MS. LOVELACE HAS CERTAINLY MADE HISTORY COME ALIVE..."
—*THE PAPERBACK TRADER* ON **ALENA**

LEAVE IT TO HARLEQUIN HISTORICALS TO BRING YOU THREE POPULAR AUTHORS IN ONE COLLECTION

RENEGADES

HEATHER GRAHAM POZZESSERE
THERESA MICHAELS
MERLINE LOVELACE

Harlequin Books

TORONTO • NEW YORK • LONDON
AMSTERDAM • PARIS • SYDNEY • HAMBURG
STOCKHOLM • ATHENS • TOKYO • MILAN
MADRID • WARSAW • BUDAPEST • AUCKLAND

If you purchased this book without a cover you should be aware that this book is stolen property. It was reported as "unsold and destroyed" to the publisher, and neither the author nor the publisher has received any payment for this "stripped book."

HARLEQUIN BOOKS

ISBN 0-373-83310-5

SEIZE THE WIND
Copyright © 1995 by Heather Graham Pozzessere

APACHE FIRE
Copyright © 1995 by Theresa DiBenedetto

THE ROGUE KNIGHT
Copyright © 1995 by Merline Lovelace

All rights reserved. Except for use in any review, the reproduction or utilization of this work in whole or in part in any form by any electronic, mechanical or other means, now known or hereafter invented, including xerography, photocopying and recording, or in any information storage or retrieval system, is forbidden without the written permission of the publisher, Harlequin Enterprises Limited, 225 Duncan Mill Road, Don Mills, Ontario, Canada M3B 3K9.

All characters in this book have no existence outside the imagination of the author and have no relation whatsoever to anyone bearing the same name or names. They are not even distantly inspired by any individual known or unknown to the author, and all incidents are pure invention.

This edition published by arrangement with Harlequin Books S.A.

® and TM are trademarks of Harlequin Books S.A., used under license. Trademarks indicated with ® are registered in the United States Patent and Trademark Office, the Canadian Trade Marks Office and in other countries.

Printed in U.S.A.

CONTENTS

SEIZE THE WIND
Heather Graham Pozzessere

A Note from Heather Graham Pozzessere

There's just something about a renegade, something special, unique and exciting about those who live on the edge of danger.

Because I'm so very fond of renegades, rogues and the like, I'm delighted to be taking part in this anthology. Rogues bring us the greatest adventures, so it seems, even if they have a tendency to be pirates, cutthroats and thieves. Renegades, feared and reviled by those against whom they make their stands, are still those who make the changes in life, who sometimes battle grave injustices. And then again, whether a man be a hero or a rogue most often lies in the eyes of those who behold him. Nathan Hale was a traitor to the British, a hero to the Americans. Since we did win the war, Nathan remains a hero. Throughout history, honest men have straddled that fence, being both heroes and rogues.

For my story, I've chosen a time when legend has left us with a similar truth we come across now and then— sometimes the outlaws are the ones with the most integrity, while those in power are abusing authority. In short, I give you an honest rogue. A renegade, yes, who will live by his own rules to his death, but one who meets his match in a woman with more than just a little of the outlaw spirit herself. So welcome to a time when the forests are dark and green, mysterious—and dangerous. When knights ride off to battle the Infidel in the great Crusades, and the land is lawless. And the only help lies with…

Renegades and rogues.

Of both the masculine—and the feminine!—variety.

Heather Graham Pozzessere

Chapter One

Far North of London, England
In the Reign of Good King Richard, Lionheart
(The Absent Good King Richard, Lionheart)

"Halt!" came a dreaded cry.

The Duke of Manning's party came to a quick pause, the four guards in helmet and mail, their swords drawn, moving awkwardly about on their huge stallions in the narrow trail to discover from where the command had come.

The forests, these days, were simply filled with outlaws.

At first, there was nothing to be seen. They were in the densest part of the forest, riding upon trails where none would dare come without a guard. The Duke of Manning, however, was a cocky fellow, and he had decried the outlaws of the forest, damning them and claiming that he could best a few wild peasants himself with one hand tied behind his back.

Despite his boast, he hadn't come into the forest with the wagon that carried his soon-to-be bride. He had left the matter of her conveyance—her person and her property—to these four fine figures upon horseback, Sir Waylong, Hugh de Frieze, Genovese St. Montmarte and young Alain de Lac, all of them masters of the joust and proved and seasoned in battle. The problem here was that they could see no one to battle.

"There you are, my good men! Now, leave the wagon behind and move on to your master, and no harm will come to you."

"Leave the wagon!" Sir Waylon, the oldest of the guards, with iron gray hair and a temperament to match, repeated in his crusty voice, outraged. "What fool command is this! Show yourself, you rogue. And quickly. Or cease your prattle and let us pass. Leave the wagon, indeed! Leave the wagon that carries my Lady Kate at the command of talking trees?"

At that moment, the man who had waylaid them chose to make his appearance, leaping down from a low branch of the tree. He was tall and well muscled, yet startlingly agile. When he stood, his size could have rivaled that of any of the guards. He was dressed in black from head to toe, breeches, boots and tunic—and mask. His concession to defense was composed of light chain mail—painted black, as well—that covered his tunic. He wore a swath of black cloth over his head, hiding his hair, tied at his nape. The mask was a piece that covered eyes and nose, and, combined with the black cloth upon his head, kept his identity a complete mystery.

He swept the men on horseback a bow. "No talking trees, my good fellow. But a man who warns you to ride—and thus preserve your lives."

"What talk from a single braggart!" Genovese, young and brash, cried back quickly. "Why, I shall decorate the wagon with your head as we proceed to Manning!"

"Come try, then, my friend!" invited the man in black.

Genovese quickly turned his heavy charger, swinging his sword to bear down upon the man in the trail. He leveled his sword with vigor as he approached, the speed and impetus of his animal adding to his favor. Yet the man upon the ground quickly weighed these things and swung his own sword in such a fashion as to not only deflect the blow that was about to come his way, but to cause his opponent to become unseated, as well.

Genovese fell upon the ground with a mighty crash of steel and metal. As he started to rise, the man in black cracked him firmly upon the head with the flat of his sword, and he fell again. This time, he did not move.

"I take great pains not to kill," the man in black said casually, "since this poor fellow is but in the employ of a wretched lord who would seize what is not his while the king is away. The Duke of Manning is the one playing lackey to the young prince. This fellow here will awaken, I think, within the hour. However, he will have a dreadful headache."

"A headache, indeed!" cried Sir Waylon, furious now. Genovese was a Florentine, a man considered to have skills beyond compare. "Well, we will see to it that he does awaken to the sight of your rogue's skull upon a pole, and therein will lie his cure!"

Sir Waylon's fury did him in. He bore down too quickly upon the black-clad man, and thus was just as easily unhorsed, since his opponent did not rely on muscle, force and bulk, but rather on quick and easy movement, knowing how not to oppose the weight that came his way. Sir Waylon was brought down.

Likewise, he was dealt a blow to the head.

And so silenced.

Hugh de Frieze looked to Alain de Lac. "It is madness that we oppose this forest monster one by one."

"Madness truly! An intelligent fellow among the roster!" cried out the mysterious forest outlaw with something like relief and pleasure. "Four of you might have taken me, at that. And now you are two. This isn't a joust, fine fellows. There is no one to whom to prove a single man has the greatest glory.

Come then, come and take me. Else take your fallen and depart. The wagon will be mine."

"What manner of man would leave a maiden to the likes of you?" Hugh demanded.

"She is in no danger. The love of her suitor will be proved, for I will simply help myself to what dowry comes with her now—and will ask, of course, for a payment in gold for that most precious dower of all, the sweet maid's very person—and she will be returned to a man who must simply love her above her property value."

Alain de Lac shook his head sadly. "Good fellow, you speak well, surely you must have some birthright that would save you from this wretched life you've chosen to live here in the forest! Outlaws hang—"

"And in-laws just the same!" The stranger laughed. "Prince John would be the death of us all, and you've not seen it yet."

"You'd have done well to fight *with* the king when he gave battle in the Holy Land, rather than *against* the prince here! If you seek riches, you should seize the gold and jewels of the Infidels, rather than preying upon rightful Christian lords!" Alain warned.

"Ah! Therein lies the question. Just who are the *rightful* Christian lords?" the rogue queried softly. "Remember, good men, our rightful Christian lord, King Richard, lies languishing in an Austrian castle, prisoner until ransomed. Prince John seems quite slow to collect the necessary ransom, don't you agree? Ah, well, surely I cannot expect to win you to my way of thinking quite so easily. The day wanes. Do what damage you will to me, or be on your way!''

They could not, of course, leave a lady, and therefore the two glanced at one another one more time, spurred their steeds and bore down upon their opponent. It seemed a good plan, one on either side of the standing man, pounding hard against the terrace, attacking him simultaneously. He could not unhorse them both.

But he could. Just as the horses neared him, he began a mighty swing, cracking his sword around with such force that he knocked first Hugh, then young Alain, down upon the ground. Hugh groaned, groggily trying to rise, crying out as he set weight upon his broken right arm. As he realized his predicament, he heard a moan of pain escape from Alain. The moan died out as Alain clamped down hard on his jaw, determined that though he had fallen, he would not whimper.

''All right, you jackal!'' Alain cried out. ''You've done your damage! Take the riches from the lady's coffers, but I beg you, leave the damsel herself. You have the sound of an educated man, for the love of God—''

''Sorry about the leg, but it is disjointed, I believe, rather than broken, and though you'll be sore, it is really far less dangerous than that poor fellow's arm," the rogue said, kneeling down beside Alain. "I did ask you to leave, remember? Joshua!" he called suddenly, and was joined by a man as big as the walls of Jericho, who leapt down beside him from a tree branch. "Give a pull of this man's leg, will you, to set it back?"

Joshua grunted, taking hold of Alain's leg with both his massive hands. Alain, despite his bravery, let out a shriek that threatened to split the heavens.

Then he passed out.

"You've killed him!" Hugh cried.

"Not at all," said the rogue. "Joshua, we now need to set these men on their horses and steer them from the forest."

"Aye, as you say," Joshua agreed carefully.

As if he lifted feathers, Joshua placed the fallen knights upon their steeds, seemingly heedless of the weight of the chain mail, helmets and plates that added to the already admirable bulk of the men who wore such armor. Hugh rose unassisted, groaning as he tried to protect his injured arm and mount at the same time. "I'll give you a hand, my man—" Joshua began, but Hugh would have none of it.

"I'll be back!" he shouted furiously. "I'll be back with scores of men. You'll pay for your thievery— your arrogance and your impudence."

"Well, we shall see you then, shan't we?" inquired the rogue. "Take him on out," he told Joshua. "I shall see to the wagon—and the lady, of course."

Hugh was still blustering, swearing that all forest vermin would be hanged or worse.

The Rogue of Heffington Forest, for that was what he was coming to be called by those who whispered about the dangers of travel to the far north of London in the dense no-man's-land there, looked to the fine gilded wagon that had so recently belonged to the Duke of Manning. He took a step toward it, wondering what he would find within. Knowing Manning, he would wed a snake-haired monster, were she rich enough, with the right property. Well, whatever, he had to look to the soon-to-be bride, be she an aging gorgon or a frightened young damsel.

She'd heard about the forest men. And being determined, Kate had simply dismissed all possible fear of them. She would be escorted by four tested knights, no less. No rabble of outlaws should have had a chance against them.

And she had remained quite confident.

Until she'd heard Alain's screams....

Dear God, by all the saints! What had they done to the poor man, what manner of torture had they used against him?

Run! she had warned herself. Throw open the door to the left of the road and take flight. These men of the north might well be no better than heathens. Some said they had come down from farther north, that they were the breed of barbarians who had roamed the Scottish Highlands, who had offered such fierce battle and brutality that not even the Romans could cross their lines. They were vicious, they were animals, creatures from hell, Satan's very spawn. . . .

But then . . .

She couldn't run. She wasn't leaving the wagon. She'd worked too hard and long to get where she was, there were far greater things at stake than the petty thievery of a cast of renegades, and she wasn't going to give this wagon over to any rogue or heathen. Justice lay in the future, so close she could very nearly taste it.

Alain screamed again.

She trembled violently.

There were horrors that could be offered by men. Horrors so filled with pain and anguish that death could become a gentle boon. Shouldn't she run now, and live to fight another day?

Run where?

Into the forest where the rogues lived and worked and plied their wretched trade. There was no running....

Only waiting.

She reached into the pocket within the skirt of her gown and found Lord Gregory's final gift to her, a dagger with a pearl-studded silver handle, embossed with the family crest. When the door to the wagon swung open, she would be ready.

And yet, she was not!

For it seemed she had scarcely heard the sounds of hoofbeats once again, moving along the road, when the door was wrenched open with startling speed and purpose.

And he was there. For a brief second, all she saw was a shadow, a figure looming tall and dark against the sudden brightness of the day. He was all darkness, filling the day, clad in black like Death itself, a demon risen straight up from hell. An unreasoning fear clamped icy fingers around her throat, but then she assured herself furiously that he was no demon, only a man, one tall and broad shouldered, a well-muscled knight dressed in black down to his painted armor.

A man. No more, no less.

Yet she trembled again despite herself. Her heart thundered. His face was hidden in darkness. Only his eyes peered through the holes of his mask.

Burning. Hazel gold. The fierce, fiery eyes of a demon. Touching somehow, as if they'd never let her go.

A man! she cried out in her heart.

And her fingers gripped with greater promise the pearl handle of her dagger.

Chapter Two

He hadn't known what to expect, but it was certainly not the creature he found there, awaiting him with a grim and furious expression upon her beautiful face. She was blessed with features that caused a man to pause, to forget to breathe. She was, indeed, the stuff of which legends were made. She had eschewed all headdress other than a ring of silver about her pate with a gossamer fall of soft blue fabric behind it. Her hair was a combination of the sun and the moon, a light blond, as delicate and beautiful as spun gold. Her eyes were as blue as the royal color of her gown, an object of fashion that seemed to cling to a form that had been sculpted with an eye toward absolute perfection. Her skin was ivory, translucent, her bone structure absolutely fine. She was elegant, glorious. He felt a sickness deep within him that she was intended for such a wretched excuse for humanity as the Duke of Manning, but it was not his intent to destroy the lives of others, but rather to gather the income necessary to ransom Richard from Austria.

"My lady," he began—most politely, most courteously. But before he could assure her he intended nothing but her safety, she let out a furious shriek and came flying down from the wagon upon him.

She came with startling, amazing speed. With an energy he'd neither imagined nor prepared for. In fact, she hurtled at him like some missile, some flying object catapulted out of the shadows. She slammed straight forward into him with such a fury and force that she brought them both flying to the ground.

Indeed, he barely—just barely!—had the breath and strength left to seize her wrist when he saw the dagger held within it, and to deflect the blow she would have brought against his throat. He heard laughter. Joshua had returned from his escort task and was watching the struggle with amusement. There was more laughter as his men began to drop from the trees, observing the battle here as he grated his teeth, determined to seize the dagger from the wild thing fighting with such agility and determination to stop him.

What ailed this elegant vixen? He meant her no harm, he had intended to be a gentleman....

But then, the laughter did it.

He did have a reputation to uphold, after all.

He tightened his fingers around her delicate wrist, causing her to cry out and release her weapon. With far less tenderness than he might have originally offered the damsel, he pushed her from him, rolling to lay her beneath him while he straddled her, reaching for the fallen dagger. A mistake. He had left her arms free. They were instantly flailing at him, fists slamming, nails clawing, nearly dislodging his mask, catching the bare flesh of his jaw.

He swore, startled as the words escaped him, then repeating them in earnest as he struggled against the writhing creature beneath him to capture her wrists at last.

"What are you, a madwoman, my lady? Cease and desist, and no harm will come to you—"

"Tremendous harm will come to you, rogue! You wretched snake in the grass, thief, outlaw, renegade—"

"My lady—"

"The deepest dungeon will be your fate, they'll cut your entrails from your body and strangle you with them, they'll draw and quarter you, hang you—"

"I don't think I'll much mind being hanged once I've been strangled with my own innards, my lady," he told her, both wearied and somewhat amused. She was still seething, much like a simmering caldron, ready to bubble over and lash out if given the very least chance.

"It's not much hospitality you're offering the lady," Joshua called out. "Perhaps if you'd been gentle with the lass..."

"Gentle!" he snorted.

"Do you need help, Shadow?" Joshua offered. "I do know that a little wisp of a girl can be a hard combatant!"

The men guffawed again.

"I've had it!" cried the Shadow, the Rogue of Heffington Forest. He leapt up, dragging her with him. He wagged a finger before her nose. "My lady, you will behave—"

But she would not. She had seized his sword from his scabbard. Now gracefully backed away, she was ready to go to battle once again, sword raised as one who knew how to use such weapons would raise it. And he, of course, was suddenly weaponless.

"I shall skewer you myself!" she declared.

Amazingly she was still elegant, moon gold hair now wild and tumbling down her back in glorious disarray, those crystal blue eyes of hers alive with fire and vengeance. She moved toward him, swinging with such vigor that he ducked just in the nick of time to avoid his own beheading. "Sweet Jesu!" he cried in surprise, taking a flying leap that brought him down, grappling her ankles, bringing her to the ground once again. She tried to find balance to raise the sword again, but luckily the sheer weight of it at last caught up with her. He rose, kicking the sword far from her grasp. He reached for her and she tried to flail at him once again. With absolute impatience he swore and reached down, plucking her up with no courtesy whatsoever and throwing her over his shoulder.

"Sure you don't need help?" Joshua called, laughing.

"I'm quite fine, thank you."

"Er, um, shall you then be *escorting* our guest to camp, Shadow?" Joshua inquired, his voice still filled with laughter.

"Indeed!" To camp! He was incredibly anxious to bring her to camp, to set her inside one of the warm wooden huts camouflaged by the denseness of the forest and the branches he and his men had dragged down to create a natural barrier between their haven and the trails throughout the forest. By God, he simply needed to be rid of her for the time being—before she managed to either kill one of them or bring great harm down upon them at the very least. After all, an injured rogue in the forest could do little good for an incredible cause.

"Stop!" she commanded. She tried to rise upon his shoulder, still beating against his flesh, not at all admitting defeat. "You will let me go this instant, you will return my belongings to me—"

"What belongings, lady?"

"The wagon!"

He started to laugh then, hurrying as he moved through the trees to reach his horse. "My lady, whether I take the wagon or your future husband does so, no belongings remain yours!"

Quite purposely, he walked with a jaunty gait, causing her to slam against his shoulders as he took her unawares with a quick step.

She swore, garnered her balance again.

"You're quite mistaken! The Duke of Manning is a noble and generous man—"

"I'm quite afraid *you* are mistaken, my lady. The Duke of Manning is a coward, a bore and a selfish man, my lady. But then, it seems that he is your choice, since you are so very willing to leap to his defense. Not to mention your own. When you are returned to him, you—just like any other fixture within his dwelling—will belong to him fully. I promise you that."

"How dare you suggest—"

"I don't suggest anything. I am telling you the truth quite bluntly. But don't fret, my lady, I will see to it that you are returned to your noble, generous lord. And if he is such a generous man, he may even wish to see that the contents of the wagon are purchased to be returned to your keeping."

"I cannot be kept a prisoner in this forest!" she cried.

"Ah, but you can!"

She beat her hands against his back once again. "Put me down, you oaf. Damn you, put me down—"

He did so. He had reached Windrider, his magnificent black stallion, the only possession he cherished. But then, he didn't actually think of the stallion as a creature he possessed. Windrider was, in his way, as free as the air surrounding them. No other man in the forest could ride him. Yet he came when the Shadow called his name. He served the Shadow with respect, and by something amazingly like mutual agreement.

Now, the Shadow plumped his burden of wriggling woman upon the horse's back. He stood back to mount, yet in those split seconds, she had managed to take up the reins. "Yaw!" she cried to the horse, setting her heels against Windrider's ribs.

Windrider, comrade in arms that he was, merely snorted and reared upon his hind legs, seeming to dance there until sending the ever-battling Lady Kate down to the dust-strewn forest floor.

The Shadow reached for her instinctively, praying that no delicate bone might have been broken in the fall, yet he should have known—she was not so delicate as she appeared. She swore, refusing his hand, stumbling up, ready to run once again. He caught her and tossed her upon the horse. "Stay there!" he commanded, but not trusting her, he held her even as he leapt up from the ground to ride behind her.

"Bastard!" she hissed at him.

"Fool. A stallion like this could kill you."

"Because he is like you. Because he thinks that force will seize for him all that he wants. Because he idiotically fails to realize that logic and intelligence can win the day when brute force fails. Because—"

"Indeed, yes! Do give me a speech on logic and intelligence after you have attempted to knife a man twice your size!"

"I meant to let the air out of your puffed-up sails!" she informed him. "You diabolical renegades think you own these forests, you—"

"Were we so diabolical, my lady, wouldn't a more gentle prudence on your part have served you better?" he inquired huskily. He leaned closer to her ear. "Think on it! Dare you test my temper so? For were you sweetly a meek and mild maid, I could allow you sunlight and green trees, and surely have you freed from here within another day and night. But, alas, me being diabolical and you being a terror, um, perhaps I shall have to use you."

"Use—me?" Her back was very straight.

"Ah, yes! This is the forest primeval, my lady. Druids roamed these lands, spilling blood for their sacrifices, specifically the blood of maidens stripped bare to tender and innocent flesh—"

She sent an elbow flying back into his ribs. Luckily, his black-painted mail protected him. She surely hurt her elbow more than his ribs.

"You'll not scare me!" she assured him.

"But you're already frightened."

"No, rogue, I am not."

"Now you're a liar, as well."

She would have none of it. Her voice was suddenly pure sweetness, her eyes like glittering gems as she twisted to search out his mask-covered face.

"You'd let me be free—within this camp of yours, of course?"

"You mean in the copse? Where the leaves bring the gentlest shadows, where wildflowers grow, where the air is kissed by the sweet freshness?"

"In the copse, aye, in the copse."

"It's so lovely there."

"Oh? I am anxious to see it!"

"Well, then, you must look quickly—before you are tied up in the prison hut."

The glitter in her eyes was suddenly a furious one. "I shall boil you in oil myself!" she promised, slamming his ribs again with such a vengeance he did feel the blow. "Rip out your blackguard's heart—"

"Ouch! What words to fall from the tongue of one who would appear to be such a tender damsel!"

"Oh, do shut up! And dear Lord! Watch where you ride, you will take both our heads from our necks," she cried, ducking against Windrider's neck.

Soft branches fell around them. Windrider had unerringly brought them through the trail that couldn't be seen. They passed through an alleyway of soft branches that fell back around them.

They came to the copse the outlaws called their home. What he had said about it was true. Wildflowers grew at the foot of numerous heavily laden trees. A creek meandered inward, circling around many of the trees like tendrils of soft hair. The air was kept fresh by the sweet scent of the flowers, the water and the sunlight that filtered through. Beyond the small copse, even here, the woodsmen's huts could scarcely be seen, for such a cover of brush and branches had been put up around them.

He dismounted quickly as two men and a plump, middle-aged woman emerged from the foliage to meet him.

"All went well?" a tall man inquired.

"As well as might be expected."

The tall man, with handsome features, lean face and graying hair, frowned. "Was there difficulty? Were our men injured in the quest?"

The Shadow reached up, setting his hands around his captive's waist. Before he could bring her down, she kicked out, catching him in the chest. She was primed and ready to run again, but he was prepared now for her every trick. He turned her quickly within his grasp so that her flailing arms and kicking feet were aimed harmlessly away from him.

"None of our men has been injured," he said, then inhaled deeply for the air his captive was costing him. "Lady Kate is simply less than eager to be among us!"

"Lady Kate!" the woman gasped. "Ah, and what a beauty she's grown to be, Lord Gregory's daughter! And betrothed to that jackanapes, the Duke of Manning!"

"And imprisoned here by a wretched batch of thieves!" Lady Kate cried out, greeting them all with her fire. But then she paused, staring at Beth. "You knew my father—Lord Gregory?"

"Years ago. I saw you when you were just a wee child. Lord Gregory was the finest of men."

"Ah! So now you are with the ruffians who would rob from his daughter," she snapped, still struggling with the Shadow, who struggled in return to hold her.

"It isn't your father we rob from, it is the Duke of Manning," the Shadow said flatly.

Kate ignored him, except for trying to aim another kick his way. She stared at Beth. "Who are you that you knew Lord Gregory?" she demanded.

"No one, lass, a serving wench grown into a serving woman. Born in these woods, and at times healer to many men who thought they ruled their great estates nearby, midwife to their ladies. And I'm pleased to see you, child, and to serve you."

"Beth, you needn't be serving this vixen—" the Shadow began, swearing as she caught his shin with one of her wild kicks.

"If you'd just let me go!" she grated to the Shadow.

"Gladly!"

He let her loose, allowing her to sprawl in the dirt before him.

"Gawain," he said, addressing the handsome, graying man. "And you, Thomas!" He spoke to the second man, a shorter fellow with a fine head of thick, curling brown hair. "And mostly you, my good Beth—she is your responsibility now. I haven't slept in nearly two days and will do so now!" He spun on his heel and walked quickly to the underbrush.

"Come, my poor, poor dear!" he heard Beth saying.

"Never!" declared the captive.

"Now, my lady..." Gawain must have tried courtesy. The Shadow suddenly heard a deep, masculine cry, and he smiled.

Gawain had met their captive in truth.

"Ah, but she's dangerous!" Thomas cried.

And the Shadow laughed softly to himself. The three were aware. And they would never let her go. Never.

Chapter Three

"She's gone."

"Gone?" he said incredulously.

"Gone!" Beth repeated, wringing her hands. "Yet she can't have fled far for I brought her warmed wine just minutes ago!"

He leapt up from the simple wooden bed and down mattress where he had slept, taking Beth by the shoulders.

"Just minutes ago?"

Beth nodded worriedly. "I swear, it was just minutes! She was in the far shelter. She did not leave by the door for Gawain was watching it all the while. He and Thomas have already gone in search of her—"

"On foot?"

"Aye."

"She will try to steal a horse," he said with conviction. "I had best find her quickly!"

"Your mask!" Beth warned.

"Aye! My mask!"

After giving Beth a quick kiss on the forehead that brought red roses to her cheeks, he paused long enough to slip into his black mask and tie the black band about his head, knotting it at his nape. Then, gently pressing Beth aside, he quickly exited his humble abode within their forest community. He tried to reason as their unwilling guest might have done. She had fled by a window, and she would keep close to the darkness and shadows of the huts while she looked for their makeshift stables. He silently hurried to the dwelling she had so recently vacated, discovered the window by which she had managed her escape and exited as she had done. He crept along the side of the hut, then eased to the next, and the next.

Then he saw her.

There was a hunter's moon that night. Full and glorious it rose over the forest, casting a golden glow upon the forest and everything within it. She had discovered the stables, like all else in the glen camouflaged with brush and branches. She had seen the entry, though, or perhaps she had heard the whinny of one of the horses, and she was silently and determinedly making her way to the trail amidst the green, slipping silently toward the stable.

He started off across the exposed copse, moving swiftly. He was nearly upon the stable when he sensed noise and movement behind him. He spun and was just in time to avoid being completely engulfed in a massive blanket of fur.

"Got you, my lady!" he heard.

Throwing his arms up, he fought off the burly hold upon him and the suffocating sweep of fur.

"You little vixen—" Joshua began.

"Hardly!" the Shadow protested.

"Shadow!" exclaimed the giant. "By the Blessed Virgin, my apologies, my lord! I've been following the girl—"

"As I have I. But we are hardly of a size!"

"The moon slipped behind a tree. A hunter's moon. I could not be blinded, then suddenly I was. I beg your pardon."

"Aye, Joshua, but we must move quickly now—"

Even as he spoke, she suddenly came bursting out of the stables and camouflage, dragging branches and brush along with her. "He-yaa, he-yaa!" she cried to her horse, a handsome bay mare he had taken from a very fat and bejeweled merchant who had erred across his path. She raced the mare straight at the Shadow and Joshua, causing them both to leap aside. Even as they fell—eating dust—she disappeared into the night, only the mare's diminishing hoofbeats proof that she had been there just seconds before.

"Blast!" Joshua cursed, leaping up.

The Shadow was already on his feet, running for the stables. He burst into Windrider's stall. Eschewing the use of a saddle for the sake of haste as Lady Kate had done, he was atop the stallion and racing in her wake within a matter of seconds.

"Rouse the men!" he called to Joshua. "Have them form a circle around the outer perimeter and warn the guards there already. I shall follow her and seize her long before that point, I swear!"

"She's a wily one!" Joshua warned. "She may well escape you!"

"She'll not escape me!" he stated angrily. Sweet Jesu, but the wench was causing no end of trouble! "She'll not escape me," he repeated, "but . . ."

"But?"

"If she should," he said dryly, "you'll see that the men are prepared!"

"Aye!" Joshua answered. The Shadow nudged Windrider, and they began their flight once again, following the trail Lady Kate had taken.

She was not difficult to follow, for her wild race through the forest was a reckless one. The earth was churned up where she rode, branches were broken, small trees were bent. Yet as the minutes passed, he found himself frustrated that she was horsewoman enough to keep up her pace, not knowing where she rode, yet unerringly seeming to head toward the north, toward the very stronghold of the Duke of Manning. Not that he truly feared at this moment that she would break through his barriers. There were seventy-eight men in his band of outlaws, though many of them came and went from other lives, as he did himself. Tonight, twenty-five men sat high atop the trees that encircled the dense forest, long before the lines where the simple folk of the duke's community dared walk and long before the place where his armored guards might venture, as well.

Yet still . . .

Some instinct caused him to halt. "Whoa, my good fellow," he said softly to Windrider, slipping down from his horse's bare haunches. He studied the ground and the trees and realized, feeling very much like a fool, that she had doubled back. She had ridden hard through the trail on purpose; she had led him in a circle.

He cursed himself and prayed he had made the discovery in time. He cut across her circle with a madman's speed, but then drew in Windrider's reins. The massive stallion crept through the foliage with the quiet and grace of a dancer.

The Shadow was grimly pleased to discover his beauty at last. Dismounted, she walked along a pine trail, breaking branches in a backward motion as she returned to her mare.

The Shadow slipped from Windrider's back and circled behind her. He stepped back each time she did so. "Ah, easy now, my fair lady!" she whispered to the mare she assumed to be close behind her. "You're a good creature, unlike that heathen spawn from hell ridden by that wretched forest blackguard!" She eased a hand behind her as if to pat the mare's fine shoulders.

She froze, for rather than the mare's flank her touch fell upon the leather-clad thigh of a man.

She spun, oddly seeming caught in time beneath the hunter's moon, moon gold hair spinning in the light with the most ethereal beauty. Her eyes touched his, vivid, gemlike blue, touched by the fire of fury.

"You!" she exclaimed.

"Indeed, my lady."

He bowed deeply.

She turned to run.

He caught her by her elbow but she doubled back into his hold, trying very hard to kick him where she might do the most damage, managing to get his knee solidly instead. He grunted and groaned, and when she tried again to escape him, he released her—allowing her own momentum to bring her crashing down to the forest floor. Before she could rise he pounced upon her.

"Alas! Is this the way we must carry on all our conversations?" he demanded, pinning her wrists to the sides of her head.

"Nay, sir, we need not carry on conversations at all!" she seethed.

"Not even a goodbye?" he taunted. "Have we not tried to make your stay as comfortable as possible?"

"I am not comfortable at the moment, I do assure you!"

"You bring about your own distress. You had only to accept our hospitality for a brief time—"

"I will not be a prisoner to a barbarian thief!"

"But you are, my lady. You are. And I might strongly suggest you cease your determination to be free. It is my intention to return you to the Duke of Manning in just circumstance for a bride, but lady, most times when I assume this position with a woman, it leads not to conversation, but other intercourse."

She tried to strike him, but he held fast. "Lady Kate, will you please behave nicely?"

"An outlaw, asking me to behave nicely? You are demented!"

"Fair warning, then. I will take what measures I must against you!"

"They will raise your head high on a pole above Manning Castle!" she predicted direly.

"Perhaps. But that will not save you now," he assured her, leaping to his feet once again. He reached down a hand to her. As he expected, she refused to take it. She lay breathing heavily upon the ground, staring at him. When he sighed and bent to pluck her up, she suddenly found her strength, rising and heading for her mare.

"Oh, I'm afraid that I cannot trust you to return to your guest room so," the Shadow said.

"Damn you—"

"Allow me!" He kept his words as polite and courteous as possible, then drew her against him and hiked her up by the waist to set her upon Windrider, following her up in one swift movement.

"But the mare—"

"Will return home. She *likes* it in the forest," he said.

"Poor creature. She is but a stupid animal."

Her scent was subtle, something derived from violets, soft, haunting. Had he noticed it before? Perhaps not. He had noticed her eyes, the golden cloak of her hair, the perfection of her face and form. Yet she hadn't given him much time to appreciate her truly fine attributes, since she had kept him busy fighting her every move.

Yet now...

Now as they rode...

Ah, that scent kept coming to him, seeping into him as if it had come into his blood, and wafted now throughout him, a strange taunt. He hadn't really felt her warmth until now, or realized the way she moved with each breath.

He urged Windrider to greater speed, praying that the night breeze would sweep away the heat arising within him. He'd been exhausted; he'd barely managed to catch a few hours' sleep. Leading a double life, he had discovered, could be far more exhausting than following Richard to the Crusades.

She was far more exhausting....

Indeed. She was far more trouble than he'd bargained for tonight....

She was beautiful.

She was deadly.

Yet the greatest danger had been erased. She had not escaped him, had not discovered the forest trails, had not escaped by way of them. She would never be able to lead anyone to them. They were safe, their secret place in the forest was safe.

He saw Joshua, standing guard by the trail into the copse.

"Ah, you've found our guest!" he cried, relieved. He shook his head. "My lady, the forest is no place for a woman alone in the night. There are wolves—"

"Yes, there are. Unfortunately, I stumbled upon one!"

"Were you hurt?" Joshua asked, deeply concerned.

"She means me," the Shadow said with a sigh.

"Oh," Joshua said. Then, "Oh!" he repeated once again, laughing. He saw the expression in the Shadow's eyes and sobered quickly.

"Shall I return her—"

"Nay, Joshua. I shall do the deed! See that word goes out that the lady has been found."

"Aye, my—Shadow," Joshua said.

The Shadow urged Windrider forward. When they returned to the copse, he did not set her down alone, yet kept his hands upon her even as he dismounted himself, then dragged her along with him. Her body was as stiff and hard as oak, her beautiful features set into a mask of fury and defiance.

A few men had silently stepped from the huts and stood staring at her. Beth slipped out among them, watching. Lady Kate spun around, staring at them all. Then she turned back to the Shadow.

"I'll escape you again," she assured him, head high as she wrenched free from his hold, hands on her hips as she stared at him.

"Not tonight."

She lifted an arm to indicate the men around them. "What guard will you leave on me, rogue, that I will not defy? Can all your men remain awake all night? Can any of them have eyes everywhere? The moon is full, a hunter's moon, your moon, for you are like a raptor after prey in the night, but clouds will come and blind the most predatory carnivore!" she exclaimed with taunting fury.

"Ah, well, my lady! I would no longer dream of giving any of my men the wretched task of seeing to your comfort. I intend to do so myself."

"What? And can you stay awake through the night? Can you be ever watchful?"

He crossed his arms over his chest, staring at her. "My lady, I intend to sleep deeply and sweetly, all through the night." He smiled at his men. "Get some sleep, my good fellows, except for those of you posted as guards. I will see to the lady myself this night."

"Oh, will you?"

"I will."

He caught her elbow and led her firmly through the trees and branches and moon-touched huts to the building in the far rear. "Let me go!" she insisted, apparently alarmed at last by his absolute determination and inescapable grip upon her. "You wretch, you can't stay awake all night."

"But—"

Beth came hurrying behind him then. "Shadow, the lass will cause you great difficulty tonight, trying to escape and the like—"

"She'll not be in such a hurry to escape again," he said firmly.

He'd reached the hut. He threw open the door. forcing Lady Kate through it. Beth hovered in the doorway.

"But why—" Beth began.

"She won't be in such a hurry to escape because she'll be naked."

"What?" Lady Kate gasped, glaring at him in outrage.

"Oh, my lady, he does not mean it, there is no finer gentleman—"

He pointed a stern finger at Beth. "Don't you tell her what I will and will not do!" he warned. "There is no more exhausted gentleman!" he assured her.

"But—"

"Out!" he ordered, and he firmly pushed Beth from the room, sliding the heavy wooden bolt on the door from within, then turning to lean against it and cross his arms over his chest.

"Well?"

"Well, what?" she demanded.

"Simple, my lady. Do you give me your clothing, or do I take it?"

"You're a madman."

"You've ten seconds."

"How dare you! Do you know what the Duke of Manning would do to you for this insult?"

"I've difficulty imagining what could possibly be worse than being boiled in oil or having my insides taken out," he told her. "Now, I mean it. I want your clothing. I'll count from ten. Then I'll take it."

"You're a fool, a wretch, a bastard—"

"Ten, nine..."

"There are worse things he can do to you! Cut off your fingers one by one before boiling you!"

"Eight, seven..."

"Burn your extremities!"

"Six, five..."

"I'll give you my shoes."

"Four, three..."

"My shoes, see? Here they are!"

She had taken her delicate leather shoes from her feet and offered them up to him.

"I want more than shoes."

"Well, you can't have more!"

"Um, what number was I on? Two..."

"You bloody thief!"

"One!"

She let out a shriek as he started toward her, then turned and flew.

But there was nowhere to go. She reached a wall, and turned, and he was there.

Upon her.

Hazel eyes burning like a demon's through the slits in the Shadow's black mask.

Chapter Four

"What if I were to give you my word that I'd make no more escape attempts?" she pleaded.

"What?"

"I'll give you my word!"

"And I'm supposed to accept your word—after you've kept me on a mad chase since I've first set eyes upon you?"

"Yes!"

"You've tried to escape every conceivable chance!"

"But I never gave you my word before."

"I can't possibly accept your word."

"Why?"

"Because you might be lying!"

"I said I'd give you my word!" she repeated, eyes narrowed warningly.

"Hmm."

"My word of honor!"

"Sorry."

"Sorry?"

"No good. I'm not at all convinced you are a woman of honor."

She was quick and powerful; only because he was coming to know her well was he able to catch her wrist before her hand connected with his cheek.

"Now really—" he began, but she shoved aside the arm he held her with and to his astonishment was already removing the delicate gold belt that rode low on her hips.

"Rogue!" she declared angrily. The belt fell to the floor. She pulled her elegant blue tunic over her head, casting it with a fury across the room. A shift that seemed concocted of pure gossamer did nothing to conceal the shape and form of her body. She wore nothing else other than garters and hose, which she dipped to discard with the same abandoned frustration and fury.

Muscle by muscle, he seemed to constrict. Nay, he seemed to constrict in places where he hadn't been aware he had muscle. In fact, his skin seemed to constrict, his heart, his limbs, his soul.

And definitely other organs of his body.

"Fine!" he heard himself snap suddenly. It had a husky sound to it. A pained sound.

She seemed startled, and straightened, her last stocking still in her hand, her eyes very wide and blue with surprise. God help them both, she seemed all innocence, unaware of all that damnable constriction within him.

"That will do, my lady," he said as coldly as he could manage. "I don't think you will be so quick to leave now."

She tossed her head, amazingly regal in her near nakedness. But then, perhaps she didn't realize how firelight played havoc over her apparel. How the rippling flame just seemed to kiss the flesh beneath the alabaster of her gown. Enhance the dusky rose of her nipples. Make a haunting shadow of the golden triangle between her thighs...

"What makes you think I wouldn't be willing to run from this place as naked as the eve I was born, rogue?"

"Would you?" he inquired.

She turned her back on him. It didn't help. Golden light and shadows fell upon the length of her back, the sweeping fall of her hair. The curve of her buttocks.

She spun back. "Perhaps."

He nodded, at a wretched loss. He didn't dare falter, yet he was ready to kick himself for this torture he had brought down upon his own flesh. Nowhere to go from here except along the path he must.

He reached out a hand to her. "Come here," he said.

She arched a brow at him. "I am neither slave nor servant. You want me, you come to me."

"Witch!" he lashed out furiously, but if she wanted him there, there he would be. He covered the distance between them in two long strides, catching her arm, dragging her against him. Oh... another mistake. He had previously shed his coat of mail to sleep. He wore his black shirt and thin breeches and nothing more, and it seemed that every curve he had savored with his eyes now pressed into his flesh and form.

But this wasn't the time to show weakness. He bent, dragging her with him, and procured one of her stockings from the floor. With his teeth and right hand, he tied her right wrist to his left one, despite the fact she gasped and tried to struggle once she realized his intent. But the knot was drawn quickly and tightly, and she was left with no recourse but to stare at him, oddly trembling now that the deed was done.

"I can still escape."

"Mmm. And I should have accepted your word that you would not?"

"I had offered it freely. That is the only way that one can ever trust another's word."

"Give it to me now."

"It is no longer offered."

"Then I suggest you get on the bed—"

"What?" The single word was a gasp, a shriek, a shudder of fear and horror.

He smiled. Ah, retribution!

"My lady, I am weary, as I've told you. Now there is a very good chance I will fall upon yonder feather mattress and sleep like one dead. However, the longer I remain awake, the more irritated it seems I become. And therefore, the more acutely aware of all that is around me. More awake, more, um, what is the word? *Aroused,* I believe. Now, you can do your best to defy and torment me longer, or..."

His arm was nearly wrenched from his shoulder as she turned and headed for his bed. She crawled upon it with such speed and determination that he found himself dragged down upon her. "Oh, would you stop!" she cried out. "I am trying my best to do as you wish—"

"Lady, you cannot begin to imagine what I wish!" he snapped, struggling to lift his weight from hers, since her impetuous dash had sprawled him lengthwise upon her. He flipped over to his back on the other side of her, inhaling deeply, willing his body to forget the sweet-smelling, incredibly fashioned female form at his right.

"If you—" she began.

"My lady—shut up!" he hissed.

To his amazement, she went silent. To his amazement, his eyes closed. He drifted into a light sleep.

He awoke, feeling the slightest movement. Barely cracking his eyes, he watched as she worked diligently with her left hand, trying so very hard to untie his knot. He closed his eyes, finding it somewhat difficult to keep a smile from slipping into his features.

But then . . .

The scent of her seemed to invade his senses once again. Permeate him, flesh and blood and bone. The softness of her hair waved over his fingers, vivid images of her slim-yet-oh-so-nicely curved form began to play in his mind's eye. He felt her every motion, her warmth . . .

And felt, too, that the knot was beginning to give beneath her fingers.

He let out a growl that brought a cry of alarm to her lips. She lay down flat, inhaling, exhaling, her chest rising and falling with the exertion. He rolled, looking down at her face, her eyes closed, thick honey lashes shadowing her cheeks. He set a finger upon her chin.

"You are tenacious."

"I'm sleeping."

"You're lying."

"I will be sleeping." She cracked open an eye, lowered her lashes again and bit nervously into her lower lip. "Honestly," she whispered.

"Mmm, you will be," he agreed. He turned his body toward hers, drawing another chopped cry from her as he twisted her back to his chest and left his hand—the one that bound them together—beneath her hip. To reach the tie again, she would have to back up to him entirely, feel the fullness of his body flush against hers. "Comfortable, my lady?" he taunted.

"I'm sleeping!" she hissed.

"You talk in your sleep?"

"Apparently so."

"So you must try to untie knots in your sleep, as well, I assume?"

"I don't know what I do when I'm sleeping."

"Perhaps you try to escape while you're sleeping?"

"I can't hear you, I'm sleeping."

Ah, yes. She was sleeping. Indeed. She was... comfortable?

He was not. He was dying; he was in agony. Tension filled him. He prayed that she would not move back. She would feel every bit of tension within his body. Protruding from it.

But she would not escape from him, that was a certainty. He groaned inwardly, laying his head down. He was startled to realize that he was praying.

Dear God, please don't let me come upon such hostages as this again. Dear God, please . . .

This time, it took a very long while to fall to sleep again.

She remembered being in the great hall as the men within it spoke.

They didn't see her; she stood behind one of the huge tapestried chairs that flanked the fire. She shouldn't have been in the hall then, and she was well aware of the fact. She should have been in the nursery with Elgin and the baby, Lizbeth. But she hadn't really been afraid. Her father was a kind soul, a man with incredible patience and tolerance. He loved his wife and his children and never seemed to find them to be a bother. If he had been about his business and had found her there, he would have scolded her, but she would have wound up on his lap, and he would most probably have told her a story before sending her back up for nap time.

But her father wasn't alone. Two other men were in the hall, the one older, the one younger. They argued with her father even as he offered them wine in one of his own homes, the manor at Glenwold. The older man threw a document down before her father insistently. Her father stubbornly shook his head. The older man wagged a finger at him. "You are for me, my lord, or you are against me! If you are against me, you are my enemy. And all enemies must perish."

Her father rose furiously, saying that he would gladly battle his visitor at any time. But then he stared into his wine, looked at the man and gasped. "Murderer! Murderer, traitor, most wretched . . ."

Her father grasped the table by which he stood. He sagged against it, fell to the floor.

"Torch the place, be quick about it!" the elder man commanded the younger.

Her father was dead. She saw his face, saw his open eyes, saw the poisoned foam leaking from his mouth. She shouted his name, running to touch him.

"One of the brats!" the elder man cried. "Seize her, quickly, you fool."

She couldn't touch her beloved father; she knew it well. She ducked and ran before the younger man could reach her, tearing for the stairway.

"Leave her!" ordered the elder man. "Set the fires, and she will burn!"

She had to find her mother, reach the nursery. Get help. But as she ran up the stairs, she began to smell the smoke. She turned, whirling, to look down the stairs.

There was flame. Eating at the tapestries, lapping at the walls, engulfing the chairs and table. There was flame....

She saw them in the midst of it, the men, laughing, enjoying their handiwork. Then one of them turned and looked up the stairway at her, meeting her eyes....

The flames rose higher with an audible whoosh of sound, and she saw yellow and gold, and felt the heat, burning...

This time, she dragged him from a deep sleep. He bolted with a rush of alarm, leaping from the bed, only to be pulled back down by the tie that bound them together. She was screaming.

No doubt about it—she did scream in her sleep. She was madly fighting him with closed eyes, gasping for breath, flailing at him.

"My lady!" he called, rising at her side, shaking her shoulders. "My lady, you must waken, you're dreaming!"

Her eyes flew open wildly. She stared at him, seeing nothing at first, then slowly focusing on him. "Oh, oh!" she gasped.

For a moment, she was vulnerable. So very vulnerable, innocent, young, beautiful. He wanted to battle whatever demon she had fought within her dream. He wanted to best dragons, to hold her, protect her.

"It's all right. You were dreaming. I am by your side, lady, no harm will come to you, I swear it. Rest easy, it is over."

There was a banging on the hut door. "My l—" someone began, then cut off quickly. "*Shadow!* Dear God, what is happening?"

He took the knife hidden in his boot and hastily slit the stocking tie binding him to the pale golden beauty on his bed. He strode to the door, sliding the bolt and flinging it open. A band of his men circled the place while Joshua and Beth stood close up front. Beth stared at him and hurried into the room. "Oh, my dear sweet Jesu, what did you do?" she inquired, stunned, and staring with accusatory eyes at him.

"Do? Not a thing!" he retorted.

"My lady!" Beth sat at Lady Kate's side, noting both her lack of apparel and deathly pallor. "You— you renegade!" Beth gasped in deepest dismay and disappointment.

He strode to the room's single table, finding wine there, pouring it into a wooden goblet. He brought it to Lady Kate's side, returning Beth's stare with an indignant accusation of his own. "I did nothing. The lady was dreaming."

"Dreaming of what?" Joshua murmured lightly.

"That I know not. Unless the lady cares to enlighten us?" the Shadow said. He lowered himself upon one knee, helping her rise to sip the wine she accepted from him. She took a sip, then a swallow, then took the goblet from his hands and chugged it down. She returned the goblet to him, those beautiful crystal blue eyes upon him.

"Well?" he asked.

She leapt up, then bounced upon her knees behind Beth. "The wretch!" she whispered. "He demanded my clothing, he threatened me, abused me—"

"Dear God!" Beth gasped.

He groaned. "The lady is a liar, and you know it. The more gently one deals with her, the more likely she is to take a bite of flesh!"

To his surprise, she flushed, her lashes lowered, sweeping her cheeks. "Well, he is a wretch," she murmured.

"Ah, but he did not accost you, eh, my lady?" Beth demanded.

"No," she admitted, much to his surprise.

"Well, then," Joshua said. "I am back for my bed!" He departed the hut. Beth rose. To the Shadow's embarrassment and aggravation, she patted his masked cheek before she left the hut.

He crossed his arms over his chest, staring at his guest, still furious with her, yet oddly, once again, touched by her. Her eyes remained downcast, the tangled moon-glow web of her hair about the delicate alabaster perfection of her face. The firelight had died down to a very soft glow. Her shift seemed all the more feather light, the fabric all but invisible. Nay, he'd not accosted her.

Yet.

And still, what living male would not be tempted, gentleman or rogue?

She looked up at him suddenly. "Why do you wear that mask?"

"My lady, that is easily seen and answered. I wear it to hide my identity."

"Why? Are you someone I would know?"

"We have never met, to my knowledge."

She smiled very slowly. "It's foolish that you wear it."

"Why is that?"

"Your eyes," she said softly, her own upon his curiously. "They are striking eyes. I would know them anywhere. They are fire eyes. And oddly enough..."

"Aye?"

"Oddly enough," she repeated on a breath. "I am afraid of fire. But not of that I see within your eyes." She flushed then, as if she had said far too much. "Is there more wine?" she asked. "I'd like to sleep again. It may...help."

He went for the goblet, poured more wine in it, brought it to her. She sipped from it this time, smoothing a lock of hair. "Join me?" she invited. She smiled. He was certain that she didn't intend it to be so, but it was the most seductive smile he had ever seen.

Join you, yes. Touch you, lie beside you, fill my lungs with you, my hand, taste, touch, see, feel...

"No, thank you."

"You'll not drink wine with me? You'll demand my clothes and tie me to your person, yet you'll not drink with me?"

"I've a prisoner to watch over, my lady."

She sipped her wine and her smile deepened. "What if I gave you my word now that I'll not escape?"

"How would I know that you meant it?"

"Because I know now that you will return me to the Duke of Manning—in the same condition as that in which I arrived."

He inhaled, feeling as if his lungs and every muscle within him trembled as he did so. *Sweet Jesu, don't be so certain of that!* he thought.

"Yes, you will be given to him as you arrived here."

"I really need the goods within my wagon."

"So do I."

"But mine is a just cause!"

"And you are so certain mine is not?"

"You are a rogue, a robber, a thief. A renegade in the forest, waylaying honest men."

"Who is to judge an honest man?"

She sighed. "I cannot parry words with you so tonight. I am so tired now...."

She had finished the second goblet of wine. He took it from her fingers as she stretched out on the bed. He set the goblet on the table, his back to her. He breathed deeply, then returned to her. "Over. You take the side by the wall this time."

"Aren't you going to tie me again? I've a stocking left on the floor yonder."

"Nay, lady," he said, lying beside her.

"Why not?"

"You've given your word, haven't you, that you'll not escape?"

She looked at him, searching out his eyes. "Did I actually give my word, or suggest that I could do so?"

"I am assuming that you have given it."

"Ah!" she said softly.

She lay on her back, then turned, face to the wall, her back to him. He set a hand upon her waist, drawing her against him.

She stiffened, but then relaxed. Not a word of protest fell from her lips.

"I shall hold you rather than tie you," he whispered. "Is that all right?"

She didn't answer right away. He thought that perhaps that she had slipped quickly into a doze from the wine.

"It's—all right," she said softly.

He was completely startled when her fingers curled over where his hand lay upon her hip. "Fire fights fire, so I have always heard." Her voice was slurred. "You will keep me from the flame!" she murmured.

She spoke no more. A few seconds later, a small shudder ripped through her body. She breathed more quietly.

And slept. Just like one dead.

And no matter how tired he had been, he lay awake late, late into the night.

Until the first cock crowed.

It was morning.

Chapter Five

The creek deep in the forest was beautiful. Near the embankment, it was very shallow, one foot here, two to three feet there. Rocks were strewn along it, fine places to sit and bathe one's feet, or to lay one's clothing to dry when it had gotten wet. Trees, deep green, dense, grew by the creek, shadowing and shading it. The area was beautiful, mysterious, secretive. She loved it immediately.

Beth was the one who brought her here. When she had awakened by morning, the black-clad man, no longer such a stranger, had been gone. Beth had come, a woman more kindly and gentle than any good servant she had ever known. She'd brought her clear water and good bread and a pastry pie filled with sweet venison. She'd eaten it all and with relish, which seemed to please Beth no end.

"It's not so terrible here, my lady. You must believe that it is so," Beth told her.

"The greatest castle, the most comfortable manor, is terrible if one is a prisoner, my good woman," Kate reminded her.

Beth sighed. "You'll not be a prisoner long, lady. The master is a great man—"

"A great rogue."

Beth smiled. "A great rogue, if you will. But now that you've breakfasted, perhaps you'd like to wash by the stream. And if you do absolutely swear upon the word of the Lord in Heaven to me, I shall give you your privacy there."

So she had sworn. She had no intention of escaping this morning, though last night it had seemed that she must make every effort. She wanted to feel the crystal coolness of the slim waterway. It was delicious. She sank into the water in her slim shift, shivering as the fragile linen clung to her skin, the cold causing her nipples to pucker, goose bumps to break out upon her flesh. And still, she played in the shallows, swam out to the deeper area, then returned again to stretch upon a rock warmed by the forest green and gold rays of the sun.

Her captor was a strange man. A highwayman, convinced of his own justice! Yet...

She liked her captor. Liked the sound of his voice, his manner. His temper, his courtesy despite it. And the strangest thing of all was that...

She had felt safe with him. Why should she not? She was already in the arms of a renegade. It didn't matter. Last night, in her sleep, she had seen the flames again. Seen them, felt them. Felt the heat. But the heat had been . . . his body. He had conjured the fire with his eyes, perhaps. But after she had awakened . . .

She had felt safe. He had cast away the shadows of the dream.

How strange.

She worried about herself for a moment. She had been seized and kidnapped in the middle of the forest by ruthless outlaws and she was no longer disturbed by what had happened. But then, she had long ago given up the worry of damnation. "Revenge is mine, so sayeth the Lord," she had been taught, and under normal circumstances, that might be just and right. But her circumstances weren't normal at all, and when she had been very young, she had determined that no matter what she had to do, she was going to have her taste of revenge. She had set out on this journey *coldly*. That was the word to describe her feelings exactly. She had sat in the wagon with the jewels, rich fabrics and gold pieces bestowed upon her by Lord Gregory and told herself that she would have her revenge at any cost, and that meant going through with marriage, and the relationship that followed.

Until the Duke of Manning's death.

The blood suddenly seemed to drain through her as she thought about what a horrible person she must be, but then again she trembled, remembering how her family had died. She wished desperately that she could simply believe in God's wrath and final justice. God might wait until the afterlife to take care of the Duke of Manning. She could not.

A breeze swept by her. She didn't hear movement; no branch cracked on the forest floor. But she had a feeling that she was being watched and she turned.

He was there. The man his comrades called the Shadow, and whom the people whispered about as the Rogue of Heffington Forest. He stood casually, leaned against an oak, black mask in place, still clad in black though without his painted mail, his sword in its scabbard by his side. He seemed relaxed, arms crossed over his chest, and she thought that he might have been there quite some time.

"Good morning," she said primly, drawing her knees to her chest and hugging them to her.

"Yes, indeed, it is." He sounded quite convinced.

"And why is that?"

He eased away from the tree, coming to her, hunching down upon the balls of his feet before her. "Because you're still here," he told her. "When Beth admitted to me that she'd chosen to let you bathe alone, I was quite certain I'd soon be racing through the forest once again."

"Prisoners will try to escape," she told him.

"But you did not."

"Beth asked for my word. I gave it to her."

"Ah!" he murmured.

"I told you my word was good."

"I shall have to remember that for the future."

She drew her eyes from his, looking out on the water. She turned back to him again. "Why do you wear a mask? Are you someone I would know?"

He shook his head. "I simply prefer not to hang— or be boiled in oil or the like, were my identity known."

"You steal from people, yet refuse to pay the price—"

"I only steal from select people for a very important reason."

"And what is that reason?"

"One I can't explain at the moment. My turn. Do you know the Duke of Manning?"

She drew her eyes from his once again, alarmed to discover that it was such a difficult thing to do. "I—in a manner of speaking."

"And you're anxious to marry him?"

She shrugged. "The marriage is arranged."

"Ah."

"He is a duke."

"Yes."

"A powerful man."

"Yes."

"A rich one."

"But you're rich, as well, my lady. Lord Gregory's sole heiress."

She bowed her head, anxious to be done with the conversation. "He has a great deal of power," she repeated stubbornly.

She felt him looking at her. "Because of his friendship with Prince John?"

"Yes—and I believe he has gained numerous properties through his own—prowess."

"And you call me a thief!" he exclaimed.

She could still feel his eyes searching her out. "King Richard will return. One day," he said.

"Will he?" she asked politely, looking at him again. "He will return, and he will leave again. Richard is a warrior king. One who must keep fighting."

"Yes, but he has able administrators—"

"Who don't seem to be able to administrate over baby brother John when the king himself is imprisoned by the Austrians! Strange, isn't it? Great Christian kings, princes and knights went to war against the Infidels—and the war has ended with one Christian ruler making a prisoner of another!"

"It's strange," he agreed. "But the kingdom remains Richard's—"

"Until the king dies."

"The king is a robust man—"

"Who," she said very softly, "is said to prefer young boys to the wife he has taken."

"Your words are dangerously traitorous!" he warned her.

She sighed. "I do not mean them so. I admire the king, I am his loyal subject. But he is not here, he is not doing much to assure himself an heir, and when he dies, John will be king. It seems then that we all must see to it that we straighten out our lives before that eventuality takes place!"

He shook his head, looking at her. "You are a strange young woman indeed, Lady Kate. So very aware of politics, and so dire!'

"Again, I do not mean to be!" She needed the conversation to end. She rose quickly, then realized that her shift was clinging to her body like a second skin. "The water is wonderfully refreshing," she mumbled, hurrying past him to plunge within it. She quickly walked to the deep water in the center of the creek, leaned her head back and soaked her hair. The water was cool, the sun was hot. Looking at him, she felt the strangest sensation of the sun's rays filtering into her limbs. Warmth, suffusing her, no matter that the water was chill...

Refreshing.

She was losing her mind, she thought. Had she said the word again, had she thought it, had *he* said it? She wasn't sure. But he was sitting on her rock, doffing boots and hose, coarse wool tunic and soft linen pitch-black shirt beneath. She thought he meant to shed his breeches, as well. Part of her was terrified that he would do so.

Part of her was eager....

But he did not. Clad in the skin-hugging breeches, feet and chest bare—the mask and black cloth remaining upon his face and hair—he strode into the water, not coming near her at first, but shivering as he doused the clear cold water upon his shoulders, chest and back.

He walked toward her then. She told herself she remained so breathless from the exertion of continuing to tread water. "You're—wearing a mask in the water," she informed him.

He nodded gravely. "I am."

"But that black cap upon your head is a waste now."

"It is?"

"Well, sir, your chest is riddled with black hair. I assume it grows upon your head, as well."

"Take care. You could assume too much. I might deem it dangerous to allow you to leave the forest."

She started to smile, but a shiver seized her. "I have to leave the forest," she whispered to him.

"To marry the Duke of Manning."

"Yes."

"Surely, a rich young woman of your impeccable reputation and . . ."

"And?" she inquired, puzzled.

"Beauty," he said softly. "You're rich, you've position and beauty. Surely, someone could have arranged a more . . . pleasing marriage."

"Ah, indeed!" she said. "An arrangement should have been made to deliver me and *all* my riches to the Rogue of Heffington Forest, eh?" She spoke lightly, dousing him with a splash of water as she finished.

"Not a bad idea, my lass," he countered, shaking the water from his face and mask. "If you're actually rich enough." And with that he snaked beneath her, and she gasped, startled, as he caught her ankle and drew her beneath the water's surface.

She rose, sputtering. "I hope that mask shrinks on your face as you wear it!" she taunted.

He caught her by the hand, drawing her against him. "You haven't told me—"

But he broke off, hazel eyes on her, the thought having flown from his tongue. She didn't wonder at all why he had suddenly gone speechless. She felt speechless herself. The shift she wore did nothing to prevent the burning sensation that now seemed to leap from his body to hers, from hers again to his. The rough feel of all that ebony hair on his chest seemed to tease her breasts mercilessly, and in turn, her breasts seemed to swell. Embarrassingly. She could see the rise and pucker of her nipples, just above the water's surface. She could feel the tension in his body, the constriction of muscles. She knew full well she should be struggling, pushing away from him, doing anything possible to free herself from his touch....

But she could not. Her mind refused to work, her limbs refused to respond. She stared into his eyes, thinking that she would recognize them anywhere again, that they were the source of the fire within him, the heat sweeping into her. The source...but there was more than the source. There was the feel of his chest, the rise and fall of it. His hands, holding her. So this was...

Desire, she told herself. Passion. Longing, aching, craving, needing . . . something.

Passion and desire were dangerous, she reminded herself. She heard the minstrels' tales of star-crossed lovers, and she'd thought men and women silly to want to die over thwarted love.

She was not in love. She barely knew this man.

And yet . . .

She knew him deeply in a way that could not be logic or understanding within her own heart and mind. And what difference did that make? She had been willing to wed the Duke of Manning and accept all that came with being his wife until . . .

His death.

She was a horrible person.

No . . .

Maybe.

She pushed away from him, breaking what spell of silence had held them together. He instantly let her go. She remembered that it was too deep here for her to stand. She began to furiously tread water once again.

"What . . . was I saying?" he asked her, those hazel eyes still burning into hers.

"I, um . . ." Her words were cut off when she suddenly cried out. A cramp, so vicious it felt as if a

knife were piercing her, suddenly seized her wildly
pumping calf.

"What is it?" he demanded, alarmed.

"My leg..."

"Something has bitten you?"

"No, no...it just hurts. Terribly. I can't swim, I
can't..."

She couldn't stay afloat, which became obvious as
the end of her sentence came out in a stream of bub-
bles. He reached for her, drawing her instantly into
his arms, against his chest. He carried her quickly
back to the embankment, back to her rock. Sitting
her down, he took her calf between his hands, rubbing it strenuously.

"Wait!" she gasped, nearly passing out from the
pain. "Please...you're killing me!"

"I swear, it will be better."

"But I will be dead!" Yet even as she spoke, the
ungodly pain eased from her limb. She exhaled on a
long sigh, meeting his strange hazel eyes.

"Better?" he inquired with a crooked smile.

"Yes. But I'm dead."

"You speak well for one decaying."

"And you speak well for a rogue."

He'd released her leg. She felt his eyes, and knew
again that her shift did nothing to conceal her. She
looked down quickly, alarmed when the heat seemed

to return to her, when she couldn't breathe quite normally, when she feared again that this was a taste of wanting...

A man. This man. A masked rogue who had seized her in the forest. An outlaw, a renegade.

So much worse than you, hmm, Lady Kate? she mocked herself.

If she was to be touched, this was the man she would want to touch her.

She thought again that she was losing her mind, feeling such intense emotions for a stranger. A man who wore a mask. He could be hideously scarred.

It wouldn't matter.

"Well!" he said, rising suddenly and swiftly. "I've business about."

"More people to waylay and rob?" she asked politely.

"The payment of your ransom," he informed her.

"Ah!"

"I know that you are anxious to quit our company."

She lowered her head in silent agreement.

"I'd hoped to make arrangements today, but it seems you'll be among us another night. Do you still swear that you'll not attempt to escape again?"

She hesitated.

"I swore to Beth that I would not do so now—"

"Swear to me that you will not do so. And I will swear to you that I will see you safely given over to the Duke of Manning—as long as that remains your wish."

"It will remain my wish," she assured him, determined not to meet his eyes.

"Swear to me. Give me your word."

She didn't look his way. "I swear, I give you my word. If your word is given in turn."

"It is."

She didn't notice that he had left her until she turned to look back to where he had stood. He had gone on a silent tread. She felt the breeze stir, and she was cold. She found her gown and swiftly slipped it over her head, shivering still.

Not much later, Beth came upon her. "Poor dear! You're shaking."

"I'm still damp, so it seems."

"Ah, well, that's easily remedied!" Beth said cheerfully. "Your trunk of clothing has been brought to the hut, you can change into something dry and warm."

Kate was startled to realize that her masked captor had already returned something that was hers. He was, indeed, an intriguing man.

When dusk fell, she sat before the fire in the hut that might have been a hunter's lodge belonging to any great lord. Though it was simply furnished, it had been strongly constructed. The chimney had been well built to take the smoke from the place and leave the warmth inside. She had been surprised to find herself exhausted that afternoon, and she had slept. And though she had gravely thought over her own purpose throughout the day, her nap had been dreamless.

Or free from nightmares, rather. Before sleeping, she had untangled her hair and dried it before the fire. Her brushes and combs had been returned along with her trunk of clothing. She had found herself a fresh linen shift, and a warm woolen gown that sat low upon her shoulders and breasts. A somewhat daring gown.

Yet one she had decided to wear.

Now, brooding and barely awakened from her sleep, she heard the noise of revelry behind the wooden walls of her prison within the forest. Someone played a flute, someone laughed. Others joined in the laughter.

She had sworn not to escape.

She had not sworn that she would lose all sense of curiosity.

She slipped out of the hut, coming through the haphazard array of the other small living quarters. She paused when she reached the clearing before the

buildings, for there tables were laid out, piled high
with plates of meat. Gourds of wine, beer and mead
were set out, as were wooden goblets. But though
there was music and laughter, and though men milled
about speaking and drinking, their feast did not seem
a wanton one. Not the type of drunken melee one
might have expected from a band of outlaws.

Yet even as she watched, she heard someone call
out that "the great lady" had come.

And she watched with a disturbing jab of discom-
fort as a wagon came into the copse and her black-
masked captor stepped quickly forward, sinking low
upon one knee as the door to the wagon swung open
and a woman emerged.

She was swathed in black, as well. She did, indeed, wear such a cloak of black, her head well
veiled, that Kate could see nothing whatsoever of her
face. Yet as she came among the men, they all
cheered, making as much of her as they might of a
queen. She, in turn, was charming, greeting each
man, calling each by name, then lowering her voice
as she chatted longer.

Wine was brought to her, a seat was drawn for her
at the table. The Shadow was given the place of
honor at her side. He took her hand; they spoke ear-
nestly. She drank her wine, then accepted a large
trunk brought out by the men.

Huge Joshua opened the chest. Kate gasped, seeing that it was filled to the rim with gold pieces and precious gems that sparkled vividly even in the soft glow of moonlight.

The Shadow turned, and Kate clamped her hand over her mouth, closing her eyes tightly even as she rued her own carelessness at allowing that rush of air to escape her. She flattened against the hut by which she stood, then realized that no matter how quiet the sound she had made, he had heard something, or perhaps even sensed something.

She couldn't be caught here, she thought.

She pressed against the outer wooden wall of the hut and opened her eyes, ready to rush back to the hut which was her prison.

Yet she could rush nowhere.

For her very first move slammed her against the rock hardness of his chest.

And she gazed into hazel eyes that seemed to sear her with a gold-tinted fury.

Chapter Six

"You gave your word you would make no attempt to escape!" he exclaimed angrily. His arms were braced around her, palms flat against the wood. She realized, as she stuttered for an answer, that though he wore his mask, the black cloth that he had previously banded over his head and hair was gone. She had been right. His hair was dark. Very dark. Rich, thick and flowing.

"You gave your word!" he repeated.

"But I'm not trying to escape—"

"You're not where you're supposed to be."

"I heard the music, I—"

"Were you invited out to join us?"

"No, I wasn't!" she hissed. "I was rudely ignored. But if I had been trying to escape, I would have gone the other way, as would anyone with half a grain of sense!"

"So you were spying on me."

"Oh, you egotistical lout! I was doing no such thing!" she snapped. She shoved against his arm, sliding beneath it to escape his hold and start back for her prison hut. She wasn't surprised to realize that he was walking behind her, following closely. He might claim to accept her word, but he didn't seem prone to believe she'd simply return to her hut for the night.

"You were spying!"

"I wasn't! I don't care what wretched revelry you and your band choose to engage in. I—"

"You were trying to escape?"

"No, damn you. I—was thirsty. I would have enjoyed some wine—"

"There's wine in your lodging quarters, my lady."

"Perhaps there are those among your men I enjoy."

"Oh, really?" he thundered.

"Don't you have a guest?"

"My guest is in the process of leaving. If she were not, she would understand my present difficulty." They had reached the hut. He pushed open the door and nudged her inside with little gentleness. The fire built earlier was crackling warmly in the hearth, casting a subtle glow of light upon the room.

"There is nothing to do with you except watch over you myself like a nursemaid!" he declared.

Kate stood stubbornly just inside the doorway as he walked over to warm his hands.

She ignored his last statement. "Is she your wife?"

"What?" he demanded, spinning back to her.

"The woman here. Is she your wife?"

A slight grin curled his lips beneath his mask. "No, she is not my wife. Whatever would make you think so?"

"You were giving her all your ill-gotten gain!"

"Ah." Dark lashes lowered over his eyes. "I see."

"You wear a mask, hiding your identity. It's quite possible to assume that you are a wealthy man leading a double life. Perhaps a noble fallen upon hard times who must rob from the rich to save his property."

His eyes were on her again. "You didn't fully see the lady?" he inquired.

"And if I did?"

"Foolish question on my part," he muttered. "You would not be asking such questions. Well, my lady, since you are so anxious to get on with your own life and marry the Duke of Manning, you should be grateful that you did not recognize my guest."

"Why? Who is she?"

"It is none of your business, my lady," he informed her firmly. "But suffice it to say that had you recognized her, I'd not have been able to release you. Now, didn't you say that you were seeking some wine? Ah, with company you cared for! Sorry, I'm the only one present!"

"All the more reason for the wine," she murmured, gazing at the door. She was suddenly burning with curiosity to know who the woman had been. He could not seriously mean that she would remain a prisoner here if she was to know the identity of his guest.

He poured wine, offered her a wooden goblet, then drained his own before seating himself at the foot of the bed to draw off his boots and hose.

"Is she your...mistress?"

"Kate!" he said with exasperation. "I cannot tell you her identity. Drink your wine like a good hostage, grow tired and please, for both our sakes, go to sleep."

"Hostages are not supposed to be well behaved."

"Then pretend that it is so."

"Why?"

"Because the consequences will be dire if you do not!"

"Oh? What will those consequences be?" she demanded. "Shall I be in some manner tortured or tormented?"

"Kate, were I to make up for all the torture and torment you have caused me . . . damn you, my lady! Drink your wine!"

She drank her wine, feeling its warmth suffuse her. She set the goblet down, then sat upon the bed, studying his back. So she tortured and tormented him! Well, he had chosen to seize her wagon.

Kate mused, "She couldn't have been someone actually needy. She came in too fine a wagon."

He rose impatiently and poured more wine into her goblet. She stared at him rebelliously. He lifted the goblet to her lips. "Drink."

"You are an impudent man," she said regally.

"And you had best be a quiet woman. Soon. Drink, my lady, that is what you require!"

She'd soon be wearing the wine. Though she hadn't intended to obey him in the least, she found herself drinking it. Again, the warmth seized her. A warmth she wanted. A great restlessness had taken hold of her. She was angry with him. And ridiculously, she was jealous. She didn't want to recognize the emotion, but she did. She wanted to ply him with questions. She wanted to force answers from him. Her mood was frightening. She even longed to argue or fight with him. . . .

Just so long as he remained with her. By her. Close to her.

"Tired?" he asked her, aggravated.

"Not really."

"Well, we are going to sleep."

"Do you sleep with all of your hostages?" she inquired.

He hesitated, staring at her. "I haven't taken that many hostages. However, all my other ladies were just that. Mild mannered, eager to await their ransom. Not a one of them continually tried to wage war against a kni—against a man twice her size. Or tried to run into the forest along with the wolves!"

He took both their goblets and returned them to the table, drawing his black shirt over his head. He stood before her as he had earlier, barefoot, bare chested, clad only in his breeches and mask.

"You take the inside, my lady," he said.

"Why? I've sworn not to escape."

"Because I've said that you must go there."

"You have no rights over me."

"My lady, there is always the possibility that I may have to move quickly in the night."

"Am I to strip?" she asked coolly.

"Only so far as you would care to do so," he told her.

She kicked off her shoes, then discarded her stockings. On a wild, wicked impulse, she drew the wool gown over her head, then stretched her length on the outside of the bed in her linen shift, where he had determined he would sleep.

She gasped when she felt firm hands upon her, lifting her to draw up the covers so that they might settle beneath them, then setting her down where he had commanded her to be. His touch was quickly gone and she was left to stare at the ceiling. The fire was dying out. The shadows on the ceiling and walls were long and dark.

He turned his back to her. She could hear the audible grating sound of his teeth.

"You didn't answer me!" she whispered. "Was that woman your mistress?"

He flipped over again, up on an elbow this time, staring down at her in the darkening shadows. "I warned you that you don't wish to know the answers to your questions. I cannot imagine Lord Gregory's daughter leading the life of a forest dweller!"

She lowered her lashes. For a moment, time rushed back again with painful clarity. She could remember being blackened with smudge, running. She had been burned, and she was in pain, but the horror within her heart went so much deeper. And she had run into a man on the hill, staring into the wind. The man had been Lord Gregory. She had never met him before, but there had been something in his face, some pain and kindness there, and she had managed to tell him, and beg him to come back with her....

"Poor lass, poor wee lass! But this world can be filled with wretched men! You can't go back there, child, don't you see? They will want you dead, as well. Your father's title is what that murdering imp of Satan is after, and if he realizes that you are alive..."

Lord Gregory had made his decision then. "Listen to me, child. My own dear little Kate lies dead this morning in her room. You must become Kate, become my own. I know that your good father will guard my little one in heaven, and therefore, I will guard you here on earth."

Well, she had been Lord Gregory's daughter from that day on. In every sense of the word. She had loved him dearly. He had helped her grow. In time, she had come to protect him, as well, to guard his interests, to keep his fortune and estates together. She had worked terribly hard, knowing all the while that she would have her revenge.

But not while he lived. Still, the desire for justice had been so strong within her! *No matter what it cost,* she had to reach Manning.

And still...

That strange streak remained with her this evening. The urge to press and make demands, to hear his voice . . .

To remain close.

"Whether I know if she is or isn't your mistress gives me no earthly idea of her identity," Kate said.

Outside, a cloud had perhaps covered the moon. Inside, the firelight filtered low. They called him the Shadow, and he seemed a shadow now, a presence in the darkness. One that seemed to overpower all else in the room. She could feel him, breathe his scent. He was watching her, she knew, in the darkness. And he saw more than she could.

"She is not my mistress."

"How generous."

"My lady, what mistress could you imagine who would allow her lover to disappear on the trail of a beautiful young woman, and hold her prisoner in his bed through the night?"

"Perhaps she believes in your honor. Perhaps—"

"Perhaps you should cease prying."

"Perhaps I am curious—"

She was startled when she was suddenly silenced in a way she had not imagined. His mouth suddenly molded upon her own, bringing with it a shattering, evocative liquid heat.

He did not hold her, he did not force her to lie still. Yet had chains bound her to the bed, she could not have been any more his prisoner. He tasted of wine, of the forest, of the creek, of the pulse and desire that had riddled her throughout the day. His mouth moved with pure seduction, lips commanding and coercive, tongue so insinuative. A brief desperation seized her, and she knew that he would leave her be now, if it was her choice. She played on dangerous ground. There would be no hesitant lover's kisses here, the game they played would be for real and she was frighteningly aware of that fact and still, she had no desire to move, no will to stop the ardor of his kiss, which grew more impassioned with each passing second.

Now he did hold her. Hands upon her arms, lips upon her throat. Tongue teasing, finding a pulse point. Lips falling against the thin linen material of her gown, finding her breast beneath it, taunting the nipple with wicked little licks until he took it fully within his mouth.

Her fingers wound into his hair; she trembled like an autumn leaf blown upon the forest floor. Even as his mouth caressed and seduced her, she became aware of the full length of his body, the wall of his chest against her abdomen and hips, the length of his legs, the swell of his sex. Feeling him seemed to spiral a new wave of sensation throughout her, something twisting, writhing, finding root in an intimate, secretive place she had not known could be so awakened....

She burned. Were she made of bubbling, boiling oil, she could feel no more alive, her blood heated, her limbs alive. His teeth grazed her flesh. His hand moved over the curve of her hip, slipped beneath the hem of her shift, stroked against the bareness of her flesh. She nearly shrieked as the startling sensations ripped throughout her, yet she choked back all sound until he was above her, whispering against her lips, "You are quiet now, my lady."

His mask remained in place. He stared down at her, and despite the darkness, she could see the hazel-gold glitter in his eyes.

"Quiet now, when to speak might serve you well!"

To speak...

She could not begin to do so. He kissed her again, his lips just brushing hers. Again. Again. Still searching out her eyes.

"No protest?" he demanded.

"Perhaps... you're an honorable man."

"Honorable men have their limits. Sweet Jesu, I have found mine!" She felt the pad of his thumb against her lower lip, felt the touch of his lips once again. His tongue, entering her, his hands... upon her. The shift was wound around her waist. She wasn't aware that he tore it, yet it was suddenly ripped asunder. His naked flesh was fierce against her own.

She played no game! she reminded herself. What happened here was real. He had commanded her to speak, to protest, and she could suddenly find no words. Her arms snaked around him, her fingers threading into the inky darkness of his hair once more as if she could hold tight while some wild, reckless ride took place through the night, dancing across the wind. Again he touched her, again and again. A palm rubbing over her breast, hand flowing over her hip, fingers stroking her thigh. His eyes on hers, while that same erotic touch entered within her intimately.

She tried to twist and turn, unwilling to meet his eyes, his gaze. His demand. "You will have me now, my lady?"

She murmured nothing, trying again to bury herself within the spill of her own hair, within the strength of his body. His voice was suddenly harsh.

"You have told me it's your wish to be turned over to Manning as his bride."

"Aye!"

His face came close, eyes gleaming beneath the mask. "No force here, my lady. No rape, no rudeful use of a hostage. Despite what tomorrow will bring, you will have me now?''

She gasped, dismayed that he would wring such an admission from her. Yet she felt him, felt the fierce heat of his body, the taut strength and demand of it, the feel of his touch within her own. No coercion, but seduction! she longed to cry out. For his touch moved within her, rotated, played, discovered . . .

Indeed, aroused, seduced. She couldn't breathe, couldn't reason . . .

''No!'' she cried out suddenly, but his lips found hers.

''Yes!'' he whispered against them.

''Yes!''

''Ah, lady!''

Then again his lips were everywhere. Kissing, seducing, demanding. His hands moved and manipulated her. Brought her against him, against the force of his chest. She yearned, she longed, she ached. The night was filled with darkness, with shadow, and yet within her there was a bursting light. It was madness, such sweet madness. She tossed, she writhed. She twisted from his most intimate caress and was dragged back to it, choking, gasping and yearning again, decrying his intimacy, yet climbing ever higher atop a precipice. . . .

He paused, rising above her, thrusting apart her thighs with the force of his knees. Staring down at her again. "You've called me rogue, my lady, but I give you this—one word, and I will turn away."

"Please..."

"Please what? Have it that you are forced by a renegade? Nay, lady, it will be of your doing as well as my own, yet from this point on..."

She shivered violently. "I have said I—"

"Yes?"

"That I will have you."

"Say that you want me."

"You are a wretched highwayman—"

"Indeed. Say that you want me."

"Thief! Abductor of innocents—"

"My sweet innocent, say that you want me."

She whispered.

"What?"

"I want you. Damn you..."

It was all; it was enough. She wasn't quick enough or prepared enough to still her shriek when he first thrust into her. He stilled it with his kiss, with his gentle words. He didn't cease his invasion, yet held so still so long, cradling her, then moving ever so slightly, rocking...

Creating a rhythm, thrusting deeply, withdrawing slowly. Again... slowly. Slowly. Until...

He began to move like the night wind. Shadow upon shadow. Within her again and again, creating a tempest that screamed within her. The yearning began again. The desperation deep inside. The desire to touch fire, touch a star, feel an explosion. She ached, and knew that surcease would come. And still she reached, and writhed and danced with the Shadow's rhythm. Felt him, felt him inside her. Filling her. One with her, thrusting, stroking, slow, fast, slow...fast, faster, faster...

The heavens split, and starlight spilled down upon her. That for which she reached was tasted. Its sweetness filled her, permeated her, seized her with such volatile strength that she was barely aware of his hands still upon her, his force, his shuddering, the final sweep within her that brought waves and waves of liquid heat coursing from his body into hers....

He fell to the side, lay there. Staring up into the darkness above them.

"Damn you!" he said huskily after a moment.

It wasn't what she had expected.

"Why?" she demanded furiously.

"Because now I am a defiler of an innocent! And this mask is itching me."

"Take it off!" she whispered.

He spun on her again, bronze body glistening with a sheen of perspiration. "Would you have me take it off? Would you remain here in the forest then?"

"I—can't!"

"What if I force you?"

"You would not!"

"How can you be so certain?"

"Because—"

"Because why?"

"Because you wouldn't even...you wouldn't..." She felt her cheeks growing flushed, nay, the whole of her body reddening. "I did bring this about!" she admitted. "Yet you would have given me any escape tonight."

"Perhaps. And perhaps things will not change. Perhaps I would not be so generous again."

She stared at him. "You don't understand. I—I must go on to Manning. I made a vow."

He groaned. "A vow would mean nothing to the likes of Manning."

"It is my vow."

"Then don't suggest that I shed the mask again."

She turned away from him, suddenly shivering. His warmth was gone from her. He lay stiffly at her side. She tried to fight the misery seeping into her, and hold tight to moments of splendor she had discovered.

"Why are you so angry with me?" she whispered after a moment. "I..."

"You what?" he asked curtly.

"I wanted you," she said simply. "You are unique, you are honorable... and I wanted to touch something that I might never touch again...."

Her voice faded, yet by the time it had died away, he had pulled her against him. He held her close, his stroke against her tender as time passed, as the embers in the fire died even lower.

Then subtly, that touch changed. And the passion returned, and the demand. He seemed ever more urgent now, leading her along a windswept trail of wildness and hunger, pulling her to a brink, bringing her down, sweeping her so high she thought that she would die when the explosive sweetness shuddered through her once more.

Again, he held her. Again, time passed. She awoke to a cock crowing, and realized that he lay awake by her side.

"Is it still your desire to be returned to Manning?" he asked her.

She looked away from him. "I have to be returned to Manning!" she whispered.

She didn't look into his eyes, but she felt his disappointment, felt it as it came over her in great sweeping waves.

He rose upon her, and she had no recourse but to meet his glittering stare. "Then I shall have Manning's bride one more time, and this morning, my lady, I'll truly not give a damn if you're willing or nay!"

Chapter Seven

He had left her. Made love to her with both passion and tenderness, no matter what his threat, yet then...he had left her. Without saying a single word.

Beth had come to tell her later in the day that her escort from the forest had been arranged. The Shadow had not demanded a ransom for her, Beth explained, but since she was a lady with a considerable good family behind her, she was free to take her clothing, but the rest of her dowry would remain behind.

As the morning passed, she felt more and more like crying. When she wept, she grew furious with herself. She was disastrously hurt over his treatment of her, when he was her abductor! She told herself again and again that he was a villain, a thief and an outlaw. He'd no right to judge her. Even if she hadn't been betrothed to the Duke of Manning, what right had he to imagine that she would join a band of renegades?

But she would have, she realized. She would have stayed with him, and given up her title, land and position, if she didn't have to find justice for the past.

She couldn't have fallen in love with him.

But she had.

And it hurt desperately that he was so disappointed in her.

In the early afternoon, Joshua came for her. He and the others would ride with her to a certain tree in the far north of the forest, and there be met by the Duke of Manning's men.

"Where is the Shadow?" she asked when he escorted her out.

"By the creek, my lady, but we must hurry—"

She ran quickly toward the place where they had laughed together. He was there, indeed, mask in place, one booted foot against a root as he stared out over the water with unseeing eyes until he heard her, and quickly turned to see her, frowning as she ran toward him.

"Whoa!" he murmured, catching her when she would have fallen against him.

"I don't want to go, I have to go. I know I can't make you understand. But I would never betray you.

I don't understand what you're doing here, but I—I believe in you."

He smiled very slowly beneath the mask. "Stay!" he said softly.

"By God, I swear, I wish that I could!" she told him.

He pulled from his finger a silver ring with a single small whitish stone within it. "Moonstone, for we met upon the hunter's moon," he said huskily. Then he began to speak quickly. "If you should ever need me, there is a man named Peter who tends the horses at Castle Manning. See that he brings the ring to me. I will be with you."

She threw herself into his arms once again, holding him tightly. She stared up into his face. "I will remember your eyes always."

He kissed her. Very long. Very hard. She trembled as he held her. Trembled, and remembered.

At last, she broke away from him and ran to the wagon where Joshua and several of the other men were waiting to begin their ride through the forest. Beth was there, waiting to hug her fiercely before seeing her into the wagon. "This isn't right. It isn't right at all," Beth fretted.

"I have to go," Kate insisted. "But I thank you deeply for your concern, and God knows, perhaps our paths will cross again one day."

Joshua closed the door to the wagon and they started out. Kate pulled the drape and looked out, disturbed to see that Beth was watching her go with distress still puckering her kindly face.

Kate leaned back in the wagon. It was madness, all madness. The outlaws seemed so good, and the nobles could often be so evil.

And who, she taunted herself, was *she* to judge either?

She didn't know how long they rode; she had leaned back in misery throughout the journey. It was evening when the wagon pulled to a halt and Joshua tapped upon the door before opening it. "Manning Castle lies ahead, my lady. Though we won't be far if you fear danger, we leave you here so that Manning's men do not betray this trust and seek to hang us all."

Manning Castle.

She bit her lip, accepting Joshua's massive arms as he helped her from the wagon. She stared through breaks in the trees and could see the fortress that rose high upon a moated hill. It had originally been one of King William's castles, built by the conqueror toward the end of his realm in his never-ending struggle to rule the people he had bested. Normans—fresh off the conquering field—had been seneschals of the castle for the first fifty years. Then the original line had died out, and in 1160 the title of Fifth Duke of Manning had been given to a distant cousin of Richard's father, Henry II, for services in battle.

That family had died out, as well.

Comte Phillippe Rousseau had then received the title. And after him, his son and namesake.

The castle was a bastion with walls that gleamed in the rising moonlight. A moat circled it, a drawbridge granting the only entry. Perched upon its hill, it seemed almost mythic, like King Arthur's fabled home. A place of enchantment, perhaps. The lands surrounding it were rich. Crops flourished. Sheep and goats thrived.

"My lady?" Joshua said, clearing his throat.

She smiled and winked at him. "Nothing can harm me now, good Joshua. I've already been accosted in the forest, you know."

"Ah, sweet lady, if only you knew . . ."

"I wish I did know, Joshua. What is it that he cannot trust me to know?"

"I fear it's not for me to tell, my lady."

She stood upon her tiptoes and kissed him on the cheek, offering him a massive hug. "I can't believe I am saying this! I will miss you all sorely."

"Walk deep into the forest, and you will need miss us no more!" he assured her.

"I have to go," she said.

Joshua smiled. "What is it that you cannot trust *him* to know, my lady?"

She smiled, lowering her head. "Go quickly, Joshua. Those men the Shadow injured may be with the Duke of Manning when he comes. I'm sure he'd gladly hang the lot of you!"

Joshua gravely remounted his giant gelding. She smiled at him, Gawain and Thomas, who had been her escorts here. They all looked at her with the greatest sorrow, then turned their mounts. In seconds, they had disappeared into the forest.

A timely retreat, for in just seconds, she heard voices.

"We must move quickly now if we'd take any of those wretched fellows."

"Lady Kate!"

Horsemen burst into view, so many of them that at first Kate could not ascertain their numbers. They were all armed and in armor, mounted on huge destriers, well-trained war-horses.

She saw then that the man who had called out to her was none other than Sir Waylon. He rode at the side of a younger man.

Manning.

Powerfully built, he sat his saddle tall. His eyes were a startling blue, his hair a corn silk blond. He was lean and hard, a striking man. Yet there were curious twists to his mouth and chin, a glitter about the eyes. She wondered if the evil in him was apparent, or if she just saw it through the mirror of his eyes, lurking in his soul.

"Lady Kate!"

She was to wed him, yet she had met him very few times. She had set her bait, greeted him as a lady must and let it be known that Lord Gregory had left her wealthy; her dower portion of his estate was extensive. She was aware that she had been something of a prize within the marriage game. She hadn't a title comparable to Manning's, but she had great wealth, no pockmarks, all her own teeth, and she was relatively young.

Often, healthy, strong lords, young men prone to a young man's fancy, wed women twice their ages, just as young lasses were often given over to doddering old widowers. Ah, but such was the structure of their feudal society, where both wealth and power were forever sought upon various quests.

"My lady, my dear, dear lady!" Phillippe Rousseau, Duke of Manning, said, leaping down from his destrier, hurrying to her. He took both her hands within his own, searching her for any sign of harm. "That this should have befallen you! The forests will be cleared of these wretched outlaws who try to rule the country! I swear, I will find these fellows who seized you and they will pay a deadly price, I do so swear it! Tell me, lady, were you harmed?'' he asked.

She wondered if his concern might be real, or rather, if he didn't rue the fact that something intended to become his might have been used by another.

"Nay, my lord, I was not badly treated, merely held until arrangements were made for you to come for me here,'' she told him.

Manning nodded with irritation, glancing up at Sir Waylon. "I had heard tales about these outlaws. That they were curiously chivalrous at times. My men have assured me that their leader spoke to them with civility—until all but crippling them. Still, they are thieves, mannerly rogues, but outlaws just the same, and hanging will be far too good for them when they are caught. And I will catch them. Sir Waylon and I have been mapping out the forest. It will just be a matter of time before I find their stronghold. But you will discover that you have chosen a man of action, my lady. I plan to hang them for you before our wedding, which will take place next Saturday.''

"My lord, perhaps these men are living in hard times, and rob those in better circumstance than themselves to survive. Please, you mustn't seek to find them on my behalf!''

His eyes glittered; his lips twisted. He smiled in a curious way that brought back memories, that nearly made her cry out loud.

"Oh, I will find them and hang them. When I have had done with them. I will find them, retrieve what they have stolen from me, and they will pay."

That smile! That look in his eyes . . .

She could almost see flames, smell the smoke, the scent of burning flesh . . .

To her distress, she discovered that the world seemed to be wavering. She never fainted, never passed out. She was strong and willful and cunning when she needed be.

But still . . .

The world swam.

He caught her. Phillippe Rousseau caught her. She instantly became very much awake and aware.

Her skin crawled!

Oh, God, she had thought that she could do this! That she could actually wed him if need be, become his wife to await the proper moment . . .

But that was before. Before she had discovered passion and longing and tenderness, wanting, craving, aching.

Before she had known the Shadow.

"I'm quite fine," she cried out, steadying herself, loathing the fact that he held her still. She couldn't wrench from his hold, repugnant though it was. She could not!

He sat her atop his destrier, mounting behind her. Again, it seemed that her skin crawled with vermin.

She had ridden so with the Shadow.

But now...now she felt the loathing. Felt she might be sick if the ride went on too long.

But it did not. Soon they had come past the fields beyond the castle walls. Ridden the sweeping green slope. The drawbridge was lowered, and they trotted into the courtyard. A groom rushed forward to take the horse's reins. Phillippe Rousseau brought her down from the horse, carrying her.

She pressed against him, desperate to gain her own feet. "I am fine, my lord!" she assured him.

"You have been through great distress. I'll see that you're brought directly to your room, that warmed wine is brought to you."

She forced herself to smile. She entered the castle keep with him, trembling as she came into the great hall, saw the huge table there, the massive chairs before the fire, the wolfhounds gathered there. An older man in a green-and-gold livery came forward, his head bowed to Phillippe. "Your lady has come. All is made ready for her. My lady, welcome to Manning Castle. I am Evan and will seek to serve you in any way."

The world was spinning again; she would not let it do so. Evan had clouded blue, weary eyes and a tired, worn, sad face. She wanted to reach out, touch his cheeks.

"Thank you, Evan. I am exhausted, and would like to rest in my room."

"With your permission, my lord?" Evan said.

"Aye, show my lady her rooms. Kate, you must rest. You seem so very weary. Tomorrow, you will meet our priest and see your new home."

"As you wish, my lord," she murmured. She lowered her head, anxious to follow Evan away from him.

"Wait!" he commanded suddenly.

She paused. She felt his hand upon her shoulder. He turned her. Again she met his eyes. She shuddered inwardly, and prayed her revulsion would not be obvious for she realized he intended to kiss her.

"A kiss for your betrothed," he said, lifting her chin.

His touch, his lips...seemed all but blasphemous. Dear God, but there was something so salacious about him! Something in the way he looked at her that seemed far more indecent than any intimacy she had shared in the forest.

He is a murderer, she reminded herself. *A foul, cruel murderer who did not care about the agonizing fate he cast upon a score of people.*

A murderer. And he kissed her. As if he would devour her. His hands were biting upon her. His power seemed brutal. She feared for a moment that she would be raped then and there in the hallway.

But he suddenly drew away, breathing heavily. "You are a beauty!" he whispered. "A temptress, a morsel of sheer perfection! So I would have our marriage beyond hint of any taint. The sons you bear me will be legitimate issue."

Again she forced her lips into a smile. His face was so cold! A mask, twisted, created. She had to get away from him. "Aye, my lord!" she said, her voice very low. "Our marriage must be legitimate, legally consummated when the vows are stated. A week is not a long time, my lord."

He smiled. Yet even so, the look upon his face was rapacious. Evil. What would he have planned for his bride? She had to get away!

"My lord, I am exhausted," she murmured.

"Evan, take her upstairs. She will need to rest well this week. I will not have her weary for her wedding night."

At last she was able to flee from him, following Evan at a rapid pace up the stairs.

So rapid, she almost passed him by.

"Lady Kate!" Phillippe called from below.

She paused, biting her lip, looking downward.

"It's good to see you so at home. One would think you know the place already!"

She laughed. Was the sound of her laughter as uneasy as the quivering feeling within her? She turned again, knowing then that he would watch her until she completely disappeared along the final twist of the stairway leading to the rooms above.

"One would think you knew the way, my lady!" Evan said, panting and wheezing slightly at their pace.

"Ah, Evan, it is just that I am so very weary," she answered.

"Your room lies just ahead."

"Does it?" she asked, coming to a sudden, dead halt and staring ahead.

"Aye. Once, those rooms were the nursery." He cocked his head and smiled a wistful smile. "When the old master was here! He and his lady loved their wee ones, so they did! Alas, what God giveth, God taketh . . . still, my fair Lady Kate, you are a ray of hope. Perhaps the sound of young laughter will fill these cold hallways once again."

He pushed open the door. The room was a nursery no longer. A large bed sat atop a dais, and a massive trunk sat at the foot of the bed. A lady's dressing table with a beautiful mirror was across from the bed, while a washstand and screen stood near the window.

"Will you be comfortable here, my lady? Is there anything that I can get you?" Evan asked.

She shook her head. "I will be quite comfortable here. Perhaps you would be so good as to tell me where the duke's chamber lies?"

"Yonder, across the hallway, is the master's set of chambers. Now, as it has always been. Aye, lady, I was born here, I'll die here. The bed remains the same there as the day I was born! Now, your wine mulls over the fire, there. The pitcher is filled with fresh water. If there is anything else, my lady?"

"You have thought of everything, Evan."

He bowed his head. "I hope you will be happy."

She nodded.

He left the room, closing the door behind him. She leaned against it.

Happy.

Silent tears streamed down her cheeks as she stared into the firelit room.

Chapter Eight

Her third night at the castle, the Duke of Manning hosted a feast to introduce his intended bride to the lesser nobility and gentry residing at nearby estates.

The great hall was filled to capacity. Kate had sat with Evan part of the day, helping him with seating arrangements. There were numerous counts, viscounts and barons among the guests, and several knights and their ladies, not to mention the clergy and younger sons of wealthy noblemen.

Kate had little interest in the occasion herself; she didn't think she'd be anxious to meet any man who was a friend of her intended husband.

Throughout the time she had been at the castle, she had been torn. Amazed by the complexity of the memories that haunted her, dismayed by the power Phillippe seemed to hold. She quickly realized that many people within his household despised him. But he was the master. And he was obeyed, and protected.

One of his men tasted his food at all times before he ate—he could have no fear that he might die by poisoning. His guards and knights were lawfully in his service and duty-bound to obey and protect him, and he was never alone. Indeed, as he dressed for the evening's festivities, she was at war with herself. What had she imagined? That she would come here, and that he would obligingly walk near a parapet and perhaps even fall from it for her, so that she would not even have to lift a finger to do the deed? Keep her hands free from blood?

And keep her from the hangman's noose?

She had set out with courage and resolution. Now it seemed clear that her only hope would be to slay him while he slept. And she would only have that opportunity...

If she went through with the wedding. The blood drained from her at the thought. But time was marching on. And every day when she walked the halls within the castle, she could remember. Her father's gentle voice as he read aloud. Her mother's laughter...

She could do whatever it took.

She dressed in silver, a veil of it falling from her head, her tunic and shift the same shimmering color, embroidered with delicate golden threads. When she heard the first arrivals in the hall below, she hurried down. She was anxious that Phillippe not come for her. It was best to keep her distance from him. Though he didn't seem to care that others saw him touch her, he was worse with his roaming hands and lascivious kisses on those few occasions he had been alone with her.

Alone...

Except for his nearby guards.

Tonight, men and women gathered everywhere within the hall. Phillippe found her quickly, taking her arm possessively. "Our estates have not been so far apart that you might not already be acquainted with many of our guests, my dear."

"Perhaps. I'm afraid we seldom entertained, especially in later years. Lord Gregory was sadly ill for a long time, as you are aware."

"Of course. Come here. Ah! My dear, Count and Lady Langley."

She nodded, dipping slightly at the introduction. The count was young, with eyes that quickly appraised her. Lady Langley was shaped like a bean pole and had sadly bucked teeth, but she offered Kate a friendly smile, and Kate returned it quickly. "Once you've wed and made the castle your home, I hope we'll see one another frequently. We've a manor not far to the east," Lady Langley told her. "It offers little in comfort compared to the castle, but we do have a wonderfully warm if small solar. It's a fine place to work upon tapestry."

"I thank you for the invitation," Kate began, but Phillippe was already moving on. She met old men and young men. Rich men and men with sagging fortunes. She moved about the hall continually.

There was one couple she did not meet. They were both tall and dark. The woman was beautiful, slender, with almost exotic features and an incredibly graceful way of moving. The man wore a plumed hat that angled well over his face. She could see only that he was powerfully built, yet agile.

Somehow, the pair always seemed to be elsewhere when she was moved about by Phillippe.

At last it was time to dine. People were seated at the tables, arranged in a horseshoe formation carefully, by rank and favor. Toward the end of the meal, Kate noted that the extremely handsome dark-haired couple was seated low down one of the prongs of the horseshoe.

She loathed beginning a conversation with Phillippe, but she leaned closer to him and forced one of her frozen smiles. "Who are the young man and woman far down the line there?"

"Where—ah, there! The man is Count Aryn Lakewood. You will not associate with him."

"But you've invited him here!" she said.

Muscles tightened in his jaw. "He is lesser nobility, long descended from a Saxon family that somehow managed to keep its title, while losing all else. He is nothing."

"But then—"

"He is one of the most talented swordsmen alive. I have asked him into my service and he has thus far refused my offers. Mark my words. I will have him."

"Why have you asked him to ride for you if you so despise him?"

Phillippe stared at her. A vein pulsed in his throat. His hand fell upon hers and she nearly cried out, for it seemed that he would soon crush bone. "You must be aware, my beauty, that I take a wife for her riches and her person. Your destiny in life is to serve and please me, fair lady, not to question me!"

She snatched her hand away, furious, dazed, humiliated.

At the first possible opportunity, she escaped the head table, desperate for a moment's freedom. She left the great hall and the keep itself behind, running to the stables. There, in the darkness and shadows, she stroked the noses of giant destriers, speaking softly. "He does not let a bride remain fooled, even before he has slipped a different noose around her finger.''

"So why would a bride take such a man?''

The question, coming from the darkness, startled her. She swung around.

It was Count Aryn himself. He leaned against a far stall. She recognized him by the plumed hat, despite the shadows and darkness surrounding her.

She did not respond to the question. "How dare you spy on me, my lord!'' she said indignantly.

"I did not come to spy.''

"Then why—''

"From that hall, my lady, I needed air.''

She watched him curiously. "Phillippe is the duke, your overlord,'' she said. "Why do you refuse to serve him?''

He walked past her. She could still see nothing of his face, except that it seemed finely enough sculpted. He scratched the nose of a bay mare. "He is not my overlord.''

"But—''

"My property is small, ancient to my family, yet granted to me by the dowager queen, Eleanor of Aquitane. I serve her and the king. Now, I have answered your question. You have not answered mine. Why do you marry Phillippe?''

"It is my will to do so.''

She still couldn't see his features. Yet she sensed something. Sensed his . . . disappointment.

"Perhaps you should return to your wife."

"I am not married."

"That beautiful woman—"

"Is my sister, Rowaina. Good night, my lady. May your—dreams—be pleasant."

He bowed to her, then strode from the stables with a long gait. She looked after him uneasily, wondering still if he might be in Phillippe's employ, if someone might have guessed more about her than was apparent.

She hurried to the keep, swiftly finding her way into the great hall. There she mingled with the crowd, greeting those she had so recently met. She was startled when she met Phillippe's eyes across the hall.

They were the eyes of the man she had seen so many years ago. Eyes that had been gleeful at the sight of fire, of death.

He came to her, taking her arm. "Where have you been?"

"Among your friends."

"I did not see you."

"Perhaps you did not look hard enough."

"I have decided that the wedding must be tomorrow. I can wait no longer."

"It cannot be tomorrow!"

"Why?"

"I have not—said my proper prayers!"

"Then the day after. No later. We will wed, and you will be mine."

"But—"

"It will be as I have said, my love, for your beauty has possessed me. Unless you would be my mistress before becoming my wife and do so this very eve, I give you only until your day of prayer is done."

"Then you will excuse me now, so that I may begin to pray!"

With those words, she escaped him, running up the stairs, until she reached her room.

Oh, God! She had but lost time. And now, now what to do?

"Did you see her, my lord?" Beth demanded anxiously, coming behind Aryn as he entered the hut, throwing down his scabbard, sword and plumed hat.

"Aye!" he said irritably, slumping into a chair before the fireplace.

"And?"

"She is still determined to marry the bastard!" he said, shaking his head in disbelief.

"Did she know you?" Beth asked softly.

"I stayed in the shadows."

"Perhaps if she realized that . . ."

"That I am poor Saxon nobility, the remnants of a once-great clan? Then she would forsake the duke, his castle and all his riches?" he asked bitterly.

"Now, my lord, you judge her harshly, I think."

"I wish I did. Beth, you tell me, why wed such a man if it isn't for gain, for wealth, for prestige?"

"I don't know, my lord, I admit," Beth said unhappily. "Except that... Well, my lord, there's something that's bothered me since the girl first came here."

"What?"

"Why, 'tis the girl herself, I think. I delivered Lord Gregory's daughter, I did. I saw the poor wee thing many times. She was a sickly lass. They had thought they'd lost her once when she was young. She was a pretty thing, sweet, but not of this world... she was almost saintly, as if she expected the angel of death to be sweeping her up any minute from the rigors of the earth. When I saw Lady Kate..."

"What?" Aryn demanded, rising from his chair, taking Beth by the shoulders. "What?"

"Oh, Count Aryn, it is so... it couldn't be!"

"What couldn't be?" My God, the woman was going to make him insane!

"They were both Kate."

"Both who, Beth? Speak to me, make sense of this now!"

She had stared at the flames, seeing nothing. Now suddenly, her eyes seemed to focus upon his. "Lord Gregory had a young Kate . . . and the Duke of Manning."

"Beth, you've taken leave of your senses! She's about to wed the Duke of Manning!'

"Not this Duke of Manning, my lord. He's an upstart, as well you know. The title was given to his father when the last duke perished—with all his family—in a horrible fire. There'd been him, his wife, three children. The flames were so intense . . . there were, I believe, twelve corpses found, yet so horribly burned that . . ."

"Wait! Castle Manning has never burned—"

"Nay, it was another of the duke's manor houses that burned to the ground. His summer home. There was talk at the time that perhaps the Rousseaus had managed to do something to the family since Rousseau was so quick to seek the title from the king— 'twas King Henry II then—for services he had done him against the French king. Oh, my lord! The home that burned was quite near to the ancestral home of Lord Gregory! But they did spend most of their time at Castle Manning. In fact, the dear child was born there, brought up there!"

His eyes stared into hers, as fiercely wild as fire. "You think that—"

"Yes! One of the Duke of Manning's children was a Kathryn, as well. A glorious little wee lass."

"Kate," he said. He glared at Beth. "By God, she does intend to marry him. She wants to do so. She is determined to get close to him. To kill him!"

"Sweet Jesu, what if she fails?" Beth asked.

She awoke to a great commotion in the courtyard below. When she came to the arrow slit to look out, she saw an older man down upon his knees, his head bowed.

Phillippe Rousseau was soundly beating him with the backside of his sword. "The beast shall have to be put down now because of your carelessness! The beast served me far better than you, my man. God! Begone from my sight before I forget I am a Christian lord and slit your throat!"

The old man tried to stagger up. He nearly made it to his feet, then he fell facedown into the dirt. A young girl, a beauty of perhaps fifteen, went hurrying to him.

Kate found herself watching Rousseau, watching his face. He smiled as he went to the girl, wrenching her up by her hair. "You haven't the time, wench, to spill tears here!" His voice lowered, yet still carried up the castle walls. "You'll serve me come this afternoon, or see him more wretchedly beaten. For now, you will see to the Lady Kate!"

He released her hair, all but throwing her back down.

The girl knelt by the old man. "Father, let me help you...."

Kate turned from the window, hurriedly washing and dressing. Within minutes she heard a knocking on her door. She opened it to find the lovely young blond girl. She bobbed to her quickly, dark eyes downcast. "My lady, I am May, here to serve as your woman."

Kate caught her arm and drew her into the room. She immediately closed the door and stared at the girl, demanding, "Does that happen often?"

Startled, the girl stared at her. She lowered her head. "My lady, I don't know what—"

"The duke nearly beat your father to death below and you do not know what I mean?"

When May stared back at her, her eyes were filled with tears. "I dare say naught against him—"

"You may say whatever you will here!" Kate assured her.

"It used to be worse!" May said suddenly. "When Phillippe's father was alive. Then they both beat us. Now it is just Phillippe...."

"Don't worry, I had occasion to meet the duke's father, as well," Kate told her. "I was delighted to hear he met a ghastly death."

"On a boar hunt. He was skewered through."

"His son was with him?"

"But I don't think Phillippe suffered any from the experience," May said. "In fact I think..."

"What?"

Tears again streamed down her face. "You're to be his bride, his wife! What if you are but baiting me, seeking to bring to him all that I know and suspect?"

"May, May, poor creature! I would rather wed Satan himself, I swear it. Finish what you were saying."

May wiped her face with the backs of her hands. "I think—I think that Phillippe somehow managed to see that his father was unhorsed and killed by the boar. He—he wanted the title and the riches for himself, you see. And he had learned all about cruelty from his father."

"He learned it at a very young age," Kate murmured. She inhaled deeply.

"If only God would..." May began.

"Aye?"

"See that Phillippe perished, as well."

"Perhaps God needs earthly assistance."

"You mean that you—"

"He is always surrounded by guards."

"I know of a potion that can be slipped into his wine," May said. "Oh, God, he would skin me alive...."

"Not you, me. You've only to bring me the potion."

"Oh, God!"

"Will you do so?"

"Yes, yes! Oh, for the sake of Peter at the very least, yes!"

"Peter!" Kate exclaimed.

"Ah, my father, Peter, is head groom."

Kate quickly looked down. Peter! The man to whom the Shadow had suggested she go.

"Will your father be all right?"

"Aye! Barely. Bruised black-and-blue about the whole of his body, he is! I'll go now for the potion."

On an impulse, Kate pulled off the ring the Shadow had given her. "Give this to your father for me. Tell him...tell him that he will not suffer long."

Kate had the vial of poison in her pocket when she went to the chapel. She was down upon her knees, her hands folded in prayer.

She didn't pray. She stared.

Thus far, the chapel had been used for but one burial, for those who had died previously had been interred in the crypts below.

But Jon Pierre Rousseau, father to Phillippe, lay within a glass coffin on the altar before her, his body gilded, forever in prayer.

The irony of her being here was such that she could not even ask God's help in the murder she was about to commit. Not that she believed God would really help her commit murder, even against such a man as Rousseau. She knelt here because it gave her time.

Yet she suddenly knew she was not alone. Phillippe stood at the rear of the small nave, watching her. "Come, lady, cease your praying to dine with me."

She rose on shaking knees, turned, smiled. "Aye, my lord. Do we dine alone?"

"In my rooms. Indeed, alone. We'll pray together, if it's your wish, that God grants us healthy sons."

Stepping into his rooms swept her back in time. She could see her parents upon the huge, four-poster, elaborately draped bed. She could see her mother's wildly flowing mane of hair, her soft white gown, her sweet smile when she welcomed her children to crawl into the massive bed and be hugged there. She could hear her father's laughter, his rich voice resonating when he told them stories, spinning tales of faeries, goblins and the like.

"Wine, my dear?" Phillippe asked.

"Yes!" she gasped, then spun around. "Yes, definitely, my lord. Do let me serve you."

She was almost blinded by tears as she reached the old oak table with its Middle Eastern decanters. She managed to place her back to him, slip the vial from her pocket, the poison into the wine.

She gave him his goblet.

"My lady!" he lifted his goblet to hers. "My bride!" he said. He took a sip of the wine, then set the goblet down, pulling her into his arms. His lips mashed down upon hers as he pressed her mercilessly close against him. She couldn't breathe. She couldn't seem to escape. His fingers were clawing into her bodice. At last she managed to wrench her mouth from his. "Tomorrow, my lord! Would you mar our marriage without the proper prayer before its consummation?"

"Tomorrow?" He swore angrily, releasing her. He picked up his goblet and she watched anxiously as he took a long swallow.

But then he paused, stared at the goblet, stared at her—and sent the goblet flying across the room to crash into the hearth. The fire burning there leapt with a hiss.

He turned on her. She backed away, her heart thundering. He stepped forward, digging his fingers into her hair, dragging her to him. "What are you doing, bitch?"

"I don't know what you mean!"

He blinked, then blinked again. "I taste it, taste the poison! But I've not drunk enough, Kate, to die, and so you will rue your attempt at this murder!" His hand suddenly flew against her face with such force that she fell, almost numbed by the intensity of the pain. "Why?" he bellowed. He stepped on her hair, grinding it so that it pulled. He wrenched her to her feet, shaking her like a rag doll, then striking her again so that she fell.

She tasted her own blood. Dazed, she looked at him. "Because I am the Duchess of Manning, and you are a heinous murderer. Because I remember my mother's screams. Because I had a sister and a brother."

"What? What bloody trick is this? All perished within that fire—"

"Nay, Phillippe. You and your father plotted to kill and burn us all to cinders, but as she died, my mother thrust me from the house to the roof, and I rolled down to a hay cart. And lived. And when the hay caught fire, I ran. And so I have waited, all my life, to come close to you."

He started to laugh. Then once again, he pulled her to her feet. "I should kill you right now. Throttle you with my bare hands. But that wouldn't hurt you enough, would it? Nay, lady. You came to be my bride. You will be so."

He threw open the door to his rooms, shouting for a servant. Sir Waylon, clanking down the hall, appeared.

"Bring the priest."

"The priest?"

"The wedding will be now."

"Now?"

"Are you deaf, old man? The wedding will be now. Here in this room! Bring the priest to me!"

He held Kate by an arm. "The wedding will take place and be consummated within ten minutes perhaps, Kate. Within half an hour, my sweet bride, I promise, you'll wish that I had killed you."

He wavered suddenly. His hold upon her barely loosened, but Kate knew she had very little hope. She surged the fullness of her weight against him and toppled him off-balance. He staggered and fell.

She ran.

She flew out the door and to the hallway, racing for the stairs.

By then he was up, bellowing to his servants. "Seize her! Seize the Lady Kate! She has tried to poison me!"

She started down the stairs. Armed men were already climbing up them. She cried out, turned and ran once more, tearing into the hallways of the castle.

Feet pounded behind her in pursuit.

Chapter Nine

There were men everywhere, she thought with dismay. Soon, they would corner her within one of the rooms.

Unseen, she ran into the second-floor solar and tore across it to the arrow slit. It appeared very narrow, she knew, but that was because of its length. She crawled into it, knowing there was a ledge that led to the parapets five feet below it.

There were voices in the room.

"Find her!"

"Seize her!"

She dropped down and crawled along the ledge. Soon she was able to drop to the parapet wall. Carefully, she crawled along it, until the walkway appeared below her. She shifted down to it, then cried out when she saw a man with sword in hand running up the wooden steps that led to the walkway. She turned to run again, certain that any second a sword would plunge into her back.

"Kate!"

She heard her name but didn't pause.

"Kate!"

A gap, a break in the masonry, suddenly stretched before her. She stopped. It was that or plunge to her death. She looked back in fear.

A man was hurrying toward her. He was tall and dark, clad handsomely in maroon breeches, mail shirt and crimson tunic, the crest upon it a raging wolf with one paw raised.

"Oh, God!" she gasped.

"Kate, it's all right. Come back to me."

She flattened against the wall. She stared at the man.

"Aryn!" she cried.

"Aye. Come to me."

She shook her head. "You may be one with them!" she whispered.

"Kate, it's me!" he hissed. "The *Shadow!*"

"What? Oh, God, I don't believe you—"

"Then stop, wait. My eyes, Kate! Look into my eyes. You told me once that you would know them anywhere! Trust me, Kate, I will protect you!"

She bit her lip, shaking. She turned, unable to do anything as he came toward her. A trembling filled her as he came nearer and nearer. And then she was looking into his eyes.

And she knew. Yes. She would have known those eyes anywhere. The eyes of the man she had come to love.

She gladly threw herself into his arms.

"How can you be here? They'll kill you, they'll—"

"I knew, Kate. Beth figured it out. And when I arrived, Peter had my ring."

"They'll still kill you, they'll—"

"My men are here, as well. And we've a secret weapon."

"It's my word against his and he holds the place—"

"I tell you—"

Kate screamed as a sword suddenly slammed against the stonework. She slid, falling against the wall, shrieking as she grabbed for some hold.

Aryn saw her fall....

And saw the sword coming his way again. Phillippe, in a rage. He barely had time to raise his own weapon in defense, parrying the blow. They fought upon dangerous ground, narrow, crumbling masonry. He struck back, desperately searching for Kate as he did so.

"She'll be my wife, she will, and you, bastard, traitor, will die!" Phillippe raged.

He raised his sword.

Aryn parried with a blow that sent Phillippe's weapon flying. In the seconds it took Phillippe to retrieve it, Aryn made a desperate dive, catching Kate's hands just when her fingers were losing their grip upon the stonework. He pulled her up, throwing her behind him.

"Stay there!" he commanded.

Even then, Phillippe was bellowing and racing upon them with his sword raised again. He missed Aryn with his deadly, shuddering blow, but caused the collapse of more of the stonework. Kate shrieked as she realized all of the wall was about to go.

Phillippe struggled to dig his sword from the masonry. He did so, turned and grinned. His macabre grin. The one he had given Kate as her house had burned.

He let out a roar and raised his sword high.

Yet he never lowered it. This time, Aryn's sword found its mark within his enemy's chest.

Phillippe Rousseau, still grinning, clutched his bloodied middle, fingers winding around the hilt of Aryn's sword.

Then he pitched forward, tumbled over and over, falling to the ground....

He landed hard. Dust spewed up from the earth.

He died grinning his evil grin.

By then many men in armor had come running to the far section of the courtyard. The wall had crumbled all around Kate and Aryn. She clutched his hand, tears suddenly streaming down her face. "Oh, my God, you can't understand how badly I wanted him dead...I was willing to die, but now I've dragged you into this, now you'll die, as well...."

"Hush." He squeezed her hand in return, then turned to her suddenly, kissing her lips. So tenderly.

"They're watching us! You'll have no chance, they'll think us worse than murderers...."

"Trust me."

"But—"

"You must trust me."

"I—"

"You must!"

"I give you my word," she whispered.

He smiled. She was able to study his face. Really study his face. With trembling fingers she touched it. Fine broad forehead and cheeks, firm chin. Those eyes she knew so well. Those full, firm, sometimes so very sensual lips...

"I trust you!" she whispered again.

"Then come down with me."

"How?"

"Joshua!" he called.

She was startled to see one of the huge figures in armor coming forward.

"We need a ladder."

Kate looked at him incredulously. In a matter of minutes, a ladder was against the wall. Aryn helped Kate down until Joshua lifted her from the bottom and soon they both stood in the courtyard. Kate stared around swiftly, uncertainly, afraid that at any second some knight was going to step forward and skewer them for Phillippe's death.

She was stunned when Sir Waylon himself came forward and knelt before her. "My lady!"

"But—"

"No buts!" came a melodic, amused voice. "Sir Waylon has been made aware—as have we all—that you are the rightful Duchess of Manning."

She would have fallen if Aryn hadn't been behind her to hold her as the woman came forward.

She was tall, very straight and certainly old. But there was a beauty about her. Tremendous pride. She moved as gracefully as a girl. Her face was long and narrow and handsomely sculpted.

Kate inhaled.

"Eleanor?" she breathed.

"Aye, the queen. Dowager queen, to be exact, since poor Henry has quite expired," the woman said, extending her hand. "Ah, but I'm still a woman with some power, since boys will be boys, and while mine who is king pays the price of his battles far away, the one who would be king tests his own strength here! Though I know that Johnny will be sad to hear that Phillippe has departed this earth—they did quite enjoy the same type of debauchery and games—he will be aware that justice has been served here today. My dear, the title that was so cruelly stolen from your family is hereby returned."

"But—"

"I do believe I said no buts. Didn't I, Count Aryn?"

"Yes, my lady, you most certainly did."

"There's truly nothing to fear. You see, King Richard will be home quite soon now. Count Aryn has been most helpful in managing to give me the last bit of needed assistance to raise his ransom."

"The king's ransom—is paid!" Kate gasped.

"I think she's going to be quite a bright girl, after all!" Eleanor told Aryn, smiling.

Then Kate began to laugh, herself. She fell to her knees, picking up the queen's—the dowager queen's—hem and placing a kiss against it. "Oh, my lady, I am ever so grateful!"

"Up, child!" Eleanor admonished. "You mustn't

be so grateful that such a horrid wrong has been righted at last.''

Even as she spoke, the castle's round, waddling priest came hurrying out to the courtyard.

"I was told there was to be a wedding! Now I hear that the duke is dead. Which is to be, a wedding or a funeral?'' he said with exasperation. He paused, seeing the duke's body splayed upon the ground. "Gone to his maker!'' There was no sadness in the priest's tone. "A funeral, then.''

"A wedding first!'' Eleanor said, clapping her hands together. "At my age and after all my years of strife, I do love a day that finishes with a happy ending! Sir Waylon!''

"Yes, my Lady Eleanor!''

"See to the disposal of Rousseau's body for the moment. I do suppose we'll have to behave like Christians later and see him properly buried. But for the moment, a wedding. That is...''

She looked at Kate and Aryn expectantly. He caught her hands, turning her to him. "Would you marry a rogue, my lady?''

She kicked him lightly. "You could have told me!''

"You could have told me!''

"Ah, yes! They're quite ready for marital bliss!'' Eleanor decreed.

"Will you?" Aryn persisted. "I am a poor man."

"It doesn't matter, does it? Since I'm a duchess?"

"It wouldn't matter who you were!" he assured her in the softest whisper.

She smiled. Touched his face. "I would know those eyes anywhere."

"Shall we get to the ceremony?" Joshua suggested, clearing his throat.

The company surged into the small chapel. Everyone. From the dowager queen to the maids, Peter and his daughter, the rogues from the forest, the guards from the castle.

The priest read the ceremony. Kate gave her vows. To love, to cherish, to honor. Until death.

There was dancing at the castle as there had not been in years. There was feasting.

There was laughter.

Finally, late at night, Kate and Aryn came to the huge master chamber. She shivered, entering it.

Aryn was quickly behind her. His whisper was at her ear. "We needn't live here. I have a home. It's far more humble, but perhaps this place holds too many ghosts for you."

She spun in his arms, shaking her head. "The ghosts are good!" she assured him. "I shivered because I might have been here with Phillippe. Because he had no right here. Because my parents were so filled with happiness, laughter, love..."

He raised her chin. Kissed her gently.

"We will fill it with love again," he promised.

He swept her up, bearing her down upon the bed. Kisses seared her lips, her forehead, her cheeks. She touched him. His face. Over and over. Molding every feature into her heart and mind. His lips found hers again. Fingers fumbled with her clothing. His own was hastily strewn between kisses, touches and caresses.

"You were stealing all that time to help Eleanor raise King Richard's ransom?" she said suddenly.

"Yes." Distracted, he kissed the pulse at her throat. Palmed her breast, rotating his fingers upon the nipple. She gasped.

"Eleanor was the woman who came to your camp that night?" she inquired, breathless.

"Yes."

His lips were against her ribs. His tongue teased them lightly. One by one. His hands...

She caught them both. "And your men?"

"Most came from my estate. Others from various nearby areas." He pulled free. Touched her, stroked her, kissed the smoothness of her flesh...

She'd wanted more out of him. More of a confession, perhaps, or at least an admission that he'd played a dangerous game.

But she couldn't quite remember what she'd wanted to say to him. Her body was filled with liquid fire. She was soaring, flying, trying to touch the moon, seize the very wind...

"You're still a rogue!" she accused him.

"Indeed!" he said, and smiled. He rose above her. Touched her face. Made love to her. Passionately, urgently, tenderly.

Later, when the moon and sun were shifting in the heavens, he turned to her and asked, "You were saying?"

She laughed.

The laughter filled the room.

She shook her head.

"You're still a rogue!" she whispered again. And curled against him.

Nothing else mattered for the moment.

After all, Queen Eleanor was their guest that night.

And the queen loved happy endings.

* * * * *

APACHE FIRE
Theresa Michaels

For all my readers

A Note from Theresa Michaels

For me, writing grew out of a love of history and reading. I have always been fascinated with the West and various Indian cultures. As I write, I try to envision both sides of the conflicts experienced by settlers and Indians.

Part of the enticement of writing Westerns is reading about the people drawn to the raw land, despite its dangers. Since men wrote most of the history books, there is little mention of the women who were part of the westward expansion. But women did file on homesteads; they also brought a civilizing influence to the West. In the Western Territories a woman had a chance to measure herself against the land. I believe women valued the opportunity and the freedom from the stifling standards of the Victorian era.

Characters are the most important aspect of a novel to me. They must be strong, vulnerable and flawed to be believable. Each has their own code of honor. And I believe strongly in the healing power of love. That belief is why I write romances.

I hope that you enjoyed reading "Apache Fire" and will watch for my ongoing Western series, The Kincaid Trilogy.

Have a great summer filled with love and laughter,

Theresa Michaels

Chapter One

Soft as a lamb's breath, the summer night's whisper barely stirred the sultry air, but it brought the scent of a woman to Niko.

The Apache stilled, his breathing instantly the same slow cadence of his heart. Honed by hunger and a warrior's skills, his lithe, taut body easily melded with the deeper shadows near the ranch's smokehouse.

He drew his knife from its rawhide sheath with the silence of smoke rising. With inborn patience, he waited for the cry of "Thief!" to break like the scream of the hawk sighting prey.

His senses alerted him to the essence of a white woman—harsh soap, stiffened layers of cloth that adorned the pale body, and sweat.

But fragrant with a woman's musky smell, just the same.

The white woman had labored this day. Her sigh was deep, and thankful for its end.

And Niko had been many moons without a woman.

From the corral came the restless shift and stir of a newly fenced group of young mares and their offspring. He had hidden and watched the white men who lived in the tightly closed small houses capture the band from the large wild herd. It was not enough that these men took the very food from a warrior's people, they stole the freedom of all wild things, as well. Was there nothing that the white men did not seek to take and lock away? He knew of none, for they did this even to their women.

She drew nearer. The moon cast its long shadow and light upon her. Niko felt the quickening of his blood. He knew what would happen to him if he was caught stealing. The soldiers would come to lock him away in their tiny dark place in one of their forts. They would curse and spit at him, naming him *savage*.

They would beat him for setting his eyes upon their women.

They would kill him if he dared to touch one.

And that was how close she had come to him. Within an arm's reach.

He was aware that she sensed something. Her hesitant step, the slow searching movement of her head, turning this way, and now back. She stared at where he stood, but did not see him.

Her hair was not the dark of the heart of the night, like an Apache maid's. As with many things that the whites had stolen, this woman had captured both the sun's long rays and those of the moon within her hair.

His fingers gripped the bone handle of his knife a little harder. He was curious to touch it, this hair that lay thick and coiled upon the back of her head.

Suddenly Niko grew even more quiet, holding air within his lungs. She had half turned toward him again, and he could look upon her face.

To the women of the Chiricahua, he had spoken many words of praise—of their skills, fine dancing, good cooking, and the ease of laughter slipping free. But as a man, he held a more honored position than a woman, and the maidens were well guarded, so his words to them were not those of a man to a woman.

Within him rose the powerful need to hear an invitation to this woman's blankets. And for him to speak lies like those of the soldiers who coaxed the young women of his people to spread blanket and legs when the lust was upon them.

Where he was dark, she was fair. Where he was strong, she appeared a new shoot, easily bent, easily broken. Soft looking, like the downy breast feathers of a newly hatched bird, whereas he was hard, like the mountains he called home.

Poised like a doe to flee, she still waited. Her head tilted to one side, listening, he was sure, for some sign that he was there. Her strength could not be measured against his. She was woman, and he, he was of the *Netdahee,* the killer warriors, chosen because of his fierce fighting skills to be of the elite of all the Chiricahua.

"I know you're here. I can't see you, but I know I'm right."

The softest whisper. The greatest danger.

She took a step forward. Niko took a step back, hugging the wood of the smokehouse. He did not want to kill her. But he would not have her call out, and see himself hunted before he had taken what he had come for.

"Please, you're frightening me. If you've come to steal again, my brother is just waiting for an excuse to go to the army. I know the people are hungry. I visited the reservation today for the first time."

He heard few of the words that poured forth from lips red as berry juice. *Steal* and *brother.* And the hated *army.* Even to himself he would not use the word for the holding of his people like cattle in pens. But he knew hunger. It prowled the bellies of the warriors, the women, and the smaller ones of hungry children. And she called them...*the people.* Not savages, not animals.

The urge to touch the soft cloth that covered her from wrist to shoulder, from neck to shoes, saw the involuntary rise of his hand. She would see him then, if he reached out, for the slash of the moonlight crossed the earth at that point.

Would she cry out and rouse those in the house? Or would she fall as one who had drunk too much *tiswin?*

This close, her scent coiled around him. No matter how shallow the breath he drew, he took a part of the woman into him.

He smelled her fear, heard her harsh breathing, and envisioned her heart pounding like the furious beating of the eagle's wings soaring skyward. A noise made him instantly alert. He looked toward the house. The door was open.

"An-gie! Angie, where have you taken yourself? Answer me, girl."

"I'm not a child, Grant," Angie Wallace mumbled under her breath. Someone was there, but her fear came from the unknown, it was not for herself.

With a shrug for the strange thought, she moved out toward the spill of light from the house.

Her brother called again. If she didn't answer him, he would come looking for her. "I'm here, Grant. Right where you can see me," she added, once more moving forward.

"C'mon in, girl. Ain't no cause for you to go prowling around at night. I warned you, it ain't all that safe this close to the reservation. Never know when them savages'll take it into their heads t' raid us."

"Please, a moment more, Grant. It's cooler out here. I won't go far. I promise." Her brother's tall, gaunt figure was outlined in the doorway, and from inside the house she heard his wife, Kathleen.

"Leave your sister be. She hasn't yet grown to hate this land."

"Cease your prattling," Grant ordered. "See you don't wander off, Angie."

She didn't answer. She had already turned back, trying to pierce the shadows to see who stood there.

Niko smiled. There was spirit in the white woman. The man called her a girl, but he heard the calm of a woman's voice.

"Are you one of the boys come to steal from us again? My sister-in-law, Kathleen, told me there had been meats missing. Please, don't be afraid of me. I know what it means to be hungry. Come out, boy. Let me see you."

Boy! She named him *child,* when he had been a warrior grown for ten turns of the seasons! Niko, his pride slighted, threw caution to the dust and stepped out from the shadows.

Her choked cry pleased him. *Boy?* Never would she name him such.

"Oh, my L-Lord, you're not…not a b-boy at all." Angie swallowed, but her mouth was still dry. She hated the stutter, but it always happened when she was nervous. Wiping her suddenly damp palms on her skirt, she was surprised she could speak. The Indian before her wasn't nearly as tall as her brother, but she had to angle her head back to look up at him. Straight black hair brushed past his shoulders. A torn cloth was wrapped around his forehead to hold it back from his face. Spying the wicked-looking knife he held in one hand as if he would lunge and rip her apart in a second, she felt a chill in her bone marrow.

Hard. It was the only word she could use to describe the strong, masculine cast of his features. Angie had a great deal of courage, and it took most of it to fight off the terror that held her. His eyes were black, piercing her with an intense look that bespoke mockery.

She took a small backward jump, but he only crossed his arms over his chest. She stopped looking at the knife. If he was going to hurt her—kill her—he would have acted quickly.

On her visit to the reservation earlier, she had seen the women and the hollow-eyed children. She had not seen one man. What her eyes beheld now was not the savage that Grant described, of painted face and breechcloth. He was dressed in the colors of the earth. The lean, rawhide-tough appearance came from a double-breasted nut brown linsey shirt such as her brother wore. Buckskin pants clung to his narrow hips and flat stomach. She glanced at the knee-high moccasins that helped him move so silently, then up at his face.

Goose bumps fled in the heat of a rising anger. The mockery in his eyes had spread to the smile of full lips. It annoyed her that she thought his smile pleasing, but it did soften his straight, hawklike nose and the broad slant of his cheekbones.

He was a handsome man. The moment the thought formed, Angie felt uncomfortable. *Not a man. A savage. A heathen Apache who would slit her throat in the turn of a moment for no more reason than she was white.*

Kathleen's words. Kathleen's fear.

It suddenly became her own. Had she lost her mind, to stand here like a helpless victim? But men, all men, thrived on making fear their weapon. Nodding to herself, she made up her mind.

Niko had no thought to kill her. She was not a girl, as the man had called her. She looked at him with the eyes of a woman. Eyes that revealed the curiosity of a woman for a man. He thought she had spirit. She had not given sign that he was there. A strange white woman, this one. Fear had been in those eyes, too. She had snatched it away and swiftly hidden it.

"You have come to steal from us, haven't you?"

He did not like the word upon her tongue. Before she could know his intent, Niko grabbed hold of her shoulder with his free hand, spun her around and locked her against his chest with the gentle pressure of his knife against her throat.

She did not cry out. She did not fall against him as one drunk on *tiswin*. Like a woman of his people, she waited, taut as a bowstring, quivering like an arrow newly struck to its target.

What was he to do with her? His belly growled with hunger, and he slid his free arm over the slight rise of her breasts to hold her slender waist. It shamed him that she heard the weakness in his body.

But that shame was small compared to the fire in his loins as the heat of her body seeped into his. He groaned, closing his eyes for a second, breathing deeply of the woman's scent that had enticed him from the first.

Angie's rippling quivers turned to violent trembling. She could *feel* him. Even through the layers of clothing that protected her body, she could feel the swift change in his.

His fingers had tightened against her side. The cool metal of his knife barely touched her throat, but she couldn't swallow. He angled his head lower, and the fine, silky-soft black hair brushed her cheek.

His breathing was labored.

Hers was lost somewhere in lungs that couldn't drag enough air inside to keep the black lights from dancing in front of her eyes.

The threat of thievery didn't matter.

He was dragging her backward, toward the smokehouse.

She had to do *something*.

Chapter Two

In her mind, she screamed. A mewling cry escaped her lips.

She saw herself fighting him off. The feel of the knife against her throat kept her still.

His lips touched the bare skin of her neck. Panic sent a surge of blood pumping through her body. She could not think of what he would do to her.

It was all that filled her mind. A suffocating helplessness warred with her refusal to allow fear to win.

She forgot about the knife and tried to kick him.

Impeded by skirt and petticoats, fooled as she was into thinking she could make quaking limbs obey, it was a futile attempt.

He would use the knife now. She would die before she accomplished all she had dreamed about.

His hips canted forward, and with the aid of the arm around her waist, he lifted her. Her feet dangled between his spread legs.

Angie had never fainted in her life. But a black void beckoned to her now. The need to fight seeped from her body, and she sagged limply against him. She didn't pray. Prayers had proved useless. All her prayers and pleading, begging and promises, hadn't saved her child. She had come west to her brother with the hope of healing the raw wound that death had left behind.

For her curiosity, her defiance of Grant's warnings, there would be no healing. No chance to pick up scattered pieces and rebuild them so that she could go on living. She was going to be raped and killed.

His sudden turn pressed her flat against the rough wood of the smokehouse. The growl of his belly made her wonder if he intended to eat first. The sheer stupidity of the thought made her struggle against his hold.

She did not want to die.

"Open."

Open? What? It took several times of repeating the word before she realized that he had spoken in English. She couldn't ask what he meant. Harsh and grating, his voice was an insidious whisper against her ear, repeating the order.

Niko took one step back to allow her room to pull out the peg that latched the door. Like a flower denied life-giving rain, she wilted in his arms. He had meant to frighten her so that she wouldn't cry out. It was not his intent to leach the spirit of her as the sun leached moisture from the earth.

With his knife hand, he made a quick shift, and pressed the bone handle against her lips. His thumb found a soft niche between the seam of her mouth. His arm slipped. The weight of her breasts rested on his forearm. Sweat beaded on his flesh. He did not want this woman with the smell of rain in her hair.

"Open the door, *iszáń.*"

Raising an arm numb with fear, Angie fumbled with the latch. How much time had passed? Would Grant come looking for her? No, he wouldn't. Kathleen would tell him to leave her be.

She only knew she had accomplished opening the door because of the overpowering smell of smoked meats. It was as black in here as the shadows outside. But he couldn't hold on to her and get what food he wanted. He would have to let her go. Courage was what she needed to wait and then make her move to run.

"So much," Niko muttered, judging the wealth of meats by dizzying smell. He had wasted enough time with the white woman. He was as aware as she had to be that the man would come to look for her soon.

He needed his hands free to gather enough food to make this raid worth his time. He was a warrior and a hunter, not a gatherer. That was left to the women. And his thoughts came back to what he should do with the one he held in his arms.

Hunger prowled his belly. A wilder hunger prowled his body. He should think of the injustice that had brought him to this pass. Anger over his people's treatment at the hands of whites was the thing to fan into flame, not the fire this woman stirred in his blood.

"To move is to die," he whispered against the small shell of her ear.

With the flat blade of his knife pressed against her nose, his hand still covering her mouth, Niko slowly slid his arm from her waist. His breaths were harsh, as if he had run a long way, and he heard the sound of them melding with her own panting breaths. He waited for her to move. He took a step back, needing to distance his body from hers.

His acute hearing picked up the restless stir of the horses in the corral. There was no more time. "Fill the sack."

Angie clutched the rough cloth shoved into her hand. She couldn't see a blasted thing, but she felt him remove the knife and hand from her face. The tip did not touch her skin, but a mere movement of air as he trailed it down her chin, following the centerline of her throat, and down, farther still, between her breasts, was a potent threat. The moment she knew he had removed the knife and himself, she forced shaking limbs to move. Hanging from the rafters were hams, sides of bacon too heavy for her, and joints of venison and beef. A well-stocked larder, she recalled telling her brother. He would kill her if he knew that she was helping an Apache steal from him.

The Apache would kill her if she didn't.

He was strong. He was dangerous. And he was here. Grant, thank the merciful heavens, was still safe inside the house.

Angie struggled to fill the sack. She no more thought of asking for his help than she had of refusing. The rough burlap must have held grain, for it was large, and she filled it mostly with hams, since those were the easiest for her to handle.

"It won't hold any more," she said at last, feeling the sweat that had drenched her. The air was too close. Fear of what he would do to her still held sway so that she couldn't breathe normally.

"The *iszán* did good," Niko said. He stepped up behind her, and from his cloth belt took two of the strips of rawhide that he carried. "Stand against the wall." The brush of her skirt against his leggings made his manhood swell painfully. Too, too long since he had lain with a woman.

"Wh-what—" Angie had to stop and swallow repeatedly to get moisture back in her mouth. She couldn't even ask a coherent question. "Me? Will you . . . please, j-just g-go."

The rustling of the sack was all she heard, and then he stood close to her again.

"It is good *iszán* fears. *This time* Niko takes meat for his people." In a flash, he slid the edge of his knife under the button at her throat. He caught the small, pearl-like button before it fell. "Now you breathe."

Breathe? Was the man crazy, as well as dangerous? He was too close. She could feel the heat of his body. And what did he call her in his language?

A warble came from somewhere outside, and she sensed his attention turned from her.

"Angie!"

"Oh, God, it's Grant! He'll kill you!"

Niko did not need her to tell him this. He knew the danger of lingering. Matizo had warned him twice now from where he stood guard over their horses. It had been his choice to leave his Henry rifle with his *siquisn*. But Matizo was a novice warrior, and the lone survivor of his family. He could not risk his being hurt or caught.

"Lift the sack."

His snapped order caught Angie by surprise. If her life depended upon it, she couldn't lift the heavy sack. *But your life does depend upon it.*

The will to live lent her strength. The fact that he had tied the sack closed gave her a way to grip one end, but at best, Angie could only drag it a few feet.

"Weak. Soft. White *iszán.*" Niko spat the words like a white man's curses. But the anger was for himself. He reached out, and with his long, strong fingers gripped her hair. With a yank that cut off her whimper of fear, he had her against his body. "You wish his death?"

She had no need to ask who. Grant's shouts, calling her name, were growing louder. The slight shake of her head turned into a violent movement that she couldn't seem to stop as terror took hold. His voice was hard, cold, so that now he sounded the savage

"You no cry out."

"N-no."

Niko had to leave. It wouldn't be long before the man came to the smokehouse in search of this woman. He did not understand why he did not strike her to silence, or bind her mouth. He could not make sense of his reluctance to let her go.

Angie was frightened. Curiosity had gotten her into tight corners before, but never with her life at risk. Why didn't he let her go? She didn't have enough spit left to call out to Grant. Even if she did, she wouldn't pit Grant against this man. *Savage, Angie, he's a savage.*

"Usen has gifted the *iszán* with wisdom." Niko touched her cheek, his fingers brushing the tears that fell. And he knew he could not hurt her, could not take her. He would not be named by the white man's curse. *Savage.* He would not do to this woman what had been done to the women of his people.

Never would he see the broken, bleeding body of a woman hurt by his hand. It was enough that he carried those images of his mother, his sister, and others he would not name.

He moved quickly then, slinging the sack over his shoulder and slipping outside. He kept to the shadows as much as he could. Matizo would be waiting, ready to ride.

Darting past the corral fence, he whispered noises to the horses. He did not want to think thoughts of the woman.

The blast of a shotgun roared and split the night into the frightened screams of women, the milling, panicked sounds of the horses, and the man's yelled warnings.

Niko did not stop his flight. He did not look back. Once he found the path through a small strip of woods, he knew he was safe. The white man had no dogs to set upon his trail. It was the reason he had chosen this outlying ranch to raid.

Matizo was already mounted when Niko reached him. He caught the braided horsehair reins that his brother tossed to him. With care and patience, he secured the sack, talking all the while to his black, who stamped restlessly and turned his head repeatedly to investigate the strange bundle on his back. There was no need for Niko to hurry now. He knew the whites' ways well. They would not be hunted this night. The fears of the white men were many when they came into the lands of his father. They were afraid of the dark of the night, and the night belonged to the Apache.

Niko smoothed a hand over the black's powerful neck, offering thanks to Usen that he, his brother and their most precious horses were safe. These men who came to claim land none could own would kill the people, calling them dogs, but they all coveted the Apache's horses.

"Why were you so long, *siquisn?* The moon sits heavy in the sky."

Niko grabbed the black's mane and swung himself up behind the tied sack. Had he been long with the woman? He thought it moments, moments he had not wanted to end. With a rough shake of his head, he forced himself not to think of her.

"Ride, little brother. We fill hungry bellies this night. The time does not count."

Matizo echoed his brother's wild cry, kicking his bay into a gallop. Only once, as they topped the rise where they had hidden to wait and watch the ranch below, did he turn to see the blaze of lights filling the Anglos' buildings. Like stick figures, three stood in the clearing, but the night breeze carried no sound to him.

He counted ten turns of the seasons, and never had he felt this chilling dread come upon him.

"Niko," he called out, his voice soft, as he drew his horse closer to his brother's. "Never return to this place. It holds *ditko* for you."

"Are you still in your cradleboard, Matizo? How would bloodfire hurt me? Is not my name of fire? Coupled with that of Mother Earth? Do you question that the very spirit of my name will protect me?"

"Never do I question the wisdom of the spirits that chose to name you Earthfire. And may the spirit of White Painted Woman and the Thunder People protect you always, my brother." Matizo spurred his horse ahead.

Niko let him go. *What touched his brother in this place?* Was this the sign that Matizo was ready to choose his own path? With a heavy heart, he rode on. Warrior or shaman. So it had been said of his brother. For himself, there had never been a choice. The deaths of his family had set the trail he was to follow.

From the tucks in his cloth belt, he took the button he had cut from the woman's clothes. Controlling the black with the press of his knees, Niko opened his shirt and lifted out his medicine bag. He opened a small space in the deerhide bag and slipped the small, white button inside with all the signs of protection and luck he had gathered over the years.

The fire in his loins had but eased. He could not promise himself that he would not go back to the woman who made him burn.

Chapter Three

Sleep eluded Angie. From the moment the Apache had left her alone, she was bewildered by the strange feelings that had beset her.

Drawn to the single window in her small room, in hopes that a breeze would cool heated skin, she looked out at the paling sky. Kathleen was already moving about the kitchen, and she should be dressing to help her, but in the two weeks since she had arrived from Warren, their small hometown in Michigan, she had never tired of watching the sun rise.

She thought of the watercolors packed away, for this sight reminded her of painting with them. The slow spill of lilac shades gave way to hues of gold and orange. In minutes the sky seemed filled with a fiery sun, and with it, the heat of the new day.

Nee-ko. She repeated the word he had used, wondering if it was his name. What was wrong with her?

Her thoughts were filled with the man, not the terror he had made her feel. It shamed her that she had lied to her brother and his wife, after all their kindness to her.

Angie turned from the window. The single bed had belonged to her nephew, but Ross was now a soldier stationed at Fort Bowie. There had been another son, lost to fever a few years ago. It was one reason why Kathleen had understood the grief she felt with the loss of her own child. Death had taken all she had within two years. First Tim had fallen from the barn roof and broken his neck. Three months later, she had awoken to find Amy dead in her cradle. She brushed away the instant tears.

And she had left husband and child buried side by side, to find a way to heal herself.

Her thoughts should be solely on ways to accomplish it, not on the thief who had stolen meats Grant intended for sale to the sutler's store at the fort.

The image of the hollow-eyed children on the reservation came to mind. Was it so terrible that he stole to feed their hunger? She was a charitable woman, brought up to help those in need. Who was needier than the Indians who were forced to live on lands that had been stripped clean of game by settlers and soldiers alike?

By not condemning him, she felt guilty of betraying her brother. But guilt was a well-worn cloak that burdened her shoulders. Perhaps it was time to strip it away.

Her mind made up about what she intended to do, Angie hurried to dress.

Niko sat with his *Netdahee* brethren, high above the Apache encampment. Each of the ten warriors had told of their successful raid, bragging of the food they had brought to their people. Hidden below, in the wickiups, was the sustenance to keep them alive.

There had been no celebration to welcome home the warriors. There would be none of the dancing, the recounting of bravery, that there had been in the past. None dared whisper or show the food gathered by the thieves they had been forced to become.

For twelve years they had been fighting, squeezed between the Mexican army on one side of the border and the never-ending swarm of whites on the other. Of the four bands of Chiricahua—the "true" band led by Cochise; the Warm Springs or "red" people named for the band of red clay worn by their warriors; the Nednhi, led by Juh, whose stronghold lay in the Sierra Madre of Mexico; and the Bedonkohes, who claimed the territory of the headwaters of the Gila River and whose wily minor leader, Geronimo, was feared by the whites—none had escaped the wrath loosed upon them.

Cochise, with his belief in Indian agent Tom Jeffords, called Red Beard by all, had led them to the reservation. But Cochise was sick and old, and the hate grew to see the Chiricahua wiped from memory. Just as he should escape the memory of the woman's scent that he still held, and the feel of her skin and hair upon his palm.

"Niko? Has Usen taken your thoughts, *skeetzee*? You do not hear me call."

Rousing himself from where he sat beneath the cool shade of the piñon tree, Niko looked across the small fire at the warrior who spoke.

"My thoughts are ever my own, Dezyo." The long tooth for which he was named gave him a lopsided smile. Niko quickly remembered then what day this was for his friend. "You have decided, then, who you will court for a wife?"

"Will you come with me to speak?"

"You have asked. It is done, Dezyo."

"I have chosen One Who Laughs to be my wife."

"Ah, Dezyo, a poor choice this," Four Toes called out. "You do not want a woman to bring laughter to your blankets."

"Aiee, Four Toes has the right way of it. You want a woman who will bring heat to your robes each night."

"What would you know of a woman's heat, *Tói?* None will share their blankets with you."

"It is I who will not have a woman. I have made promises to Child of the Water that, like the fish I am named for, I will ever swim against the white tide that overruns our lands."

"As have we all," Niko added, rising to put an end to the talk. "Come, Dezyo, we will look over the horses to choose the best ones."

They walked together, comfortable with the silence, to the herd of horses that belonged to the *Netdahee.* When their band formed, they had agreed that all the horses would belong to them, so none would stop Dezyo from choosing any. But Dezyo knew which was a warrior's favorite mount, and these were not the ones he looked over as his marriage gifts.

Dezyo seemed to want his approval, so Niko examined the two sturdy bay mares, whose bloodlines were a mix of the wild mustangs and the fine horses the Spanish had left behind.

"Her grandmother will be pleased with the horses."

"I have a fine blanket for you, Niko. It is only right that you accept my gift to talk for me."

Sliding halters on the mares, they each led one down to the encampment.

Niko listened as Dezyo made note of his value as a husband, knowing what was wanted for One Who Laughs. He interrupted him once to ask, "Will she meet your offer with favor?"

"I have spoken to her several times. She does not run from me. Many times, I think, she has sought me out. But I have not touched her. I would not dishonor her so."

"Then I will do my best to sing your praise to the old one." Niko watched his friend leave him at the edge of the encampment, for it would not do to have him seen now. Leading the horses between the wickiups, Niko called out greetings, and answered those directed at him. He smiled, but would not answer when asked where he went with the horses. They would all know soon enough.

One Who Laughs lived with her grandmother at the far end of the encampment. Niko spied a buckboard, his gaze quickly looking over the mules in the traces. From the missing spoke on one wheel he identified the wagon as one belonging to Mary Ten Horse. She was the old woman's sister, married many years past to a trader who had paid ten horses to take her to wife. His steps quickened, for Mary laundered at the fort, and she often brought news of the soldiers' plans.

Leaving the horses tied to the wickiup, Niko called out, "Greetings, old one. I have come to talk of a grave matter with you."

"My dwelling is yours, Niko. Come sit by my fire."

Niko bent low to slip inside the tightly woven brush opening. He nearly tripped over his own feet when his gaze locked on the woman. He stilled once he stood tall, but his eyes never left hers. What did she here, among his people? But he could not ask, for this was not his wickiup, not his family, for him to question the visit by a white woman. He had seen no sign of the soldiers who often came to lay blame, real or false, upon the men.

The old one, eyes rheumy in a face creased with age, motioned him to sit.

Niko was torn. He had the urge to flee *her* presence, this white woman who leveled such a steady gaze upon him, but he thought of his friend, waiting to know if his suit was accepted.

"Does the presence of my sister's guest anger you?"

"My words are for your ears, Grandmother. Not those of an Anglo *iszáń*."

"She is a woman, Niko, whose tongue speaks straight, and she has found a place by my fire."

"Then I will leave until I lose the anger that one such as she finds welcome here."

Angie did not understand the words they exchanged, but she heard the anger in *his* voice. She was sure that Nee-ko was his name. Mary Ten Horses thought her idea of sketching the hunger on the faces of the women and children of the Apache a good one. Mary had lived among the whites long enough to know that all were not evil, all were not good.

She had to bite her lip to keep from calling out to him, to ask him to stay, for her fingers longed to capture the proud cast of his features. She watched him leave, then listened to the rapid-fire exchange between the sisters.

But she couldn't understand a word, so her thoughts turned to Niko again. She discovered there wasn't any difference between the way an Apache expressed his anger and her brother's clipped, harsh voice. Thinking of her brother reminded her that time was fleeing. He had agreed to take her with him to the fort this morning, but he didn't know that she had talked Mary into coming out to the reservation again. Grant had not been pleased to know he had to wait to see Major Sumner, but other ranchers had been raided and had come to file their complaints.

It was rude to interrupt, but Angie had no choice. She touched Mary's arm to draw her attention. "Please, forgive me, Mary, but I will have to get back before my brother misses me. Ask her if she will speak to Cochise for me."

"Already I have asked. My sister wishes to know what you will do with these—"

"Sketches, Mary. I will draw the faces to show the hunger of the people. Many of the newspapers back East will pay for these. It will show many whites how the Apache suffer."

Mary repeated her words to her sister, listened to the old one's question, and relayed it to Angie.

"My sister asks if you have no hunger among your people, that you concern yourself with ours?"

"There is much hunger. Children beg in the streets. But I am here, not in the cities, where men care more for the money that lines their pockets than for the cry of a hungry child."

The old one raised her hand to still Mary's tongue. She heard the truth in the voice of the young white woman, saw the caring that sharpened her features. "Tell her I will speak to Cochise. He is gone with Red Beard to have the agency moved to Fort Bowie, to stop the treachery of Anglos. They will not listen. Never they listen. I promise nothing."

The old woman's direct dark gaze and slow nodding head gave Angie her answer before Mary spoke. It was hope, and now she had to convince her brother to allow it.

"You will wait outside for me."

It was not a request, but an order, from Mary. Angie thanked them both before she stepped outside.

She hadn't realized until that moment that she harbored the hope that Niko would wait. It didn't take the brains of a peahen to understand the meaning of the two fine horses tied to the brush. Why should she care that he had come courting? He was young, and handsome— She stopped herself.

He was dressed as he had been last night, but now the sun shone on the ebony sheen of his shoulder-length hair, and revealed his dark gaze, which sent strange curls of warmth through her. He stood silent for so long, Angie thought he would not speak to her at all.

And when he did, it was not to ask the question she expected, why she was here.

"You have sewn another button on."

Her hand rose to her neckline. "I had to. In the midst of the confusion last night, no one noticed it missing, but either my brother or sister-in-law— that's who I live with—would have remarked on it."

"You did not speak of seeing me?"

"No. I...said nothing." Last night she could have sworn that he didn't understand much of what she said, and spoke very little English. But now... She was distracted by the small boy who wandered close and stood smiling and looking up at him.

It wasn't until Niko hunkered down close to the boy that Angie saw the silver-and-turquoise earring he wore. If anyone had told her that a man could appear so masculine and wear an earring, she would have scoffed at him. But she couldn't imagine anyone poking fun at Niko.

"This is Little One," Niko said, drawing the boy nearer to the V of his thighs. "He will take a name befitting a man of the Chiricahua when he is older. But he will have no father to stand ceremony with him."

To the boy Niko smiled, but Angie heard the underlying bitterness in his voice. It prompted her to say, "He is one of the reasons I have come here. I want to draw the faces of the children and show people what is happening here." She couldn't help staring at the gentle movement of Niko's hands as he cuddled the boy. Hunger for her own child sent pain through her, and she turned away.

"Are you so poor in love, *iszán*, that you see shame in a man giving it to a child? Do you see evil in the ways of my people, that a warrior holds a boy?'' He rose and, with his smile still in place, sent the boy off. "Look at me. Is this what you have come to show? Will you twist what you see into more lies against us?''

Chapter Four

Angie steeled herself to face him. She couldn't stop the tears from falling down her cheeks, nor did she try.

"Tears? Have my words brought them to your eyes?"

She searched his eyes for scorn and found only a deep concern. Honesty was the only answer she could give him.

"No. Not your words. I was touched here," she said, lifting her hand to her heart, "that you are proud and strong, yes, strong enough to show love and gentleness to a child. That is a strength all its own. Not many men would be so open before a woman."

Niko looked away from her. Once again she watched him with the eyes of a woman for a man, and he knew, in his heart of hearts he knew, he should walk away from her now. There had been sadness in her gaze upon the boy, and a longing, as if she, too, wished to hold him. He had to be wrong. She was white. Her pale hands would not touch the skin of an Apache. Not willingly. Or would she? Like the winding movement of a snake, the question wove itself into his mind, raising the heat of his blood, bringing to life the fire in his loins.

"You will not come back here. There will be no drawings made. I will forbid it."

"Forbid it?" His harsh grating tone stated that he would snatch away the rope she needed to cling to before she drowned in a sea of guilt and grief.

"No! You will not do this to me. I need—" She broke off and stared at the implacable set of his features. She couldn't tell him about Amy. She couldn't speak of it to anyone. Her shoulders sagged beneath the weight of her burden, and the fight left her.

She held the hope that the old woman would talk to Cochise. But were the Apache men any different from the whites, who would always listen first to a man's words? She didn't think so.

A far-off cry rang out. Niko spun around as whispers spread. He saw for himself the rising cloud of dust and the glint of the sun's rays on brass buttons. Soldiers. He hated the bold way they rode into the camp. The woman was forgotten in the face of this new threat to his people.

He was alone, for Dezyo had long since returned to the others. Old women and young children were all that remained in camp. The young women tended the hidden patches of corn. Twice now the fields had been discovered by Anglos bent on their destruction. The warriors who hunted, and the others that kept watch over the horses, would come at a signal from him, but he would not give it. Any sign of resistance would be seen as a threat against the soldiers.

Niko would not flee. He even walked out to the clearing where they had to stop their horses.

Angie was right behind him. When she saw that they were soldiers from the fort, she looked for her nephew. Dismay filled her when she recognized her brother riding with them. What was Grant doing here? While she silently asked herself, she noticed the leader of the small patrol. Corporal Eric Linley had been invited to supper twice since she arrived, despite her pleas to her brother that she wasn't ready to think of marriage.

"Stand away," Niko ordered, but of necessity his voice was very low.

"There she is!" Grant yelled, spurring his horse to the front. "And that's the filthy buck that stole her!"

"He didn't steal me." Angie ran forward, crying out, "No one stole me. I came on my own, Grant." She tried to grab hold of his stirrup. Shocked, she felt his foot lash out at her. She stumbled back, vaguely aware that a few of the soldiers cursed him.

With his gaunt features livid, fury alight in his eyes, Grant dismounted and holding his reins, grabbed hold of her arms. "What lies are you muttering?" He shook his sister as if she were a tree whose fruit he wanted to jar loose. "What happened to you? Tell us what he did. You ain't got to fear—"

"B-but I'm not a-afraid!"

"I seen you. Stop lying for that heathen savage, Angie. You were close to him. My own eyes ain't lying to me. You were *talking* to him."

She ignored the pain of his fingers biting into her arms, and his look of warning. Grant had never lost his temper with her. But she couldn't keep quiet about this. Her brother was wrong.

"Grant, just listen—"

"Your sister speaks the truth," Mary Ten Horses said, walking toward them as fast as her girth would allow. "She rode here with me, to visit my sister."

"Then what the hell was she doing with that damn buck!"

It wasn't a question. Angie tried to pull away from him, but he wouldn't let her go. "Grant, stop this," she pleaded. "Yes, I spoke to him. But that's all. You're acting as if—"

His slap rocked her head back and immediately silenced her. Stunned that her brother had raised his hand to her, Angie didn't see Niko lunge for him until it was too late.

The sheer force of Niko's tackle ripped Grant's hands from her arms. Before Grant could recover, Niko took hold of one hand, bending and twisting his fingers until Grant released a howl of agony and went down on one knee.

Niko never thought of pulling his knife. This was a dog that should be kicked to the earth. His foot lashed out, but the moment he was unbalanced, six soldiers jumped him.

"Stop them!" Angie screamed. She rounded on the three men who stood holding the horses' reins. "Do something," she demanded. One by one they looked away. She ran toward Eric, only to stop. "Please. Order your men to leave him be." Her appeal fell on deaf ears, for he, too, turned away.

"How can you let this happen?" Everywhere she looked, she saw the stoic faces of the Apache. No one moved. Not even the children. But they didn't look away from the horror of one man beaten by so many.

Angie couldn't stand it. She ran forward, trying to pull the soldiers off him. Her cries didn't matter. She used her fists, she clawed skin and cloth, even landed a few kicks on several men's legs.

"Have you lost your mind?" Eric grabbed her arms, yanked them behind her back and dragged her clear. "For my sake and your reputation, Angie, remember who you are. There will be enough gossip attached to this as it is. I can't imagine what got into you to behave no better than these animals."

"Animals? You call them animals? What of your men, Corporal? These are brave soldiers conquering the enemy?" She tried to angle her head back to see him, but he moved to the side. "Damn you, Eric. Damn you and those men to hell for this day's work."

She stopped struggling. The violence of the beating appalled her. Her throat was so raw she couldn't even cry out anymore.

Niko forced himself not to move. He knew he had no chance against so many. They wanted him to fight, these Anglo dogs, goaded him with vipers' tongues that insulted his manhood, his people, even the spirits that he believed in. Only once did a groan escape his lips. A heavyset soldier's boot landed a solid kick to his kidney. He tried to shove them off him, fought to rise, rage exploding inside him that *she* had to witness his shame at their hands.

He was blinded by sweat and blood. His headband was gone, and hair hung in front of his eyes. One moment he was struggling to sit, and in the next, pain roared through his head. He fell back to the warm earth.

"That'll fix the bastard." Replacing the pistol he'd used to knock the Apache out cold in his leather holster, the soldier kicked one limp leg. "Ain't gonna give us no trouble now, Corporal."

Bile rose in Angie's throat as they backed away and she viewed his broken, bleeding body. Nausea roiled in her belly. She wouldn't, couldn't, be sick in front of them.

She turned her head and met her brother's furious gaze. "Are you satisfied now, Grant?"

He ignored her and addressed himself to Eric. "I want him arrested. I demand that." He shot a glance at Niko's body. "That savage attacked me. You all saw that." He sent a searching look at the now-silent soldiers, standing in a half circle, more than one wiping blood from his mouth.

"You can't let him get away with this. If you don't haul him back to the fort, I'll go to your commanding officer."

"No." Mary came forward then and stepped between Grant and the soldiers. "I will go to Major Sumner. I cook, clean and launder for him. He will hear the truth from me."

"And me." Angie found herself released from Eric's hold, and she walked on shaking legs to her brother. "Leave it be, Grant. You're making a fool of yourself. They beat him for you." She spat out the words, scorn underlying every one. "He didn't do *anything* to me. You're the one who hit me and he came to my defense. Something," she stated, looking over her shoulder at the soldiers, "a *white* man didn't have the courage to do." Head held high, she challenged her brother with her gaze.

"You dare! After all I done for you? Trouble's what you are. I don't know why I took you in when no one else would have you. Worthless, ungrateful—taking up on the side of a filthy buck against your own brother! You'd be beggin' on the street if it wasn't for me. No one wanted a nagging witch that caused her husband's death. Giving yourself airs. You're forgetting it was your own neglect that killed your child?"

"Grant, no!"

"And now you shame me, defending an Apache dog! Get out of my sight. I'll deal with you later."

Angie fell back as if he had hit her again. Mary kept her from falling. Mary, whose arms offered her comfort when her brother turned his back on her. But Angie didn't cry. She couldn't let Grant see the wounds he had ripped open inside her. Shame? He dared to speak of shame, after he'd twisted her grief and laid bare her sorrow by blaming her?

Niko came to in time to hear Grant. A child? She had a child? No. He drifted in and out of a sea of pain. It took all his strength to will his body not to struggle when they used rope to bind his hands behind his back, then tied his ankles together. As they lifted him like meat ready for the spit, he managed to open his eyes, and saw that *she* still watched him. He named her then, mouthing the words—Woman of Sorrow, for such were her eyes that her sorrow pained him more than his own. It was the last thought he had.

No one stopped the soldiers from taking one of the bay mares that were to have been Dezyo's gift to the old one. She stood near her wickiup, mumbling to herself, but gave no other sign that she saw or heard what had happened. Angie waited for someone else besides Mary to come forth, to raise a protesting voice when they flung Niko's body over the mare's back and tied his hands and feet together beneath the horse's belly.

Silence reigned as the soldiers mounted and rode out, leading him at the last, where the dust was sure to choke him.

"Mary?" she whispered in a hoarse voice. "What will they do to him?"

"If he lives?"

Angie didn't know where she found the strength to grab the older woman's arm. "What did you say? If he lives? Why won't he? Surely they don't plan to kill him? My God, Mary, he didn't do anything to deserve death."

"He attacked a white man. That is enough. Apache have died for less."

Her soft words, spoken without any hint of emotion, acted as a spur to Angie. "We can't stand here, Mary. We'll follow them to the fort. Between us, the truth will be told. It wasn't his fault. He only protected me."

"No. This I will not do. You go to your small house."

"But you just said...you told them that you'd go to Major..."

"Mary go. Mary talk. Mary alone."

"But I'm the one who was hit. The major will have to listen to me. Mary, please, don't send me away. I need to do something to help him."

"You no listen to Big Ears. He tell you—"

"Big Ears? Who?"

"The bluecoat with hair like cow's hide."

"Eric? Eric is Big Ears?" For a moment, the twinkle in Mary's eyes distracted her as the woman nodded. Angie couldn't argue. Eric did have big ears. She was beginning to understand how the Apache named things and people. But, more, she found that they had humor in their ways. "All right, Mary, tell me why anything that Big Ears said should matter."

"Here," she said, touching Angie's left breast for a moment, "your heart is good." She lifted her hand and cupped it on the side of Angie's head. "Here, you are as one who had all reason stolen by Owl."

Just from her hushed tone, Angie knew that was something bad. But she couldn't let superstitions stop her.

Mary shook her head. "You no listen. You are white woman. You no speak for Apache warrior. Anglos make ugly words. Hurt you. Hurt you bad."

"Gossip, Mary, can't hurt me. I won't stand by and do nothing. If you won't take me with you back to the fort, I'll find my own way there."

"Take her, my sister," the old one said.

Mary's shrug told Angie she had won. But she could not spare a moment to be happy about it. She had to figure out what she would say that would free Niko. *Niko.* His name came easily to her lips. Too easily. She liked saying it to herself as she climbed up to the buckboard's seat.

Unaware that her lips were almost curved in a smile, Angie didn't see Mary shake her head.

Clucking to her mules, Mary set them on their way. *No good will come of this day. The gode had been set among them. All knew what the Gray One caused. All but the woman.* Mary glanced skyward. *Thunder People, protect your son of earth and fire. Strange are the ways of a woman's heart. Strong are the legs that carry her on her chosen path.*

Her memories turned back in time, to a summer when she had been young and strong and a bold trapper had courted her. He had fought bravely to make her his wife. To cross the land took courage. Mary glanced at Angie.

Have you the courage to cross the lines that divide us?

She would not ask.

Chapter Five

Angie's gaze passed unseeingly over the piñon and stunted oak trees, the boulders that rose nearly as high, the grasses lush from the constant summer rains. Her body swayed with each bump the buckboard made over the rocky ground. Flies and mosquitoes swarmed, and she brushed them away without thought. The image of Niko with the little boy would not leave her.

She even understood why. Her mind refused to conjure up the sight of him beaten.

It wasn't until Mary spoke of the coming rain that Angie suddenly became aware of her surroundings. In the far distance were low-lying mountains. The land easily could look the same, but she was sure this was not the way they had twice taken to come to the reservation.

She said as much, then added, "Mary, is this a shorter way to the fort?"

"This is the way we go now."

"Then it is different. For a few minutes I thought my mind was playing tricks on me."

"No ask questions. Always the Anglo must question. This way safe for you."

Despite Angie's prodding, Mary would say no more.

And Angie began to worry about where Mary was taking her.

Niko turned inward, finding strength and inner quiet. He judged by the length of time it took until the pain receded from his body how far they had taken him. His body was curved like a hoop over the back of the horse, but he did not open his eyes to the sky. He willed himself to work at the knots that tied his hands to his feet beneath the mare's belly.

Not easy was the need to shut out the voices of the soldiers who rode ahead. He knew what his fate would be at their hands. Breathing was a difficult task, not only because of the dust rising with the striking hooves of ten horses, but also because he had to contend with the piercing pain that lanced his side.

He thought of the place they would have to ride through, a narrow defile that would force them to go one by one. *Child of the Water, hear me. Send to the Thunder People for the* Intchi-dijin, *the blackest of winds, so that the Controller of Water will hear their cry and send the rains to aid me.*

Hear me. I am Netdahee. *To leave me helpless is to leave your people helpless.*

He worked at fraying the end of the rope. His silent calls to the spirits of his people repeated over and over as blood swelled his fingers and made them clumsy. Never once did Niko show any sign that he was awake, and aware.

High above the soldiers, the slurred whistled warning of a male meadowlark was heard. Niko listened as it was repeated. He waited for the soldiers to be alert to the danger that was coming to them. In his mind he smiled when no whisper was passed from man to man. He should know that the Anglos would not realize that a meadowlark was a ground hunter and could not be above them.

The place was close, then, and he had to be ready.

With his lips he tasted the first fat drops of rain. A woman's rain, for had it been male, the lightning and thunder would have shaken the earth.

Niko had to block the thought of Woman of Sorrow from his mind. She had no place in his life. In the deepest corners he heard the whispers that her life was now entwined with his. And he fought its telling, just as he fought the pain that once more surfaced.

His head bumped against rock. Now he opened his eyes to see that most of the soldiers had disappeared up ahead, through the deep cut in the rocks. He did not listen for cries. He knew there would be none. The *Netdahee* made no noises unless they wished to. Like the shadow cast by the drifting cloud, so would they move over their land.

The roaring blood in his ears made it impossible for Niko to hear. He strained anyway, listening for the thuds of falling bodies. Not a whisper of sound reached him.

Was he mistaken? Had they forsaken him? Would not his brethren come to free him?

At the head of the column, Eric lifted his arm to halt the soldiers. He half turned in his saddle and looked at the grizzled-bearded private behind him. Ben Holloward was a veteran of Indian wars. His drinking prevented him from rising in rank, but when he repeated his warning, Eric had to listen.

"I'm a-tellin' you it's too damn quiet. They're out an' around. You give the order to draw weapons, Corporal. Ain't a man jack of us gettin' back to Bowie otherwise."

Eric scanned the rocks on either side, his gaze climbing high as the stone rose. He saw nothing amiss, but he could not dismiss Ben's warning, either. "Draw your weapons," he ordered softly, waiting until the order was repeated, man by man. He couldn't see what lay before them, for the trail curved beyond the rocks.

Damn Angie Wallace and her brother for getting him into this mess! He shot a quick look over his shoulder at Grant Cowan. The man hadn't uttered a single word. But Eric saw that he, too, had drawn his gun.

"Private, pass word along to Hennisee to secure the prisoner's horse to his. The mare should be tied tightly. I don't want to lose that buck if we are engaged in an attack."

Eric waited, batting off the flies and mosquitoes that came swarming from the swampy area of the reservation's lowland. He had five months left of his enlistment, and he fully intended to have a promotion at the end of that time. Bringing in the Apache for attacking a white man without encountering problems would look good on his record.

Uneasy, he kept looking around, but saw nothing but the dreary rise of stone. Water began collecting on the brim of his cap, and he felt the rain slide down his neck, soaking both neckerchief and shirt. Thankful it was a gentle rain and not one of the wild, violent storms that came up suddenly, he welcomed the cooling of his heated skin beneath his uniform.

Word came back finally of a delay. The horsehair bridle's reins were too short to be tied to Private Hennisee's saddle.

"Then pass word back that I shall hold him personally responsible for the safety of our prisoner." Once more Eric looked around, and then he gave the order to move out.

Once around the boulders, the trail widened enough for two to ride abreast. Eric rode with Ben at his side, keeping the horses to a walk. The corporal sensed the unease that had the men behind him— men he was responsible for—fretting and sweating. His own nerves were on edge as he recalled all the black eyes of the Apache women and the children staring at him back at the camp.

The reassuring sound of harness jingling as his men formed up two by two behind him made him relax his vigilance. He gave the order to holster their weapons, and kicked his horse into a trot.

They were nearly at the border of reservation lands when a call went up from the end of the column. "Hennisee's missing!"

Already being taken southward across the reservation, Niko neither heard nor cared. Four of the *Netdahee* rode with him. The others drove a small herd of horses behind them so that no tracks would remain when the mud dried but those of many horses moving with the wind.

They had cut him free of his bonds, but Niko laid his body against that of his black, his fingers woven tightly into the horse's thick mane. Pain rode with him, great waves of it, so that he couldn't sit up and ride. He did not call out, or ask for help. It was not the way.

"It's not the right way, Mary," Angie found herself repeating again. The woman refused to answer her, just kept her mules to their plodding walk, heading, it appeared, for a small grove of piñon.

Angie sensed that something was not right, but the unease that settled around her did not make her fear it. She wasn't at all surprised when Mary brought the buckboard to a stop beneath the trees.

"Here we will wait."

"Wait? What are we waiting for, Mary?"

"You see."

And with that Angie had to be content. She pushed her wet hair back from her face, realizing for the first time that she had lost several hairpins. For some reason, it didn't matter to her what she looked like.

She heard the horses before she saw them coming across the rocky field. With the lessening rain, she was able to make out the riders leading the herd of horses.

She rounded on the seat and gripped Mary's arm. "It's Niko, isn't it? They managed to set him free."

"The Apache will never be free."

"Oh, Mary, that's not true. There are many white people who are sympathetic to the Indian's plight. There are men and women, too, who speak of the injustice. But please, tell me how they got him away. No one did anything back in the camp."

"The *Inde'* speak many ways. Niko is one among the *Netdahee,* but their numbers are few now."

"What is this word *in-de?*" Angie needed to keep her talking. She was desperate for a distraction to help her fight the rising excitement she felt as the horses drew nearer.

"*Inde'* is the name of the people," Mary answered, her eyes directed straight ahead.

"And the other, the name you said Niko was?"

"*Netdahee.* As white-eyes have their soldiers, the Apache have their own."

A soldier? Niko was a soldier for his people. Angie twisted in her seat, both hands gripping the low wooden side of the buckboard seat.

Dezyo, riding with Niko behind the others, signaled the ones behind to veer off with the horses. He leaned over to nudge his friend to sit as they approached the wagon. He knew the cost to Niko to move at all. But what man wished to have a woman see him weak?

Angie ignored the others. Her eyes were for Niko. She searched his face, seeing the bruise that darkened one broad cheekbone, the blood still running from a cut over his eye, his mouth and jaw swollen from fists. Rain had plastered his hair to his head, and his headband was gone. A jagged rip revealed the skin of his shoulder. Everywhere she looked, there were livid marks showing. But she had seen the kicks from army boots, and she knew these surface wounds didn't matter.

One of his arms was wrapped around his waist, and she saw his struggle to sit upright on his horse.

"Niko?"

"No. You will wait for him to speak," Mary warned. "Get down. It is not good for a woman to sit in the presence of the *Netdahee.*"

"But you and your sister sat. You allowed me to sit in his presence in the wickiup."

"We are of the people, and you were our guest. Now you are Anglo, and there are his warriors with him. Show him your respect. He will honor you for it."

Niko saw her climb down, and stand proud beside the wagon, waiting for him. If he could have moved his lips to do his bidding, he would have smiled to see her obey Mary Ten Horses.

His vision was clouded, but he saw that the woman's rain had darkened her hair so that the sun's long rays did not shine within the tangled curls that fell to her shoulders. His gaze touched the livid mark on her cheek, and his pain dissolved into rage that he had not moved fast enough to prevent its happening.

"Come, *iszáń*. I would talk." He wished to hold out his hand to her, to show her that she had nothing to fear from him, but the effort of speaking took too much from him. Dezyo and the others were distanced, and Mary turned to watch the rain dripping from the leaves. None would hear him but her.

"How did you get away from them? They didn't let you go. They'll hunt you now, won't they?"

"Our women only speak after—"

"And Mary has taken great pains to remind me that I am Anglo."

"To my regret." The words slipped out from the buried place within his thoughts. He knew it was the pain that forced the words free. The pain, and the need he had to leave this place.

Angie couldn't stop herself from touching the arm that held his waist. "I'm sorry. So sorry this happened to you because of me. I never meant to bring you trouble. I only wanted to find a way to help."

"Your eyes are dark with the sorrow in your heart." He leaned down to speak to her ears alone, unable to hold himself upright. "I wanted to see you before I leave."

She looked away then, toward the south. "Mexico. That's where you'll go. And your people will have one less to protect them."

"Mary tells you many things. She cannot speak for me. Go from us. Do not come back. Your child—"

She looked at him with stricken eyes, silencing him. He reached out to touch her hair. "Woman of Sorrow, I have brought you pain. There is no child now."

Angie felt herself drawn into his dark eyes, and for the first time, she shared with another the loss of her daughter.

"My little girl, Amy was her name, died after I lost our farm. My brother wasn't all wrong. She died from hunger."

"Your people?"

"Did they help me? No." *Tell him all of it,* a little voice urged. "They wanted nothing to do with me after my husband died. You see," she said in a voice laden with bitterness, "I was ill after I buried Tim. My kind neighbors came to take care of me and my baby. Kind, nosy neighbors who went through his papers and discovered that the man I had married and borne a child for was an octoroon."

She closed her eyes, unable to bear the disgust she would see in his.

"What is this word—*octoroon?*"

"They found out Tim's blood wasn't pure white. His family tree revealed a woman who had been a slave." She opened her eyes then. "Now do you understand? He was as blond as I was, as fair of skin, and they called him—"

"Not say the ugly words of the Anglo tongue. I have been called much."

"Niko!"

He glanced over to see that Dezyo had called the warning of time growing short. He would have been discovered missing by now. The soldiers would ride back to the camp with their demand for him. Already the other warriors would have gone back to the camp, ready to fight against any who would harm the old women and children.

"I would have a thing from you," he whispered.

She saw that he was struggling to draw his leg up. "What? Let me help you."

"There is a knife in my moccasin."

Angie fought the thought of his leaving, of her never seeing him again, as she drew the small knife from its sheath and lifted it to his hand.

"No. It is for you. But first you will gift me with a small curl of your hair."

His eyes held hers with a steady gaze full of unspoken things. All the words that filled his heart would remain there. Time did not allow them. But he would not go without taking a part of her with him.

The long moments stretched into a tension that sent heat flooding Angie. She moved to do as he asked, biting her lower lip not to ask the hundred questions that hungered for answers. He had not cursed her, or condemned her for the accident of Tim's birth or the death of her child. And when she handed over the curl she had sliced from her hair and saw that he tucked it inside his shirt, she felt the first of the healing she had sought begin.

"Don't let them catch you, Niko. I'll pray for your safety."

"And I will call upon my spirits to protect you always."

She begged with her gaze to know if she would see him again.

He longed to tell her he would come back for her.

There had been no shame to see her after he had been beaten, as he had feared.

Niko said nothing more. He urged his horse away from her and did not look back. To see her again was to court the need to keep her with him.

He was a true renegade now. Branded as such by the army. Never would he walk in freedom upon the lands of his fathers.

But he would come back. This he swore.

For burning into his back were the eyes of a woman who looked upon him as a man, and only a man. A woman who wore sorrow in her eyes. His people knew the loss of one child could be replaced with another of joy. There was love in the heart of this Anglo woman.

Yes, he would be back. Well and strong once more, ready to ease the hunger in his loins. For there was hunger within the woman, and it called strongly to him as the distance widened.

Yes, he would return.

Chapter Six

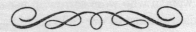

Angie should have expected it. Major Sumner refused to see her, refused to listen to Mary. The private brought word that it was an army matter now, regardless of what had caused it, and that being the case, nothing she said mattered.

Mary made no promises that she would try to talk to the major. Angry and disappointed, Angie began to look for her brother. She couldn't put off dealing with Grant any longer.

She walked across the parade ground to the sutler's, but Grant wasn't among the men inside. Angie was puzzled by the way they suddenly grew silent and watched her. A feeling of revulsion overcame her as she left the post's store. She dismissed it outside, as twilight fell, thinking they had already heard what had happened from the returning soldiers.

And likely blamed her.

Angie held her head high. She refused to accept all the blame for what had happened. The past had taught her that she couldn't change the way people thought, or alter their beliefs. She was too exhausted to try.

The livery offered the best chance to find Grant, and it was there that she headed. She wasn't sure what attracted her attention across the open ground to the commandant's office, but as she looked, Eric stepped outside. He'd know where Grant was.

"Eric!" She called him again, then walked rapidly, once more repeating his name when he didn't acknowledge her. Angie lifted her skirt and petticoats and began to run to intercept him. "Eric, please, wait for me!"

She ignored the attention she was drawing from men who stopped and stared, determined to find out why Eric refused to answer her.

"Corporal Linley, a moment, if you please." She planted herself in front of him, demanding his attention.

"Mrs. Wallace," he answered in a curt voice.

He couldn't meet her searching gaze, and despite the fading light, Angie knew that Grant had told him about Tim. It was just as well. After his behavior today, she wanted nothing to do with his narrow-minded cruelty.

"I only want to know where my brother is, Corporal."

"After the major chewed him out for instigating an incident that brought the loss of—"

"Someone was killed?"

"Private Hennisee was injured when the prisoner escaped. Thanks to you, Mrs. Wallace. As for your brother, he's long gone from here. Now, if you will excuse me, I need to see how the soldier is getting on."

He brushed past her, and Angie let him go. She closed her eyes against the disgust she felt sure was in his.

Once she had defended herself, trying to protect her innocent child against a rigid social code. Her defense went unheeded by one and all. People condemned her for loving the man Tim had been and in so doing condemned her child to die.

Lingering was no longer a choice. She'd have to find a way back to the ranch on her own. There was only one who would help her—Mary Ten Horses.

Mary had her own room attached to the commandant's quarters. It was here that she led Angie, arguing with her to stay the night. Angie refused, asking only for the use of her buckboard to get home. Reluctantly Mary agreed, even coming with her to harness the mules.

"I'll bring them back tomorrow," Angie promised as she slapped the long reins against the tired mules' backs.

"I will see you before the sun greets the day," Mary muttered.

Angie couldn't get the mules to move beyond a plodding walk. Her mind was filled with the events of the day, and she was glad her thoughts were taken up with them, for it held fear away to travel alone in the dark.

Grant's ranch was a good two hours' ride from the fort, but it seemed more like five. She startled at every night noise, giving in to the worry that began to plague her that Mary was right, that she should have waited until morning.

But all too soon the lights of the house shone, a most welcome beacon, and even the mules, scenting water and food, picked up their pace.

When she guided the buckboard into the yard and set the pole brake, Angie thought it strange that no one answered her call. Anxious now, she hurried to climb down, ripping her hem when it caught on the rough board.

"Grant! Kathleen!" The door remained closed. Angie looked around the yard, but there was no unseen terror in the shadows. She had to force herself to go to the door.

"Kathleen. It's me, Angie."

She heard the scrape of a chair inside. So someone was there, someone had heard her. She waited impatiently for the bolt to be lifted, shivering as the mountain coolness made its presence felt.

It was her sister-in-law who finally opened the door, her body blocking the way. "Angie, I tried to talk to him, but he refused to listen to me. Grant wants you gone. He made—"

"Gone? What are you saying?"

"Your brother said you shamed him in front of the soldiers. That you were with one of those savages, and even defended him after he attacked Grant."

"Grant was wrong. I only told the truth."

Kathleen shot a look over her shoulder, but didn't move from her place. "Your things are packed and in the barn. He wanted me to leave them out here, but I couldn't do that."

"Stand aside, Kathleen. Let me talk to my brother." But Angie found that her frail-looking sister-in-law was strong enough to stop her.

"He doesn't want to talk to you, doesn't want to see you, either. He just wants you gone."

"And where does he expect me to go?" Anger sharpened Angie's voice, and she welcomed its heat, to warm her against the night's cold, and an even more chilling dread that filled her.

"I liked you, Angie. I never blamed you for what happened. I grieved for the loss of your child with you. But Grant is my husband, the father of my children. I can't go against him."

There was a feeling of disbelief inside Angie. This could not be happening to her. She was to start a new life, she was to heal the pain of the past. Now Grant was throwing her out because she spoke up against an injustice? It didn't make sense, none of the day made sense.

Kathleen leaned closer. "I put together some food and a blanket for you. I wish it could be different, but you know he's a hard man when his mind's made up."

"Yes, I know. And thank you, Kathleen. I'll go now."

"Where will you go?"

But Angie didn't answer her as she led the mules toward the barn to get her belongings. How could she answer, when she didn't know?

Angie didn't discover until morning how vicious her brother could be.

She had driven the buckboard a little ways off the trail and, beneath the shelter of sapling oaks, made a pillow of one of her carpetbags, wrapping herself in the blanket Kathleen had provided. This was one morning when she did not watch the rise of the sun.

But the hard bed and her turbulent thoughts had made the little sleep she had a weary battle.

The small parcel that her sister-in-law had left her contained the bread and cheese that broke her fast. Later, Angie never recalled why she reached for her other bag. It was the one she had never unpacked, the one holding her watercolors and charcoal, the sketches she had made of Amy, and of Tim, all the precious memories she had left of her past.

Grant had destroyed them. The papers were ripped apart.

Everything was crushed and broken. Angie wept for its loss, then walked out to the land and scattered what remained. She never looked back as she drove the mules toward the trail.

It was nearly six weeks before Niko learned what had happened to her. He was part of one of the small raiding parties that crossed into Sonora, where unguarded herds were. The stock was driven to Janos, where the animals were exchanged for needed clothing and food, which was then loaded onto Indian-owned horses and packed back to the reservation through the Dragoon Mountains. Rarely was there any risk.

But Geronimo had brought back a boy from Mexico, and word quickly spread. Niko was there

when Tom Jeffords came to get the boy to return him
to his family. As ever, Red Beard was welcomed in
Geronimo's camp.

Only once did his voice rise in anger over the boy
being taken and the continuation of the raids. "I've
denied the raids to Howard, and the general is beginning to question my word. I've written to the
commissioner, too, and denied the raids to the press
and public. I can't do my job as agent and get fair
treatment for all the *Inde'* if you will not stop the
raids."

"My people are hungry. *Friendship* is an empty
word." Geronimo was short, as were many of the
Apache. His hair, parted in the middle, hung down
to his shoulders. His small, black eyes were set close
to the bridge of his nose, and his mouth was a thin,
angry slash against his coppery skin.

"If Geronimo has closed his heart to hear me, then
I can say no more. I still wish you good. I have always been a friend of the people."

Jeffords rose and motioned the young Mexican
boy to his side.

"I believe you. There are too few of your kind."

Niko heard Geronimo's last words, but he waited
near the horses for Jeffords.

"Red Beard, I would have words with you."

"Niko? I might have known you'd be here. When I heard what happened—"

"It is past."

"The hell it is. Grant Cowan put a price on your head. Said you raped his sister."

"*Inde'* no rape." Fury simmered, dangerously close to exploding. Niko looked away, swiftly regaining control. "Does the woman claim this rape?"

"Angie Wallace left her brother's house, or some say he threw her out that same night. She stayed with Mary Ten Horses for a few days at the post. They came to see me at San Simon. You heard that we moved the agency there?"

"I heard." Within him there was a need to hear more of what had happened to *her*. He had to wait for Jeffords to tell it his own way.

"Cochise is ill. This business with the raids has got to cease. I've got the commissioner on my back, the army demanding to be turned loose, and now this stealing of a boy to smooth over." He could barely make out Niko's face in the wavering light spilling from the fires.

"I know your honor, Niko. You would never have touched a white woman. She's a strange one, all right. I wouldn't have given her permission at all, but there was something about her that just wouldn't let me refuse."

"What was this thing you did?"

"I let her have the old agency house at Sulphur Springs."

"She is there, on Chiricahua land?"

"She's safe enough, if you're worried. Mary drives out every few days to see her. There's been no trouble with your band over her staying there. But you'd better keep away. I can't guarantee—"

Niko spun away from him. She was there. All this time he had worried, waiting for word of her, and she was living at Sulphur Springs. Why had no one told him?

He walked off, ignoring Jeffords's calls, his hand pressed to his medicine bag, where a button and a curl of hair were all he had of her.

He had a promise to keep.

Niko left at first light. No one attempted to stop him, for such was not the way in this renegade band. He traveled light, knowing he could live off the land as he made his way to the Mule Pass Mountains. In the heat of the day, he sought shelter and rested, but the moment his shadow was faint upon the earth, he was moving northeast again.

From the Mule Pass he headed for the Dragoons, where Cochise's stronghold lay to the northwest, but he would not endanger them with a visit until he had spoken to his brethren.

Steady rains fell, for the summer had been an unusually wet one. He was at home here, in this mountainous land with the mescal, the piñon and the oak trees. There was little of the big game left, and the spoils from the raids of the year before, stowed in caves and caches, were long gone.

How did the woman live? Who hunted for her? Who shared her fire?

The questions were a goad to spur him on, despite the danger to himself.

In natural stone bowls, he quenched his thirst with the sweet rainwater and wondered why he had kept himself from the young widows who had escaped into Mexico to know freedom with Geronimo. The answer was there, in the clear reflection of the water, for he saw not himself, but a woman who caught the long rays of the sun within her hair.

She had accepted a man, and borne him a child. Niko had respected her time of grief. As the seasons were marked by the gathering of food for the body, so, too, did time allow for other needs to flourish.

His body had healed. It was time, then, for him to know her as a man knows his woman.

Chapter Seven

He had been schooled to wait. Restless prowled his mind and body as the late afternoon slipped away. From the shelter of a shallow cave above, he watched the rain fall on the wooden building that had once housed the agency. As far as he could see across the land in the drizzle, there was no sign of life.

To lessen the risk to both of them, he had sworn he would wait for the cover of darkness to make his presence known to her. To make sure that his visit was kept secret, he had tethered his horse in a grove of oaks, and come the rest of the way on foot.

The damp of the rain did not matter. He had been cold and wet before, but never had the smoke curling from a chimney offered tempting warmth. Lantern light revealed her moving within. He resisted the strong pull that urged him to leave his place and rush down there. It was not for a warrior to be open with his feelings.

When the last of the light was reflected in the puddles below, it was time.

Niko knew the whites' practice of banging a fist upon the door, but it was not his way. He stood before the place she had made her home. "*Iszáń*, will you welcome me?"

Inside, Angie nearly dropped the pan of heated water she was holding. All day she had fought this strange feeling of excitement. To hear his voice, the voice of her dreams, brought one hand up to touch her hair. The other she pressed to still a quick-beating heart.

Lifting the bar from the door, she opened it and peered outside to see him. He stood with legs planted apart, straight and tall, his arms at his sides. She shivered despite the heat of the wood stove, and scanned the area behind him.

"Come quickly, Niko. It is dangerous for you to come here."

"Do you share your fire with another?"

She repeated the words to herself, and shook her head when she understood his meaning. "There is no one here with me. Please, come inside."

He was as she remembered, overwhelmingly male, filling her small house with his presence. Gone was the nut brown shirt. He wore the faded gray of rain clouds, tucked into buckskins.

She closed the door and bolted it, then turned to lean against the solid wood, seeing her home through his eyes as he stood and looked around.

Angie felt pride in the trades she had made with her carpetbags and some clothing. It was all she had had left. Her wedding ring and two pairs of earrings had been long gone before she arrived in the territory.

Her needs were few, her wants simple. She cataloged her possessions as he moved to touch them. A pan to heat water, a coffeepot, the frying pan. He picked up the fork and turned it over and over, as he did with the knife and spoon. His finger grazed her single plate and the handle of her cup. They were the sum of her kitchen supplies.

Her gaze followed his to the two windows, bare of curtains, of any covering. On the floor by the small pot-bellied stove was the rag rug she had started fashioning from clothes beyond repair. The shelving she had made was crude boards salvaged from one of the shacks, separated by rocks she had hunted for their flat sides.

She caught a faint smile on his lips as he reached out to touch the two baskets. They had been a gift from Mary Ten Horses. The bucket had been left behind when the agency was moved—another of her finds, which allowed her to draw water.

But he stared the longest at the blanket covering the thick pile of sweet grass that made her bed.

Niko turned to her then, and she bore his dark-eyed study with as much calm as she could muster. A most difficult task, she discovered. Her knees felt as if they would give way if she moved, her heart seemed to triple its beat, and the heat of his gaze sent an answering warmth to chase the dreary chill of the night away.

She still wore white woman's shoes, but her skirt fell against the flare of womanly hips. There was no longer the scent of the stiffened layers of clothing that had covered her the first night. She wore no cloth belt, her shirt hung outside the skirt like the Chiricahua women.

"Your hair is as straight as my own."

"I no longer have the pins to keep it in place. That's what made it curl, Niko."

"You are changed. There is peace within you."

"Is that why you've come? To see—"

"I have come to know why you live here."

Without a tinge of the self-pity she had felt those first few weeks, Angie told him what had happened.

"To be cast out is a grave matter, *iszán,*" he said when she was done. "There is no one to care for you."

She stared at the small scar above his eye, the only visible sign she found of his beating. When he rephrased his last words into a question, she stopped musing and answered him.

"I care for myself, Niko. I am learning how, and liking it a great deal."

"Then you have chosen to walk your path alone?"

"I've not been given a choice. And I've been rude to you. Please, sit upon my blanket, I'll make us tea. Mary has shown me how to collect the right herbs and grasses, and I even have some yucca buds dried for sweetening."

He sat, because she wished it. The scent of her rose from the sweet grass and the blanket, clouding his senses when he needed them clear. There was much he had to say to her, much more he wished to show her, but that would have to wait. She was eager to show off her new skills, and share with him this home she had made. He could not steal her pleasure in this.

"Mary promised to take me with the women to the mountains when they collect the chokeberries. She said that when summer ends we gather the fruit of the giant cactus, the screwbean mesquite beans that will allow me to have flour, and walnuts."

Angie knew there were more, but his grunt could have meant anything, including a desire for an end to her chatter. Since the water was already hot, it came to a boil quickly in the coffeepot, and she added small pinches of her supplies to make the tea. When it was done, she no longer had an excuse not to face him. She brought the one cup to him.

"In your house there is but one place to sit, one cup to drink, and one man and one woman. Will you sit and share with me, *iszáń?*"

"Why do you call me *woman?* My name is Angie. Is it hard for you to say?"

"It is the white name for you. I have given you my own."

Angie sat, because her legs wouldn't hold her any longer. She toyed with covering her shoes with her hem, her back very straight, while she wondered what name he called her.

Her gaze was anxious, so Niko sipped from the cup, finding the tea weak, and much too sweet for him. "It is good. Mary has taught you well." And for the first time he heard her laugh.

"Niko lies well. Mary said my tea is weak and far too sweet for an Apache."

"Niko is not Mary Ten Horses."

She fought the smile coming again to her mouth, and nodded. "Niko can never be Mary Ten Horses. I don't want you to be, but I don't want you to lie to me. Tell me why you have come so far. Did you know that my brother has lied about you and set a reward for your capture?''

He sipped again from the cup and handed it over to her. Angie saw that he had turned it for her to drink where his lips had touched. She had never shared an intimacy like this, and his dark gaze compelled her to drink as he had. When she managed to swallow past the lump in her throat, he nodded as if satisfied.

''It is an ugly thing my brother has accused you of.''

''Even with the heat of youth, never have I forced a woman to take me inside her. This thing he says I do brings no pleasure to a man and less to a woman.''

Blushing to the roots of her hair, Angie didn't know where to look. Such frank talk was beyond her.

Seeing how uncomfortable he had made her, Niko took the cup from her hand and set it on the floor beside him. ''You have no male for me to talk to. There is no one of your family to bring a gift to. It is for me to speak to you of the feeling I have. Is it the *iszán*'s wish to hear my words?''

Was it? Angie thought of the lonely nights when she dreamed of him, and the mornings when she wondered why. Did she desire him as a woman would desire a man she wanted to have as husband? It was a question she had asked herself many times in the past weeks. But she couldn't lie to herself. There was something between them, unseen, but strongly felt.

His touch was gentle as he lifted her chin so that he could see her face. "The *iszán* is not pleased to hear that I have feeling for her?"

"I am pleased," she whispered, holding his intense gaze with her own.

"The grief in your heart is no more?"

"There will always be grief in my heart for the child that I was not strong enough to protect, but I have come to accept that it was not to be. The pain is gone." She inhaled the scent of the rain on his skin, and felt the fine trembling of his hand, still touching her face. She wanted him to kiss her, and as the need sharpened, she realized that she didn't know if the Apache shared kisses.

Like the sweetest of the ripe wild berries, her mouth tempted him to taste. Niko was thankful he now wore the soft, supple deerskin breechcloth over his buckskins, so that she could not see how the desire for her brought life to his manhood, like a spark to dry tinder.

He moved to touch her, stroking the hair that gleamed like the gold the white man killed to possess. Not once had she looked away from him.

"The man that held the *iszán*'s heart, does he still dwell within?"

There was a hushed delicacy to his voice that wrapped itself around her, soft and warm and gentle, but demanding the truth just the same.

"I cared for him with the first love a young woman gives to a man. The memory remains, faded and cold—"

"Poor comfort when the winter winds blow from the mountains."

"Just so." Angie closed her eyes. "It is said that Niko has never taken a wife, though many have approached you with offers."

He smiled, and his fingers learned the curve of her jaw, the slant of her cheek, the arch of her brow. Her quickened breath became his own, her scent all he knew, as he leaned closer.

"The season had not come for me to choose." One finger stroked her bottom lip. "I have thought much about the tasting of your mouth with mine. Is this what the *iszán* wishes me to do?"

Angie once more closed her eyes. "Will you always ask first, Niko?"

"You are Anglo. I am Apache."

"No. You are a man, and I am a woman. Do the Apache kiss? I have never seen or heard—"

"It is for a man and a woman alone to show. Not for other eyes to see what passes between them."

"Then show me. I, too, have wondered how your lips would taste to mine."

From the gentle way he drew her against the heat of his body, Angie expected a tender, chaste kiss.

Niko held her gently, but felt her response, the swelling of her breasts, the quickening of an excited heart, and he kissed her mouth with all the long hunger that had built inside him.

There was fierce pride in his eyes as, with a graceful, quick turn, he brought her to lie beneath him. His hands framed her face, his lips drank her cry, and he felt the hard press of her fingers against his shoulders. Her touch told him of the desire that waited to be claimed. The need in him demanded a joining.

He tempered the unbridled hunger of his kisses till she lay shaken. Slowly he lifted his head, seeing his fine black hair entwined with the golden color of hers. In minutes he could be inside her, gloved in tight warmth, easing the agony of need that prowled his body.

Angie opened heavy lids to see him watching her. "Niko?"

He brushed his mouth over her eyes to close them.

"What's wrong? Please, tell me?"

"I have given you the taste of my lips, and have taken yours to me. For this time, it will be enough."

His lithe body was gone, taking with it the warmth that had covered her own. She saw him stand, and struggled to brace herself up on one elbow. "You're leaving me?"

"I would honor you."

"Honor me?"

"I will come for three nights, then you will tell me what is in the *iszán*'s heart."

He was gone before she understood, gone before she could utter a word.

Chapter Eight

Niko could not remember a time when he had longed for darkness to come with such impatience. All day he watched over her, smiling when he caught her stopping to search for a sign of him. She would not find any. Long before the sun greeted the new day, he had moved his horse to where no water stood from the rains and the grass grew thick and sweet.

He snared four cottontail rabbits, waiting until the breeze freshened so that the smoke of his fire would be carried high and disappear. He skinned all four, but ate only two. He intended to bring them to her later.

There was much time to think. He remembered running as a boy, his strong legs pumping hard to cover the miles while he carried a mouthful of water. He'd spit it out at the end to prove his strength, then quench his thirst. No water could quench the thirst he had now. No liquid could. His thirst was for her lips, opening beneath his own, granting him the right to plunge his tongue deep inside to imitate the joining they would share.

His hands were not idle. He cleaned and honed his knife, searched for and found wild onions, but his hands longed to touch the curve of her breast and feel the flare of her hips.

And his thoughts took him to an understanding of the steps he was taking. She was an Anglo woman. He was an Apache warrior. There would be no acceptance for her with her people again.

Time after time, his gaze drifted toward the south, toward Mexico. He could take her there. But would she accept his life-path? It was a question lost in the heat of his loins.

Lost, because he made it so.

He was unable to dismiss the thought that she came to him as rain to earth, because this was a thing forbidden to her.

Three nights, he had promised her, and he would keep this promise, too. He would show her that he had honor and would not take the gift of her acceptance of him lightly.

There was a deep depression in stone where he bathed, wishing he had his fine ceremonial buckskins to wear. The breeze dried his hair as he dressed and gathered his gifts of food to bring to her.

Angie was waiting for him outside as dusk hovered. She had bathed and changed her gown, wearing now a pale cream calico with tiny sprigs of leaves scattered over the cloth. Her hair was tied back with a ribbon stolen from her chemise, and she fiddled with it as he walked toward her. There were fluttering feelings in her belly, as if butterflies had taken up residence there.

Niko presented his gifts of food, her smile as shy as an Apache maid's, but warm with welcome. Her female grace enhanced his male strength, and he felt his spirits were smiling with them.

Angie added the rabbits and onions to the jerked-beef stew she had made, aware of Niko watching her every move. There was a mood set, that of youth and innocence and the sweet time of courting. Excitement flowed in her blood, and, as she turned toward him after washing her hands, his smile made her feel the most beautiful of women.

"Come, *iszán,* we will walk."

He did not take her hand, as in the way of the Anglo, but kept his pace even with hers as they walked away from the agency building.

"Tell me of your day."

Angie glanced at him. "My day passes one to the other with the care of my home, the tasks all women do." She couldn't ever remember anyone having asked her how she spent her day. But Niko was frowning, as if her answer had not been what he expected. She struggled to recall something special.

"Is there no beauty of the land that brings a smile to your lips?"

"The sun rising does. Each morning I watch the sky painted with colors, and each time it is different, a thing of beauty that I wanted to paint."

"In the lands of the tall grass that flows like a wide river, there are those who believe the sun is the home of a great spirit. The Apache believe it is not so. For us the sun played a great part when there was fighting between Thunder and Wind. They made floods on the land, and long times of no water. The sun spoke to them. Then they worked together once more to make the land as it should be, green with grass and water that flows for the people."

There was a peace to be had as dusk deepened, and Angie knew it was from his presence. There were so many things she wanted to know, she wasn't sure what she wanted to ask first.

Niko looked at her then. "*Iszáń* is bright of eye, and quick to smile at Niko. She is happy?"

"She is happy. Niko, tell me how you come to speak English."

"The black robes taught me. I did this to please one-who-is-not-here."

She pondered that for a few minutes in silence. Mary had told her that he had lost all of his family but a younger brother. Knowing the Apache fear of ghosts being raised when the names of the dead were mentioned, she assumed he had spoken of his mother.

Touching one hand on her shoulder, Niko stopped her. He sensed he had brought her sadness. He leaned down and brushed his lips against hers. "I would see the joy in your face once more."

"Tell me about you, Niko. What was the boy like? Was he very good?"

"Niko became good. Many times the Clown came to frighten me before seven seasons had turned."

"The Clown? I do not understand."

"We hobbled our horses far in the woods. I would sneak off to learn to ride. When I would not come back before dusk, they sent he-who-is-gone dressed as the Clown to frighten me. When I went on my first hunt alone for the deer that numbered ten times the people, he-who-is-gone told me what had been done. Does not the *iszán* have a thing to frighten the child to obey?"

"A bogeyman. We were warned to stay close to the house and to obey our parents, or the bogeyman would take us away. I used to wake up at night thinking I had heard a noise beneath my bed. I would be afraid to move for fear that he could grab me and take me away.''

"Now you are woman and know that the dark shadows of a child shall be no more. We will return, and *iszán* will feed me.''

They shared the food from one plate, and Niko, to keep the shadows from her eyes, told her stories of his childhood. Some made her laugh, and he took the smile that curved her lips into a place in his heart. She again made tea, this time a little less sweet, and they shared it in a silence tense with the awareness of each other.

As he had done the night before, he set the cup aside on the floor beside him and drew her close. *Iszán,* I must know if you come to me because this is a thing that is forbidden to you.''

"Forbidden, Niko?''

"The touching of you brings joy here,'' he explained, then lifted one of her hands and touched his forehead. Lowering it to his heart, he pressed her hand against his chest. "Feel how you make the blood quicken, *iszán*. Here,'' he whispered, his dark gaze holding hers as he drew her hand slowly down his chest, and lower still, to curve her fingers beneath his own around his manhood. "This is where you bring a fire to me.''

Her eyes fluttered closed, and she shuddered to know that he wanted her so much. Even through the layers of supple hide, she could feel the heat. The strength. The male power that made her imagine she could feel the lifeblood flowing.

Forbidden? How could this be forbidden? She opened her eyes and looked at his face. His features appeared sharper. His mouth fuller, his eyes black and hot. There was a faint, deeper color to his cheekbones. Angie gazed at their hands, fair and dark, then looked up at him.

"If this is a thing that is forbidden, it is by others. I desire a man who brings me joy here," she said, lifting his hand with hers and resting it against the side of her head. She held his gaze as steady as he had held hers, drawing his hand down to curve it over her breast. She felt the instant swell of flesh, the hardening of her nipple with this lightest touch from his palm. And she smiled to know that the fine trembling besetting her had hold of him, too.

"Niko is a warrior. But a man who touches me with a gentle hand. There is an empty place inside me that hungers to be filled."

It took great courage for her to lean closer to him, for she had never initiated a kiss before. But she wanted to with him, for him, needing to show him what words could not.

He shook with the need of her that coursed through him, but held her away. "*Iszán,* if you accept me as a man, there will be no going back. I would not let you go."

"There is nothing for me to go back to, Niko. All waits for me . . . now, with you and the love I need to give. . . ."

All day he had thirsted, and now he quenched himself with kisses that spoke of hunger, of need, of the pleasure her words brought him. The sweet grass beneath the blanket rustled and released its faint scent as he lay back and drew her to lie upon him. And with the gentleness she seemed to want, he cradled her face between his callused hands and slowly drew her head down to his.

Her mouth was soft and hungry, mating with his. For a moment he feared the power of her as she pressed the fullness of her breasts against his chest, the whole of her body straining against him. He stroked her spine, then cupped her buttocks with his hands, bringing the soft heat of her womanhood to cradle that which made him male.

He meant to be gentle. Her small, wild sounds drove him toward a savage need. Anglos had named him *savage,* and he felt one now. Hot. Powerful. Male.

Her mouth touched his neck, her teeth caught the lobe of his ear. He courted the wildness he sensed, returning each kiss, each nip that brought pleasure and the pain of denial. Niko rolled her beneath him, a primitive moan escaping his lips as his mouth trailed to her throat, kissing her flesh, then biting, soothing and hurting before his mouth once more sought hers. He plunged his tongue deeply, withdrawing, then again claiming the warmth and rich taste of her. Soon he would make the same claim upon her body.

His hands rose to tangle within the long length of her hair, holding her head still. He plundered the sweet giving of her lips, branding them his, as he branded upon his mind the sighs and moans he called forth from her.

She was soft where he was hard. Despite the weight of his body on hers, she writhed against him, the soft noises she made exciting him. Even in this, the first joining of a man and a woman, the *iszán* of the Chiricahua did not respond with abandon.

Niko felt the trembling of his body, on fire as she arched her hips. He lifted himself to one side, running a hand over her breast and hip, curving his fingers over her breast to lift her nipple to his mouth.

She cried his name, lost in a whirlwind of sensations as if the wind had caught her up and spun her around and around, always bringing her nearer to the heat of the sun.

Even through the cloth of gown and chemise, she felt the intense wet heat of his mouth suckling her. She knew it was not the sun that scorched her skin, but Niko.

Abruptly, he was gone. She opened her eyes to find him standing above her, his chest moving with his harsh breaths. Her own were heaving pants. "Why?" The one word was all she could whisper.

"Come to me, *iszán*. Without shame."

It took seconds to understand, for he was already stripping off his headband and shirt, unwinding the cloth belt, then removing his breechcloth. She rose and stood there on unsteady legs, forcing her hands to open the buttons on her gown. And as she watched him bare his flesh to her, so, too, did he watch her.

"Do you know the courage you ask of me to do this?"

"I know."

Angie stepped out of the gown pooled at her feet and bent to lift it up. Niko was beside her to take it.

"Do you know the pleasure you are for my eyes, *iszán*?"

"Am I, Niko? I want to be."

He caught her chin with one hand and stayed the hand she raised to untie the ribbon holding the neckline of her chemise.

"You are pleasure only for my eyes. Never will another see you. I will make you Niko's *iszán* this night. First I tell you I had already claimed you in my heart the day your brother struck you." He placed his fingertips over her lips to silence her. "Do not ask what I cannot answer."

His lips touched the flesh of her throat, finding the pulse that beat with a wild call of its own. His teeth caught the end of the ribbon, and he pulled the tie free. With the rolled tip of his tongue, he opened the knot and nuzzled aside the cloth that hid her from his eyes.

Before she could hold him, he dropped to one knee and removed his moccasins. And there he remained, waiting and watching as the soft, sheer cotton slid down her body to fall to the floor.

He rose, and she touched his smooth, hairless bronze chest. The move was a bold one for her, but not more so than the bold way her gaze searched his flesh, noting the scars of a warrior. His manhood rose proud between his powerful, muscled thighs, and her eyes flew to his.

Niko grinned at her look, and held his hand out to her. "Come lie with me. I will show you how we fit without pain." And when he had her beneath him, he whispered, "Like the knife slides easily into the sheath that was made for its blade alone, so will we join. Never again will an Anglo bring pain to my *ishton*. I would kill not to have it so."

"No death, Niko," she murmured, reaching for him as he brought his lips to her breast. "I want only life. Yours. Mine. Fill the empty places of my heart."

Swollen flesh sent her arching up to his hand. She cried out moments later. He drank the cries of her pleasure, filled her heart and mind with his praise. He held back longer than he thought he could as he made a place for himself between the pale skin of her thighs.

"Watch, *iszán*," he demanded, his voice husky with the need that tore through him. "Watch as we join, and no man can part."

She watched until passion sent her head thrashing from side to side. Niko was the sun, setting fire to the earth, quenched with the spill of life till the embers flamed anew.

Chapter Nine

Ishton. The woman, the beloved of all women. Angie cherished the words as she woke to find him gone from her side.

In the cool light of morning, she recalled her boldness, reaching for him as he reached for her, touching him as he touched her, until there were no secrets to be discovered.

From her memory she dragged up the faded image of her first wedding night, lying alone in the dark, feeling stifled by the high-necked, long-sleeved nightgown beneath the linen sheet and quilt. She had felt fear of the unknown, remembering only that Tim's kisses were hot and wet, his touch was rough, his flesh piercing hers before he rolled over and fell asleep.

Niko had held her within his arms, stroking her body, coaxing her to do the same. He had made her laugh when she took the same path he had explored on her body on his, telling her he would be a toothless grayhair, soft and useless to her, before she was done if he waited any longer. She had made him wait. She had a mark on her neck from his teeth. He'd never grown soft and useless. The unaccustomed aches of her body were proof of that.

She missed him. He had told her that he had broken his promise to give her three nights to decide, and would find his way to the new agency at San Simon to see his brother.

It was foolish for her to look for him, but she did, all day long. By late afternoon, worry came. The sun shone, chasing away the rain clouds that had plagued every day, and the wind sent a freshening breeze to mock her fear for him.

As twilight came, Angie began to doubt his return.

Since they had left the lantern burning all night, she lit two candles to conserve her small supply of kerosene. There was no hunger for food in her, only a hunger to see Niko again. She wrapped a shawl around her, too restless to wait inside. Pacing the area immediately around the building didn't satisfy her. She felt no relief from the tension that was building with every minute of Niko's delay.

Angie felt the need to run, but the lengthening shadows cautioned her to keep to a walk. In her mind she framed the land before her, the placement of rocks, boulders, the looming of cacti, the small shrubs. She blocked a path for herself, then followed it, wishing she could shake off this feeling of dread. Like the dark, it had crept up on her, until she couldn't fight the feeling that something terrible had happened.

No one would bring her word.

No one knew that Niko had been with her.

Why had she let him go? If she had asked him, he would have stayed with her. She knew he would. It was dangerous for him to go near the agency while her brother still had the reward for his capture. If someone saw him...

A muted sound caught her attention. She had started to dismiss it as the scurrying of a small animal when she realized it was not. And as she turned to follow the repeated sounds, she saw how far she had walked away from her home.

And the noises? They were no longer muted. She forced her eyes to close. Breathing deeply, she willed herself to look carefully at the land once more.

Metal on stone. That was the sound she heard. Who would be digging in the dark? Her senses were alert, and she took a step forward, then another. No, it couldn't have been someone digging. The sound moved closer. A horse? A shod horse moving slowly, at a walk. *The Apache don't shoe their horses.*

The fear that had been growing and growing had not been for herself.

Not until that moment.

She was angry with herself for once more having donned the light-colored calico gown. She stood against the darkness like a beacon for whoever was out there.

There was no question in her mind that no friend to her had come to pay a visit. Friends did not arrive at night, giving a feeling there was as little noise made as possible.

Who, then?

Niko rode with a heavy heart. There was no question that Cochise had grown weaker since he had last seen him. Many said he would not live out the year. There would be no peace for his people then, for Jeffords still could not get enough food. All this he had learned from his brethren, who had ridden a ways with him.

Matizo was already sheltered with several of the shamans, happy with the path he had chosen. Niko had left him with the promise that he would return.

He'd told no one of Woman of Sorrow.

What was in his heart was not a thing to share. Dezyo would have understood, for he had not waited for Niko to return, but had asked Four Toes to speak to the old one about her granddaughter. Already plans were set for their marriage.

What plans could he make? Word had come that John Clum, the agent at the San Carlos reservation, was looking for Apache scouts to hunt runaways. He would value Niko because he spoke his language. But for him to hunt his own people... He would no longer be *Netdahee*.

Was he to keep nothing of his life-path?

Within the cry of the wind he heard the call of his name, and he shivered, fear snaking up his back. There was a faint glow in the southern sky, but long had the sun set, and the moon was but a thin slice in the night.

Again the wind rose, its cry wailing through the deep crevices in the rocks surrounding him.

He slid from the black, holding its muzzle with one hand, listening as he had been taught to do, with all his being.

The cry did not come again.

But the fear deepened, coiling around his belly like the bite of a rope pulled taut, choking off air, sending streamers of pain down his legs.

His eyes hunted the darkness, seeking this fearful thing.

And he heard the cry again. Not with his ears. Within his heart. He knew then what true fear was. Not for himself.

His *ishton*. His beloved cried out.

Niko left the horse. He could make his way faster on foot over the rock-studded land. Ever had he run, strengthening his legs, building the power he needed to join the *Netdahee*.

The child had won races. The man won a warrior's glory on raids. But never had he run as quickly, more fleet of foot, than with the cry of his name on her lips, calling him....

Niko! Angie screamed, but the cry went unanswered, for it never passed her lips.

She tried to move quietly, slipping from one deep shadow to another as she made her way slowly back, toward her home.

The candles were still burning inside when she reached the back wall. Burning bright, for the glow appeared to pool outside.

Her heart pounded with fear, and sweat drenched her. It took minutes before she forced herself around the side to look in the window.

At the exact moment she realized that no one was inside, she saw that her bedding had been set on fire.

"No!" With the cry on her lips, she ran around the corner toward the door.

"Figured that'd smoke you out."

Hearing a man's voice, Angie stopped so suddenly that she tottered for seconds, trying to regain her balance. The smell of smoke, of cloth and sweet grass burning, drifted out and stung her eyes.

She choked on the sudden dryness of her mouth. The heat of the fire made itself felt. She hated the whimpering sound of terror that came from deep inside her. Hated that the man stepping out from the side of the house had heard her.

Angie recognized him. The image of Niko lying beaten and knocked out rose in her mind. She saw this man as he had stood over Niko's inert body, saw the booted foot that had lashed out with a vicious kick, and heard again this man's gloating voice as he reholstered the gun that had put Niko down.

He stepped forward and in the glow of the fire she saw his thick, grizzled-bearded face. His eyes were dark, set close together over the bridge of his crooked nose. There was no mistaking the bright, hot look of them.

She refused to be at another man's mercy. That was all that stopped her from running inside to save her few possessions. She had revealed her fear once. She wouldn't do it again. With her head held high, Angie stood her ground.

"Ain't gonna ask why?"

"You're an animal. Animals don't give reasons for what they do."

"Real brave words. Ain't gonna do you a lick o' good. I figured you'd welcome company after bein' out here alone so long. I got more savvy than that starched-collar corporal. Watched Mary Ten Horses, an' followed her. Knew you were here."

Listening to him, hearing the crackle of the dry wood, Angie knew she had to run. He was stocky, and she didn't see his horse, but he wouldn't have left it far. If he thought he had her cowed, she could buy time.

Wrapping her arms around her waist, she glanced at the fire. She couldn't help herself. She had to know.

"Why did you set fire to my things?"

"Walked inside an' found it reekin' of buck. Put me in a right sour mood, knowin' you laid with one of 'em."

Even digging her fingers hard into her sides couldn't stop the rage she felt. That he would dare take the beauty of what she had shared with Niko and make it shameful and dirty! *Niko!* she cried out in her mind.

"The only thing that's filthy here is your mind. Get out of here. You've done—"

"Ain't even started. Woman that lays with Injuns ain't no better than them."

She dodged his lunge. Her thought was to flee where he couldn't see her in the blaze of the fire. She closed out the sound of his voice cursing and muttering what he'd do to her. She wished she had not given Mary Ten Horses the gift of Niko's knife. She wished she had a gun, a weapon of any kind.

She held her skirt hem high and fled into the night. But she couldn't shut out the sound of his pursuit. *Where to hide? Where?*

She tripped and stumbled. Panic couldn't take hold. She wouldn't get away if panic ruled her. Oh, God! She could hear his heavy breathing! Too close. He was too close.

He brought her down on a screaming cry of denial.

Angie's arms were flung out straight in front of her, and her hip slammed painfully against stone. The jar rocked her head and she was stunned for seconds.

And seconds was all it took for him to kneel astride her hips and yank one arm down behind her back.

She tasted blood to keep from screaming from the pain.

Her body went limp beneath him. And she cringed to hear his gloating satisfaction.

"Don't matter none to me which end we start at."

His laughter gave her strength. She prayed he wouldn't hear the bitterness. "I won't fight you. Just don't hurt me."

"Well, I'll be damned. Like it rough, do you? Shoulda figured that. You takin' up with a buck, an' all."

Her tears fell to the earth. *Niko! Niko, forgive me!* "A woman has needs, too. Please, let my arm go. Let me turn over."

She heard the change in his breathing, smelled the raw, lusty excitement, and she wished that he weren't sober, but drunk, too drunk to feel the gathering tension in her body.

"I'll let you, but I'm warnin' you—fight me an' I'll leave you buzzard bait."

He released her arm, and she fought the wrenching pain in her shoulder to move it. He eased his weight up, just enough for her to turn over. *Wait,* she cautioned herself. *You'll know the right time to move. You'll know.*

His fingers clawed her skirt up. Angie lifted her hands to his hips. To the smooth leather of his holster. She must have made a sound, and one he approved of . . . he must think she was excited, that his jerky moves to open the buttoned fly of his pants pleased her.

Distract him! The order came from somewhere outside herself. But she obeyed it.

"Don't rush."

Thin cotton ripped beneath his fingers.

I can't do this!

Yes. Yes. She could block the feel of his heavy thighs spreading her own. Her hand lifted the flap of the holster, closing over the smooth wooden grip of the gun. *Now!*

She bucked and yanked the gun free, swinging it toward his head. She hadn't counted on his quick reflexes. He rolled off her and caught her wrist, slamming it and the gun against the ground.

With a desperate cry, she clawed him with her free hand, legs flailing. She shut out the sound of his voice, shut out pain as he slammed her hand to the ground again in an effort to get her to let go of his gun.

"I'll kill you. Swear I'll slice you like jerky for dryin'."

A shot rocked the night.

A wild, chilling cry followed.

Ben Holloward went still above the woman.

He should've known....

Ben didn't notice that she had gone still beneath him, listening as he was listening.

Slowly then, he raised his head, sniffing the air. All he could smell was the burning building. The fire would soon spread....

"Niko!" he yelled. "I know it's you! I've got your woman! Stay the hell away, or I'll kill her!"

The crackle and pop of wood consumed by the roaring fire came in answer.

Ben knew how vulnerable he was with his back exposed. Like a snake, he struck suddenly, releasing the hand that had tried to claw him, and wrapping his thick, meaty fingers around her throat.

"I'm choking her now, Niko! She'll be dead before you move."

Angie no longer fought to hold the gun. And with a cry of triumph, Ben snatched his weapon up.

Chapter Ten

Niko's foot lashed out, and the gun flew from Ben's hand.

"Dog!"

The Apache's word fell softly. But Ben balanced on the ball of his foot, swinging his body to the side and grabbing for the knife hidden in his boot. He had survived before. He would do it again. No damn buck was taking his life. He no longer thought of the woman as he crouched, ready to fight for his life.

Niko skirted Angie's body, knowing he couldn't take his eyes from his enemy. But his heart cried out that she didn't yet move. Had the dog made good his threat and killed her?

Taunting Niko, Ben backed away in a circling movement that would bring him nearer the fire and force the Apache to show himself.

With the flash of knife blade, his coppery skin glowing bronze from the blaze of the fire, Niko lunged at him.

He easily parried the first few knife thrusts the soldier dealt him as they took each other's measure.

Luring an attack, Niko feinted a retreat. His lithe body curved like the supple give of a drawn bow to avoid the downward slicing motion of Ben's knife.

With the hand that gripped the bone handle of his own blade, Niko landed a chopping blow to his enemy's lower back. The man did not cry out. And Niko had his enemy's full measure. He was not facing a novice fighter.

He spun around quickly as the man recovered and faced him.

They were closer to the fire now. Niko felt its heat. But not fear. He took his name from earth and fire. Never would fire's spirit bring him harm. Sweat beaded and rolled down the blunt, furious features of his enemy. He watched it disappear into the thick beard, and saw the mouth that curled into the snarl of an animal.

Niko refused to answer the taunts. But he smiled to see fear suddenly appear in the man's eyes.

Fear was in Angie's eyes as she came to, struggling to raise herself, and saw Niko leap high, felling the soldier beneath him. Twisting and turning, the thrashing bodies were locked in a macabre dance. They were rolling closer and closer to the spreading fire.

She couldn't cry out. Her throat felt as if the choking grip that had made her black out still held her.

Her eyes grew wide with pain. Slashes bled on Niko's chest as he rose for a few minutes above his enemy. The man's arm was a rigid force holding Niko's arm high, to keep the blade from a killing strike.

She saw the savage cast of Niko's features in the fire as he slowly forced the soldier's arm to bend. Fire licked the grasses at their feet.

A blue-clad knee rose, aiming for a blow to Niko's manhood. Again they rolled. Fire blazed high, covering the spot where they had momentarily lain, and she couldn't see them through the flames.

Unable to stand, she held her limp wrist against her chest to half drag, half crawl, nearer the fire. Her eyes watered from the smoke. Intense heat seared her skin. Before her, two figures rose, still locked in deadly combat. They were surrounded by the flames that greedily ate whatever lay before them.

Suddenly Niko stood alone. His arm was raised high, his blade was descending.... Angie looked away.

Death. She carried the mark of death to all she loved.

"Ishton! Ishton."

Niko's voice. Niko's strong arms lifting her, holding her close while he ran with her, away from the spreading blaze.

Niko, still calling her his beloved.

He carried her high above the fire, to the shallow cave where he had waited out his days. Even now that he had her safe, he would not let her go. He cradled her against him as the trembling turned to violent shivers, and did not know from whose body they came.

He kissed the tears that spilled from her eyes, despairing that she would not look upon his face. He rocked her, as a woman held her child, offering the silent comfort of his arms and the strength of his body to tell her she was safe now.

And he watched the fire cleanse the earth of all trace of the white man's buildings that did not belong upon the land of his fathers.

In the darkest part of the night, when the fire had glutted its hunger, the *Intchi-dijin* came, that blackest and most fierce of winds, and with it came the rain. Not the rain of the male, wild with lightning and thunder to shake the earth. Nor was it the soft, gentle fall of the female. Hard and steady, its force beat into the earth, and beneath his hands he felt the stir of his woman's lifeblood come to wake.

"Niko? I thought you dead. I thought you wouldn't want me."

"You are mine. Ever as my heart beats I will want you."

He touched his lips to hers tenderly, but passion flared. He twisted to lay her within the cave's shelter, covering her body with his. Her kisses were wild, and he met them with his own, knowing she kept her eyes closed, blinding herself to all that had happened but the need that flamed between them.

Ever would life chase death. And he silently bared her to his eyes, finding all of beauty created for him. Breasts soft and white for his touch, nipples hard with need. The flare of her hips, the length of her legs, the mouth that tempted and cried his name, the long hair that beckoned his hand, all were her treasures for him.

Need tangled with the violent emotions that seethed within both of them.

He gave her the fire of his spirit as he gave her his body.

She gave him a love as wild and free as her welcome for his gift of life.

"Born in fire, beloved. The woman you were is no more upon this land."

She opened her eyes then, and with her good hand drew his head down to meet her lips. "I am *ishton*, the beloved woman of Niko, until my heart beats no more."

Within the stone canyons the *Intchi-dijin* was heard, its cry echoing a warrior's glory call of battle won.

From the natural stone basin, he drew sweet rain water to bathe her. He wrapped her swollen wrist and gave her his shirt for warmth.

"Sleep now," he whispered, stroking her hair. "Sleep safe, and know that I will return for you."

And she slept, wrapped in his love, soothed by the gentling sound of the rain.

When Niko returned with the black and the placid bay the soldier had hidden, he found her still sleeping. For long minutes he knelt beside her, watching her. She stirred as he lifted her hair and raised it to his lips.

He was Apache. A *Netdahee*. And as he lowered his head to wake her to his kiss, he knew he would do what none had done before him.

"Wake for me, *ishton*. We must be gone from this place before the sun sets."

She woke with a smile and reached for him, but Niko shook his head. "I will talk. You will listen to me."

"Niko? Has something happened? Did they send—"

"No. I will tell you what is in my heart. Long have I followed the path of the warrior. The love I have for you and the need to see you safe make me speak now." With his fingertips he traced the arch of her brow, then skimmed the bruise on her cheek.

"Never do I wish to see you hurt. Never has a man of my people given this choice to a woman."

"A choice?" Fear darkened her eyes as she looked up at him. "Tell me you'll not send me away from you. I could not live with that, Niko."

"Would I cut out my heart? To speak such words is to ask me to do this."

She searched his eyes, and saw that his clear, steady gaze held the truth of his words. "Never would I ask that. I will listen."

"It is good that you learn." His smile softened the harshness of his voice. "There is a place for me with the agent of the San Carlos—"

"No! You hate the reservation. I would not ask that you live there."

"Woman! It is not for me. You would have food. You would have a place to be safe. I know the lands. Never will the white-eyes find you."

"And the other choice?"

"There is a place I could take you, across the border."

Angie struggled to sit up. "Take *me,* Niko? I was right. You plan to leave me."

"I think only of you. I would not have you hunted like an animal."

"And while I'm safe, where will you be?"

He looked away, and she followed his gaze toward the south. "Niko, while you made these choices for me, did you think that there might be a child?"

"Am I a boy, not to know what the joining of a man and a woman will bring?"

"No. You are a man, one that I love. I will not be meek and follow your choices."

He rose in a controlled rush and loomed above her. "Come," he said, holding out his hand. "It is time for us to leave here."

"With nothing decided between us?" She took his hand, gripping it, while she swore she would not beg.

As he led her from the cave, Niko looked over his shoulder at her. Proud. Anger tinted her cheeks. Spirit flared in her eyes.

"It is decided. But I will tell you this. Once I named you Woman of Sorrow. I will call you that no more."

She held her tongue to keep from asking what name he would call her now. Dismay filled her when she saw the horses. "Niko." She jerked his hand to stop him. "I can't ride."

"Then I will teach you. I will teach you all that I know." He turned and lifted her to his black, handed her the reins of the army horse and swung himself up behind her.

"Choose for us, Woman of Joy. Do we ride north?"

She angled her head to the side to look up at him. His eyes gazed upon her with love. "South," she whispered. "We will ride south to freedom."

Weeks later, Corporal Eric Linley reported that his searches for Private Ben Holloward had turned up nothing. He reminded his commanding officer that rumors of gold on the reservation's lands had surfaced, and they both knew what gold fever did to the men who caught it. *Deserter* was marked across Holloward's record.

Linley left then to attend the service being held by Grant Cowan for his sister. The gravestone was inscribed with her name, the dates of her birth and her death. The grave below was empty. Nothing but charred wood remained of the abandoned agency buildings. It was assumed that wild animals had carted off her bones. None were found.

And in the months that passed, the rumors persisted that Apache had stolen white children, those of the Mexicans and even other tribes. Unless proof was given, these rumors were always dismissed by the army, just as the whispers of a woman living among them high in the Sierra Madre were dismissed, too.

It was said that her hair held the captured long rays of the sun and the spill of a full moon's beams. And in her eyes there burned a fire. An Apache fire of love.

*   *   *   *   *

THE ROGUE KNIGHT
Merline Lovelace

To Al, the handsome rogue
who stole my heart so many years ago
and still holds it in his hands,
with all my love...

A Note from Merline Lovelace

After twenty years as a military brat and another twenty plus years as an officer in the air force, I cheerfully admit to a decided partiality for warrior heroes. There's just something about strong, decisive men of action that turns my bones to mush—and makes me chuckle with delight when those fierce warriors are set back on their heels by an equally strong, adventurous heroine.

If you enjoy this tale of a Crusader whose unexpected return creates havoc in one very determined heroine's heart, I hope you'll look for my next historical, *Lady of the Upper Kingdom,* set in ancient Egypt during the time of Alexander the Great.

I always appreciate hearing from readers and can be reached at P.O. Box 892717, Oklahoma City, OK, 73189.

Happy reading!

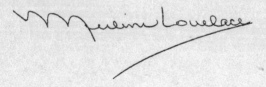

Chapter One

'Twas a rescue such as the troubadours sang of.

A lone knight came charging down the narrow forest track and barreled his mount into the band of thieves and cutthroats that surrounded Joanna. Swinging his sword with deadly efficiency, he slashed his way to her side just as her palfrey stumbled and went down. He threw aside his shield and wrapped his free arm around her waist, yanking her out of her saddle and away from the hands that grabbed at her skirts.

Joanna's breath whooshed out as the band of steel cut into her middle and pinned her against the knight's side, but she continued to kick at her attackers and stab her jeweled dagger at any hand that came too close.

Using his sword and his mount's vicious, slashing hooves to deadly effect, the knight cut a path through the outlaw band. Within moments, they were free and thundering down the narrow path.

"My escort!" Joanna shouted, her fingers clutching his surcoat for a hold as he dragged her to a precarious seat across his thighs. "We must go back and aid my escort!"

"They are down." His deep voice sounded distant, disembodied, coming as it did through the narrow opening in his great helm. "The last man fell just as I rode into the fray. By now the bandits will have cut their throats and all but picked their bones clean."

Joanna threw a frantic glance over his massive, mail-clad shoulder and saw he spoke the truth. Thieves swarmed like flies over unmoving bodies clad in the distinctive blue and gray of Greystone Keep. She swallowed, then faced forward once more. No stranger to the violence that plagued England in these perilous years, Joanna was nevertheless badly shaken. 'Twas the first time the bandits had struck this close to home.

With King Richard, known as Lionheart, so much abroad and his barons grown unruly in his absence, the bands of thieves and mercenaries who roamed the forests and preyed on unwary travelers had become near unmanageable. Still, Joanna had thought her escort of a mounted knight and ten men-at-arms sufficient for the short journey to town. She felt a twist of pain at the thought of Sir Avery, gruff old Sir Avery, going down under the weight of the men who had dropped from the trees upon him, like stones from the heavens. Her mouth grim, she said a silent prayer for his soul and those of the men with him.

The heavily armored war-horse stepped in a rut and dipped its shoulder, causing Joanna to clutch at her savior's surcoat to keep from sliding off her shaky perch. Once more a mailed arm encircled her waist, this time lifting her over the wooden pommels to settle her more securely in the saddle. Joanna felt the hard wall of his chest against her back and the unyielding strength of his arm about her middle. Wrapped thus in the safety of his body, she fought off the shock and fear she hadn't had time to experience during the attack. Tremors racked her, and she blinked furiously to hold back a sudden rush of tears.

By the time the winding track cleared the thick forest and the square tower of Greystone Keep appeared in the distance, she'd regained control of her emotions. When the knight drew rein outside the barbican, Joanna identified herself to the guard in a voice that wobbled only a bit.

They clattered over the drawbridge that spanned the ditch, then through the gate and into the outer bailey. Men-at-arms came running. Sir Eustace, her senior vassal, appeared from the inner yard and strode forward to lift her down from the saddle. Only when she reached out to put her hands on his shoulders did Joanna realize she still clutched her bloodied dagger in one fist.

While the knight dismounted, Joanna quickly told Eustace what had occurred. Whirling, he called to the captain of the guards to mount a troop at once.

At last Joanna turned to the man behind her.

He stood at his ease beside his mount, his great helm tucked under one arm. Sweat flattened his dark hair, worn shorter than the current fashion. Nor did he favor a beard, as did most men, who aped the king's style. His face was lean, and so bronzed by the sun that the fine white lines webbing his eyes stood out in stark contrast.

Joanna glanced at the heraldic charge embroidered on his dust-covered black surcoat, but didn't recognize the device. 'Twas some kind of fantastic two-headed dragon, carefully picked out in silver thread that glittered even under its layer of dust.

"I know not who you are," she said at length, "but I thank you, sir, for coming to my aid. I am Joanna, lady of Greystone. I bid you welcome to the keep."

He didn't move, didn't change his expression, but it seemed to Joanna that his gaze sharpened on her face. He studied her for a moment, then lifted his head and surveyed the crowded yard. His blue eyes, narrowed against the hazy afternoon sun, skimmed pond and stables, dovecotes and mews, and lingered on the massive square tower that loomed beyond the inner wall. Constructed of the uncompromising granite that gave Greystone its name, the keep was stark and unadorned by any softening stonework. At last his gaze returned to the woman before him.

Joanna waited for him to identify himself, as courtesy demanded. When he did not, she raised one brow.

"Will you not tell me your name, that I might thank you properly?"

"I am Ivo," he said at last.

The shock of the attack paled beside that which Joanna experienced now. The ground seemed to heave under her very feet, and she took an unsteady step back.

"But...but you're dead!"

Her eyes wide with disbelief, Joanna stared at this apparition from the netherworld. He bore little resemblance to her husband, Lord Fulk, she thought wildly, although their kinship was distant enough that Joanna shouldn't have expected similarity of face and form. And, indeed, there was none.

Where Fulk had been somewhat well fleshed, and pale from all his hours at prayer, this knight was tall and tanned and, as she remembered from the way he'd lifted her so easily, well muscled. Where Fulk's smile had been gentle and loving, even when he corrected a misdeed or admonished an erring servitor, this man's lips curved in a slow, feral grin that sent a sudden shiver down Joanna's spine.

"I am yet of this world," he drawled, "although I doubt not Fulk will be most unhappy to hear it. Do you summon him, lady, and tell him Ivo has returned to settle his debts."

The hard expression in his eyes confirmed his identity as nothing else could have. This was indeed Ivo, whom she'd heard so much of in her brief marriage. Ivo, the wild youth whose many misdeeds had sorely troubled her saintly husband. The young rogue who'd stolen a sword and Fulk's best mount and ridden off some ten years or more ago, hiring himself out as mercenary to any and all with the coins to pay. The same black knight who'd gone crusading, not in search of forgiveness for his many sins, but in expectation of plunder! He'd met his fate at the siege of Acre six years ago.

Or so they had all thought.

Now, as if from the dead, he'd come back to Greystone Keep to settle with her husband.

Drawing in a slow breath, Joanna met his unwavering gaze. "I fear I cannot summon Lord Fulk," she said with only the slightest catch in her voice. "My husband died of a colic to the stomach last summer, after partaking of a dish of boiled eels."

Behind their screen of dark lashes, Ivo's eyes took on a silvery sheen, until they glittered like the slate tiles that were forever sliding off Greystone's roof and crashing down on unwary servants and the hapless pigs rooting in the yard.

Joanna's warm heart contracted at the bleakness she saw in their depths. For all the harsh tales told about him, Ivo was obviously pained by the death of the man who had raised him. She took an impulsive step forward and laid her hand on his arm.

"I'm sorry," she whispered.

"As am I," he replied, after a long, silent moment. "I had much looked forward to being the one to send him to his just rewards."

Joanna's mouth dropped. She gaped up at him, sure she could not have heard him aright. Her utter astonishment brought a grim smile to his face.

"'Twas what sustained me these many years, lady, the thought of putting a lance or a sword through his gullet. Assuming," he added dryly, "he could be goaded sufficiently to take up a challenge of arms. Fulk was ever one to retreat to the chapel and pray while others fought his battles for him."

Joanna snatched her hand back, not sure whether she was more shocked by this man's claim that he came back to do battle with his kinsman or by the aspersions he cast on her husband's piety.

The buzz of excited exclamations behind her stilled the angry reply trembling on her lips. She glanced over her shoulder, seeing avid interest on the faces of the crowd gathered around them. Men-at-arms, stable hands, kitchen maids and a scattering of lords and ladies from the keep all stared openmouthed at the drama unfolding before their very eyes.

"Ivo!" someone whispered excitedly. "'Tis Ivo!"

"Ivo's back," another echoed.

"The rogue has returned."

A red-faced, hulking knight pushed his way through the crowd and strode forward to stand beside Joanna. The senior and most persistent of her unwanted suitors, he glared at the intruder.

"How do we know you're who you say?" Sir Arnould demanded. "King Richard himself saw the one called Ivo fall at Acre!"

The dark-haired warrior's gaze flickered over Arnould's uncombed beard and grease-stained surcoat. He didn't bother to respond, but the casual manner in which his hand moved to rest on his sword belt caused a ripple of fresh murmurs. Of a sudden, the balmy midsummer-afternoon air wafting about the bailey seemed to take on a decided chill.

With a calm she was far from feeling, Joanna interceded. "I am lady of Greystone Keep, Sir Arnould. I will deal with this."

Lifting her chin, she pinned the knight before her with a cool look. "'Tis not meet that we discuss such matters here. Attend me, if you will, inside the keep."

She spun on her heel and led the way inside Greystone's huge, timbered great hall, then headed for the stairs to her private solar. It was only when she reached the first step that the reality of the situation struck Joanna. She stumbled, all but tripping over her heavy skirts.

When Ivo reached out a hard hand to steady her, she stole a quick look at his face. The cynical amusement she saw there told her that he, too, had grasped the irony of their circumstance.

Despite her brave words, despite her calm assumption of authority, Joanna was no longer chatelaine of Greystone Keep! Fulk's only kinsman, Ivo, was heir to his estates. He was lord of this manor, and 'twas he who should be issuing commands, not her.

A wild surge of emotion washed over Joanna. Relief, joy, dread, all chased themselves through her veins, one after another, like hounds coursing a hare. Swallowing, she shook off the knight's hold, lifted her skirts, and led the way up the stairs.

Ivo followed more slowly, his face impassive. During his years in Outremer, he'd learned to hide his thoughts, as well as his physical reaction to any pain, any pleasure. Yet despite his hard-won control, his hands were balled into tight fists.

Damn Fulk.

Damn him to the depths of hell for dying before Ivo could send him there.

With iron determination, he forced himself to breathe in an even measure. He'd long ago acquired the ability to push the cold, deadly anger to the back of his mind and focus instead on what was before his eyes. In this instance, it was a slight figure robed in blue wool.

Fulk's wife.

A second son, destined by birth and by inclination for the Church, Fulk had reluctantly assumed the honor of Greystone upon the death of his older brother in battle. Just as reluctantly, he'd taken responsibility for a rascally five-year-old Ivo, son of a distant kinswoman who'd died birthing him.

Ivo's lips twisted in a cynical smile. For all his preference for spiritual matters over temporal ones, the man had at last taken a wife. And such a wife.

When she identified herself in the yard, Ivo had noted little more than huge, forest green eyes in a face still pale from the attack, the sheen of golden braids under a gauzy veil, and a somewhat determined chin. Then, his thoughts had all been on the coming confrontation with the man he'd once called by the courtesy title of Uncle.

Now, he noted with instinctive masculine appreciation the thickness of those shining braids, her long, slender neck, and the sway of rounded hips outlined by a girdle of woven gold and silver threads.

Remembering the feel of those same curving hips against his loins, and her courage while Joanna had held off her attackers, Ivo shook his head. In his wildest dreams, he could not imagine such a woman married to Fulk.

Lady Joanna opened the door to the small room that she had referred to as her private solar. Ivo recognized it at once. 'Twas the same chamber where Fulk had handled the keep's affairs. He glanced around with a wry smile, remembering the many times he'd been summoned here in his misspent youth to account for some wrongdoing or other. The stone chamber hadn't changed much. The same faded tapestries still hung on the walls. The same locked chest no doubt still held Greystone's accounts. And the same view of the rolling Sussex countryside Ivo had escaped to so often beckoned from the high, arched window.

While Lady Joanna lit candles with a twist from the fire banked in the hearth, he strolled over to the window. Fading summer twilight showed green, fertile fields, and an opalescent sea shimmering in the distance. The small fishing fleet that supplied much of Greystone's revenue lay at anchor in the stone-lined harbor.

For a moment, the years fell away. Idly Ivo wondered if the well-endowed fisherman's wife who had introduced him and the armorer's son to the pleasures of their manhood still lived in one of the thatched cottages beside the sea.

"Are you really Ivo, who was nephew to my husband?"

He turned slowly to survey the woman standing before him. A wash of color rode high on her cheek, contrasting with otherwise smooth, pale skin. Her eyes, huge and thick lashed and so changeable a green that they reminded Ivo of the emerald waters just off the coast of Cyprus, regarded him steadily.

"Were you really wife to the one I once called uncle?" he countered, leaning one hip against the stone sill.

Her flush deepened. "Aye, I was."

"Forgive me, lady," he offered after a moment. "I meant you no insult. 'Tis just that I have difficulty imagining Fulk ever taking a woman to his... bosom."

"To his bed, you mean."

Ivo arched a brow at such blunt speaking. Less and less could he imagine this woman as his kinsman's wife.

"'Twas not Fulk's wish to wed," she admitted stiffly. "But when you were lost to the Infidels, he knew he must beget an heir."

"Did he do so? Do you fear that I have come to dispossess your son, Lady Joanna?"

Her dark lashes, surprising in one so fair, swept down to cover her eyes. When they lifted once more, Ivo felt an unexpected tug of sympathy at the shadows in their depths.

"Nay, I have no son, or daughter, either. You do not dispossess anyone."

The shadows lightened, to be replaced by a slow glimmer of satisfaction. "Except for the suitors who have battened on me and on Greystone these many months. They will not be best pleased at your return."

"Particularly the suet-faced one below?"

"Particularly him."

They contemplated one another for a moment, his eyes thoughtful, hers curious.

"Where have you been these many years?" she asked at length.

Ivo considered the many answers he could give her and discarded them all. Instead, he simply shrugged. "I took a spear during the siege of Acre and went down. Against all odds, I survived and was taken by the Saracens."

He paused, watching her closely.

"When I recovered, I was sold in the slave markets. Since then . . . I've been in the East."

Her face contracted with pity. "Oh, my lord, if only we had known. To think you've been a prisoner of the Infidels all these years."

When he made no comment, she continued, almost shyly. "Well, if you are indeed the one called Ivo, you're the answer to my prayers."

He'd been called many things in his past, by many people, but never had he been labeled the answer to anyone's prayers. Crossing his arms, Ivo regarded the woman before him. By the beard of Allah, she was a winsome creature, with her great, gleaming eyes and ripe lips. For the first time in his life, he felt a stab of envy for Fulk.

He didn't like the feeling.

Straightening, he speared her with a hard look. "Aye, I am indeed Ivo."

"Thank the Lord."

Her low, fervent prayer brought him forward. Curling a hand under her chin, he tilted her face to his.

"You give thanks for the deliverance of one sworn to vengeance with your husband?"

"My husband is beyond your vengeance. Whatever wrongs Fulk did you as a boy, trying to curb your evil ways, he has settled them with God."

"Think you that's why I came back? To gain revenge for a few whippings?"

"What else could it be? You left Greystone while still a beardless youth. My husband had no word, no message from you, in ten years and more."

"He told you this?" Ivo growled. "He spoke to you of me?"

"Everyone spoke to me of you," she replied tartly. "Your dissolute past is the stuff of legend in the castle and the surrounding villages. When you were lost at Acre, Fulk went barefoot on pilgrimage to Canterbury to pray for your redemption."

The thought of his uncle donning the pilgrim's cross to pray for his soul made Ivo's fingers tighten on her chin.

"My lord!" she gasped, her hand coming up to cover his. "He prayed most heartily for you! Even today the priest says the masses Fulk ordered for your soul."

Her touch was light on his hand, as soft as the brush of a silken veil, but it cut through the anger that tested Ivo's rigid control. It also sent a shaft of awareness slicing through him. Loosening his hold, he stroked his thumb, once, twice, along the flesh of her lower lip.

" 'Tis beyond saving," he murmured, "this soul of mine."

She tugged her chin free and stepped back, a flush once more painting her cheeks.

"If not yet beyond saving, then very close to it," she snapped. "I will of a certainty include you in my prayers when I retire to Lessingham."

"Lessingham?" Ivo searched his memory. After a moment, his dark brows drew together. "Isn't that the convent Fulk endowed, where the nuns chant matins to the sting of the scourge?"

The color faded a bit in her cheeks, but she said only, " 'Tis a most holy place."

"And you would retire there?"

"'Tis what my husband most wished for me."

Ivo muttered a vile oath. Since he did so in Arabic, his words, if not his tone, were lost on Joanna. Frowning a bit, she continued.

"It greatly sorrowed Fulk that we had no children, however. Despite his wish that I take sanctuary with the holy sisters, he made me promise to wed again after his death, to provide Greystone an heir."

She paused, drawing in a deep breath. "Now that you are home, Greystone has its heir. I need not take another husband and may hie myself to the convent."

After six years in the East, Ivo was no longer sure of many things in this world. But he knew without a trace of doubt that this woman did not belong among the fanatics at Lessingham. Not this vital, vibrant woman with sunlight in her hair and a well of compassion in her heart.

In this, at least, he could foil his uncle, as Fulk had foiled him by dying. From a dish of boiled eels, yet! Stifling his disgust, Ivo shrugged.

"You must do as you think best, of course. But you should know that I am not come to claim Greystone. I want it not, nor do I intend to swear allegiance to Richard for it."

"What?" Her shocked exclamation bounced off the stone walls. "But... but you must! Your ancestor won this keep fighting with the Angevin kings against Stephen's false claim. You cannot just... forfeit it.''

"I can."

"But the revenues! The tariffs and fees I've been so hard-pressed to collect!"

"I don't need them."

Her eyes narrowed, then skimmed his length. For the first time, she seemed to take in the richness of his surcoat under its coating of dust, the fineness of his mail. Her lower lip jutted out as she pondered this unexpected turn of events.

Ivo watched the play of emotions chasing across her face. Consternation, disbelief and a touch of irritation all surfaced, as though she couldn't quite decide whether to believe him. The openness of her countenance both amused and intrigued him. He'd been too long in another world, Ivo decided, one where women were schooled to show no emotion, no thought, except for their lord's pleasure. That this one slight female should so fascinate him with her changeable expressions was a sign that he'd not yet adjusted to this world he'd returned to.

"What about the people?" Joanna demanded, interrupting his musing. "The serfs who work your lands? The vassals who owe you service or scutage in lieu of service? You can't just abandon them."

"I can. They'll work the land and pay their service, whatever lord holds their living."

She flapped a hand, angry now. "I disbelieve this. You walk back in here after all these years and dare to refuse the responsibilities that are rightfully yours?"

"Aye, lady. As do you."

"I?" She drew herself up to her full height, which put her nose at about the level of Ivo's shoulder. "What are you speaking of? I've held Greystone against all who would take it, including that greedy clutch of so-called suitors below stairs. I've done my duty by it."

"Yet you would abandon it now, and retire to a nunnery."

"'Tis yours!" she exclaimed, exasperated. "The keep is yours!"

"Nay, lady. Greystone was never mine. It was Fulk's, and he left it to you to provide an heir. 'Tis you, not I, who are bound by your promise to him."

Chapter Two

Several hours later, Joanna paced her bedchamber. She was exhausted from the stresses of the day and emotionally drained from comforting the families of the fallen, yet sleep eluded her. She'd shed her veil and robe, and wore only her shift. The linen swished against her ankles with every agitated turn.

The women who shared the spacious bedchamber kept a wary eye on her as she roamed from one end of the room to the other, then back again. 'Twas rare indeed that Greystone's lady showed anger or disquiet, but when she did, all knew to stay out of her way. They busied themselves at the various tasks of preparing for the night.

Straw pallets rustled as they were rolled out on the thick rushes. Wooden shutters banged shut. A maid climbed on a stool to set a glowing ember to the huge, fat candle that served as a light for any who needed to use the garderobe during the night. The women murmured among themselves as they worked, and more than once Joanna heard Ivo's name.

Ivo! What manner of man was he? she thought furiously. How could he simply deny all claim to Greystone?

He'd refused to bow to any of her arguments, refused to allow her to move her belongings out of the main bedchamber, refused even to occupy the lord's seat at high table at the evening meal.

When she joined him at table, he'd taken one look at her face, drawn after her visits to the families of the slain men, and told her to seat herself. Unthinking, she'd slipped into the high-backed wooden chair she'd assumed since Fulk's death. As soon as she realized her error, Joanna had jumped up, but Ivo had already been sprawled in the chair next to hers. Waving her back to her seat, he'd proceeded to spear the choicest morsels for her from the dishes brought by the goggle-eyed pages and ignore her low-voiced, increasingly desperate arguments.

Joanna made another turn of the bedchamber, an uncharacteristic scowl on her face. How could he refuse his responsibilities, his birthright, his king? Were all those stories about him true, the ones she'd always only half believed?

At least some were true, Joanna decided with a fresh spurt of ire—the ones that recounted his youthful prowess with the women of the area. Even now, the maids sighed and giggled and offered gushing comments about his reputation, his glinting blue eyes, and his other, more masculine accoutrements.

Her pace slowed, and Joanna reached up to press her fingers against her lips. To her consternation, her flesh tingled where his thumb had stroked it. A sudden heat coursed though her, followed almost immediately by a wave of mortification.

After all these years, she thought in despair. After all this time, she'd not learned to control her wantonness. 'Twas why she'd hesitated so long to take another husband. Why she'd taken full advantage of King Richard's absence on the Continent to prolong her widowhood.

If Fulk, kind, gentle Fulk, had been shocked at his young bride's eager responses, she shuddered to think how another man might react. Fulk had curbed her girlish passion by pulling her from their marriage bed and leading her in prayer hour after endless hour, but another husband might well have beaten her, or resorted to some of the more disgusting instruments devised to control a woman's lust.

Joanna stared blindly at the tapestry on the wall before her. Its glowing colors were dim in the flickering candlelight. Sweet Mary, she was sure she'd overcome the weakness of her traitorous flesh. After that initial period of shamed confusion with Fulk, she had accepted that she was indeed the daughter of Eve. With conscious effort, she'd suppressed every urge, every curious thought. For the sake of their immortal souls, Fulk had carefully avoided any hint of carnal passion during their infrequent couplings. Joanna hadn't felt a yearning for her husband's touch since shortly after they were wed.

And yet... And yet a rogue knight had but to run his thumb along her lip, and her skin flamed.

Joanna turned and groped her way toward the huge, carved bed. Sliding under the coverlets, she tugged the heavy curtains closed and lay in the smothering darkness.

She had to convince Ivo to remain at Greystone. Only then could she in good conscience retire to Lessingham. Only then could she be sure that she was no longer subject to the mortifying weakness of her flesh.

Fingers of gray light snaked through the heavy bed curtains before she finally hit upon a solution.

Ivo had a fondness for women. Everyone acknowledged it, whispered about it, laughed over it.

Fine! Then it must needs be a woman who would bind him to Greystone.

'Twas time he married, anyway, Joanna told herself. He must be well past his third decade, although the lines that gave such character to his face could be the result of his experiences in Outremer.

Joanna's generous heart, at once her greatest gift and greatest weakness, contracted. How he must have suffered at the hands of his captors! No wonder he felt adrift, unready to assume his place in the land of his birth. He'd been so long in the clutches of those who abused him, he had yet to rediscover his roots.

Aye, a wife was what he needed, she decided, throwing off the coverlets. Tender, loving companionship to erase the memory of those awful years and—

"Are you awake, lady?"

The low, timorous voice penetrated the thick bed curtains. Pulling them open, Joanna stared at the young maiden standing beside the bed.

The daughter of a minor baron, Lady Alice had come to Greystone some years ago for training. She was sweet and unassuming and held a special place in everyone's heart. If she was also somewhat plump, 'twas no mark against her, not in this time when men measured their wealth by the number of dishes they could lay at table.

"How old are you now, Lady Alice?"

"I've passed my sixteenth summer."

Joanna slid out of bed and took the girl's hand. "Do you still grieve over the loss of your betrothed, the one you were to wed last year?"

Lustrous brown braids swayed as Alice shook her head. "Nay, lady. I met him but once, at the ceremony where we exchanged pledges. He sent me gifts and kind messages on my name day, and once a nightingale in a gilded cage. But in truth, I can scarce recall his face."

Joanna bit her lip. For some strange reason, she was reluctant to put into action the plan she'd so recently formulated.

Then Alice heaved a most unmaidenly sigh. "My betrothed was handsome, as best I can recall, but nothing like Sir Ivo. Now there's a man."

A trifle shocked by the knowing gleam in the girl's doelike eyes, Joanna loosed her hand and moved toward the washbowl, set on an ornate, carved chest.

"Mayhap 'tis time I spoke to your father about another betrothal," she said, a hint of coolness in her voice.

"Oh, aye," Alice breathed. "'Tis time."

With a light step, the girl moved to open the shutters, letting in the dawn and a fine, curling mist. With the sea not a mile distant, such morning wetness often dewed the keep's walls. It made for cool summers, but also for aching bones and horrendous chilblains in winter.

While a tiring woman laced up Joanna's surcoat of rose silk, embroidered along the hem with the gold griffins of Greystone, the lady of the manor considered the other women entrusted to her care. There were several of marriageable age who were not already promised, but none came close to Alice's sweetness of disposition.

Joanna knew a moment's disquiet at the thought of entrusting such a gentle girl to one of Ivo's reputation, but quickly brushed it aside. Of all the tales told of him, none included brutality toward women. Quite the opposite, in fact.

Her mind whirling, Joanna stared unseeing into the polished-steel mirror while her maid braided her hair and coiled it over her ears. With deft skill, the tiring woman anchored a delicate veil of a shimmering rose hue on her mistress's forehead with a circlet of beaten gold.

Standing, Joanna wrapped her girdle around her waist, then knotted it about her hips. To it she attached the pouch containing her most precious possessions—the illuminated Psalter that had been Fulk's betrothal gift and a tiny pair of gold scissors. Out of habit, she reached for the heavy chatelaine's ring of keys. The bits of metal jangled, reminding Joanna with a start that they were no longer hers to possess. They belonged to Ivo, or to the woman he chose as wife.

And he would choose one soon, she decided with renewed determination. Lifting her chin, Joanna swept down the winding tower staircase, which led direct from the lord's chamber to the great hall. She would begin her campaign right after morning mass and a bit of ale and bread to break her fast.

She found Ivo in the outer bailey, putting his mount through its paces before a delighted crowd of stable hands, men-at-arms and admiring kitchen wenches. Joanna stopped halfway across the yard, transfixed by the sight.

The black stallion was magnificent. Big and barrel chested, as was necessary in war-horses bred to carry heavily armored knights into battle, it nevertheless possessed an astounding grace of movement. The animal appeared to float on the air as it lifted first one hoof and then the other in an intricate, measured prance.

But if the horse was awe inspiring, its rider was even more so. Having left off his armor and surcoat, Ivo wore only tight-fitting braies and a shirt of some soft white material that looked too fine to be linen. Dampened by the morning mists, the shirt clung to his superbly muscled body. Joanna watched him move as one with the horse, and felt a little lurch in the pit of her stomach.

Holy Mother, she'd best get this business done quickly, and get herself to the nunnery!

Unclenching fingers that had somehow curled themselves into fists, she waited until Ivo swung down from the saddle and strode toward her.

"God grant you good-morrow," she said in greeting.

"And you, lady."

Although he kept his voice steady, Ivo felt an intense and unexpected pleasure at the sight of the woman before him. She reminded him of the caliph's magical garden, where the blooms had all been crafted of precious metals. Under its short veil, her hair shone like burnished gold in the sunlight. The rose of her gown was no match for the delicate color that adorned her cheeks, or the lush tint of her full lips.

With a wrench, Ivo realized that those same lips were speaking to him.

"...and 'tis a matter of some delicacy."

"What is?"

She frowned. "What I would speak with you about."

"My pardon, lady. You have my complete attention."

Now that she had it, however, she appeared not quite certain what to do with it. She glanced about the busy yard, then nibbled on her lower lip a moment.

"Will you walk with me in the gardens?" she asked at length. "I would speak privately with you."

His interest now thoroughly engaged, Ivo shortened his stride to match hers as she led the way to the walled garden. Like Greystone Keep itself, the cultivated area was stark and utilitarian. It seemed smaller than Ivo remembered, thinking of the days when he was used to sneak inside to filch apples and pears. And of the nights when he'd filched other, more succulent forbidden fruit in its dark corners.

He sniffed at the delicate scent of mint and thyme that filled the air, almost hidden by the odor of manure used to fertilize the beds. 'Twas a far cry from the gardens he'd grown used to in the East, Ivo thought wryly. No flowers bloomed here. No fountains flowed with musk or rosewater, nor did any gilded boats float on ponds filled with a mercury brighter than polished silver.

He propped a boot on the corner of a stone bench and waited while Joanna settled herself. After plucking at her skirts for a few moments, she lifted her head.

"I wish to speak to you about marriage, my lord."

He nodded, experiencing a sharp relief. "So you've changed your mind about Lessingham?"

"Not my marriage, sir," she said stiffly. "Yours."

"Mine?"

"Aye, I . . ." She paused and glanced up at him quickly, as if struck by a sudden thought. "You're not wed, are you? You didn't take a wife in the years since you left Greystone?"

Ivo hesitated, his mind weighing the possible reasons for her question. "I was a long time gone," he replied at last, "and spent many years in the East."

Joanna cursed herself for a fool. Why hadn't it occurred to her that Ivo might already be wed? Wondering how she was to extricate herself from this embarrassing coil, she almost missed his next words.

" 'Tis the custom in the East to take several wives, by the way. Four is the prescribed number."

"Your pardon, my lord?"

"Four. The Koran allows a man to keep four wives in his harem."

Joanna's mouth opened and shut several times. "Harem?" she managed at last. "You...you kept four wives...in a harem?"

"A man may also keep as many concubines as he can support." His lips curved in a slow grin. "And I could support many."

Her jaw dropped once more. When she caught sight of the wicked glint in the depths of his blue eyes, Joanna closed it with a snap.

She'd heard the fantastic stories brought back by the crusaders, of course. Tales of exotic animals and rich palaces and women trained to give men secret, scandalous pleasures. She'd even heard that Frankish lords who settled in Sicily and in the Holy Land adopted many of the more outrageous customs. But Ivo was the first man she'd ever met who confessed to having more than one wife. *And* several dozen concubines.

Not sure whether or not to believe him, Joanna pursed her lips. "I thought you said you were a prisoner of the Infidels. Are all prisoners allowed to keep harems?"

The teasing glint faded from his eyes. He leaned a forearm across his bent knee and studied her face, as if debating how much to tell her, how much of himself to reveal. Unaware that she did so, Joanna held her breath.

"I was, in truth, a prisoner at first," he said finally. "I still bear the scars from those early years. But when the caliph of Rabat purchased me, he promised me my freedom if I would serve him faithfully for four years. In that time, he sought to enslave my mind instead of my body and made every effort to convert me to his ways."

Joanna's pity was considerably more restrained now that she knew some of the circumstances of his imprisonment. Still, she felt an instinctive rush of sympathy for one forced to shape his thoughts and ways to suit another.

"The caliph was a very learned man," Ivo continued slowly, speaking as much to himself as to her. "His private library held thousands of illuminated manuscripts. He employed a small army of scribes to make copies of the Koran and other great books. Those he gave to public libraries, so that the poor could read the holy words. He had one of the scribes teach me the ancient Kufic script so I, too, could read the books. In time, he included me among the ranks of his *nadim*."

"His *nadim?*" Joanna prompted when Ivo fell silent.

"His trusted companions. All the princes of the East choose artists, scholars, men of letters, as companions. Their job is to amuse the caliph with discussions of the holy book, or with literary debates and games such as chess and mah-jongg.'' He smiled at her blank look. '' 'Tis a game from China, played with ivory pieces.''

For long moments, Joanna could only gape at him. Then silent laughter bubbled up inside her chest. Despite her best efforts to contain it, it spilled out, low and musical, and totally unexpected, if the expression on Ivo's face was any measure.

"Forgive me, my lord," she said, gasping. '' 'Tis just that I spent so many hours on my knees at those endless masses Fulk had sung for your soul. And all the while *I* was praying, *you* were reading books and playing with ivory pieces . . . among other things!''

She gave another little giggle, so girlish in sound, so seductive in its effect.

'Twas at that precise moment Ivo admitted to himself that he desired her. There, in that unpretentious little garden, with the scent of manure rising about them and the echo of her laughter almost lost amid the raucous chatter of the starlings in the fruit trees. Ivo saw the merriment sparkling in her green eyes, the rise and fall of her breasts under the rose-hued robe, and he wanted her.

As he'd trained himself to do, he controlled each muscle, each sinew, so that he showed no sign of the sudden stab of heat that shot through his loins. And, as he'd learned to do in order to survive, he focused on the object before him.

Unaware of the silent battle being fought within the man who regarded her so intently, Joanna mastered her mirth.

"Do you still maintain these many wives in this harem you speak of? Not that such marriages would ever be recognized by the Church, of course," she added hastily.

"Nay, I claim no wife," Ivo replied, his gaze on her face. She had the most inviting lips, he decided. Full and curving and made to be kissed.

"Then I would ask you to consider marriage with Lady Alice."

It took a moment for her words to penetrate. "Who the devil is Lady Alice?"

"She resides in my household, and lost her betrothed last year. She's young and sweet, and most compliant."

Ivo straightened slowly. "You brought me here to discuss marriage to some girl I've never laid eyes on?"

Another chuckle escaped her. Where just a few moments ago her merriment had thoroughly delighted Ivo, now it irritated him greatly. While he had been contemplating what it would be like to kiss those smiling lips, she, apparently, had been scheming to marry him off so that she could retire to her damned nunnery.

"Well, you do seem to be short a few wives right now," she pointed out. "Mayhap this time you should take a gently reared, God-fearing maid to wife. One who would serve you well as mistress of Greystone Keep."

"Nay, lady, the only woman I seek at this point is one who would serve *me* as mistress."

Joanna blinked at the silky menace in his tone. What on earth had she said to raise his ire?

"Just think on it," she suggested in a placating tone. "You're...what? Passing thirty years? 'Tis time you—"

"Enough!"

"But my lord—"

She broke off, gasping in surprise, when he reached down and curled his hands around her upper arms. Before Joanna could protest, he'd hauled her up against him and lowered his head until his breath warmed her lips.

"When I wish to take a wife, I will so inform you."

Her heart pounding, Joanna splayed her hands against his chest and stared up into eyes that seemed to taunt her, almost to challenge her. Beneath her fingertips she felt his thin, damp shirt and a broad expanse of heated male flesh. Something sparked within her, something sudden and sharp and searing in its intensity.

When she understood it as desire, a wave of shame washed through her, quenching the spark completely. She jerked out of his hold and stumbled backward.

The taunting gleam in his eyes faded. He stepped toward her, frowning. "Did I hurt you? 'Twas not my intention."

"No, no..."

She held out a hand to stop him, then forced herself to calm. "I'm...I'm sorry if I pressed you unduly about Lady Alice."

"Aye, and so you should be."

She bit down on her lower lip, unwilling to give up her only scheme. "But I wish you would consider her."

"Joanna..."

The low growl sent her back another step. Then she lifted her chin.

"Truly, my lord, do you but meet her, you will see she is just the wife for you."

Chapter Three

"Your pardon, my lord. Lady Joanna bade me bring fresh linens for you to don after your bath."

The squire detailed to attend Ivo paused in the act of sluicing a bucket of rinse water over his lord's head. Opening one eye, Ivo peered at the plump, blushing maiden who stood before him, a stack of linens clutched to her generous breasts.

At his appraising look, the tide of color in the girl's face deepened, but she stood her ground. To Ivo's considerable amusement, she conducted an inventory of her own. Since he was at that moment ensconced in the huge wooden tub that served any and all of Greystone's inhabitants who could be coerced into it, the girl saw a good bit more of him than he did of her.

His mouth curved. "Are you by any chance Lady Alice?"

He wouldn't have thought it possible, but her blush deepened yet another shade. "Aye...aye," she stammered, crushing the linens still closer to her chest.

The squire rose to relieve the girl of her burdens. "Here, lady, I'll take those."

While the two of them smoothed the wrinkled clothing and laid it on the bed, Ivo eased back against the tub's rough side. Despite his relaxed pose, a dozen possibilities streamed though his agile mind. He hadn't lain with a woman for some time now, not since the willing wench who'd welcomed him back to England's shores. This maid, for all her stammering and blushing, had the kind of full, generous curves that would fill a man's arms quite satisfactorily. Moreover, her brown eyes held a gleam that belied her shyness.

That she was no doubt a virgin, and of some rank, didn't bother him unduly. He'd seduced few virgins in his checkered past, although he'd allowed himself to be seduced by several. Ivo suspected, however, that if he sent the squire away and took this pretty, plump bird to his bed, Lady Joanna would be here with the castle priest afore either he or Maid Alice achieved release.

The thought of the lady of Greystone banished Ivo's passing interest in the girl. Since their session in the garden this morning, he'd had time to consider Joanna's sudden determination to marry him off so that she could bury herself in a convent. And to reflect on her reaction when he'd taken her in his arms.

No stranger to either his own or a woman's passion, Ivo had seen the desire that had flared so briefly in Joanna's eyes. And he'd seen, as well, the wave of shame that suffused her face when she wrenched herself out of his hold. It hadn't taken him long to unravel the mystery of why this warm, compassionate and thoroughly bewitching woman should be ashamed of her own sensuality.

Fulk.

His pious, ascetic uncle, who abhorred all weaknesses of the flesh.

His saintly uncle, who'd tried every means known to man and God to cure an adolescent Ivo of what was then a growing but as yet unfulfilled interest in kitchen wenches and dairymaids.

When prayers and penances and fasts failed to lessen Ivo's involuntary youthful hardening, Fulk had ordered foul dosages of potions infused with herbs valued for their antiaphrodisiacal qualities. To this day, Ivo could hear Fulk's voice citing the virtues of rue, which, according to the first-century pharmacopoeia he'd consulted, was good against serpent biting, and, either eaten or drunk, extinguished geniture.

And when the herbs didn't curb the now-defiant youth, a much saddened Fulk had ordered Greystone's torturer to beat the baseness out of his young charge. Ivo had endured whippings before without losing his cockiness, but this one had been especially brutal. With a strength born of fury, he'd torn the lash out of the torturer's hands, wrapped it around his burly neck and all but strangled him. Taking a sword from the armory, and Fulk's best mount, Ivo had left the keep the same afternoon.

If Fulk had worked so diligently to extinguish his nephew's natural appetites, Ivo could well imagine his reaction to a young and sensuous wife. In his pious way, Fulk had no doubt decreed that desire had no place in the marriage bed, which was intended for procreation only. And thus damned Joanna to a frozen hell on earth.

A sudden, fierce need to be the one to release her from that wasteland coiled in Ivo's belly.

"Do you wish me to assist you in your bath, my lord?"

Ivo slewed his head around. Alice stood beside the tub, hands demurely folded in the long sleeves of her robe, eyes downcast.

"Did Lady Joanna ask you to do so?" he asked with a slight frown.

Normally, the chatelaine of a keep oversaw the matter of bathing, which presented the opportunity to check for diseases and festering wounds that might need tending. 'Twas a courtesy provided to all guests, although generally not one delegated to unmarried maidens.

"No, she did not," Alice replied, slanting him a most unmaidenly glance.

Ivo considered how best to rid himself of this girl so that he could focus on the woman who was coming to dominate his thoughts. Recalling the conversation in the garden, he raised one brow in query.

"Did Lady Joanna mention that I am used to the ways of the East?"

Alice's brown eyes widened. "No, my lord."

"The women of there are most skilled in tending to the bath."

"Th-they are?"

"They are."

Tepid water sloshed against the sides of the tub as Ivo sat up and jerked his chin toward a tooled-leather pouch that held his belongings. "Inside that bag is a flask that contains a special oil. Go fetch it, and I will tell you how you may make use of it."

Some five minutes later, Lady Alice rushed from his chamber, her face an impossible shade of red.

Ivo grinned at the openmouthed squire. "'Tis something for you to think about when you have a few more years under your belt, lad."

The youth swallowed, then grinned back. "Aye, my lord."

Ivo had just pulled on his chausses and was attaching them to his braies when the door to his chamber flew open. Joanna, her face thunderous, stalked in.

"What in the name of the Holy Virgin did you say to Lady Alice?" she demanded. "The girl is all but incoherent, babbling about heathens and oils and unnatural vices."

Ivo shrugged. "When she offered to assist me in my bath, I..."

"When she *what?*"

"She offered to assist me in my bath. Wasn't that what you intended when you sent her to my chamber?"

"Of course not! I wouldn't allow a maid in my keeping to tend a knight alone! I but desired her to bring fresh linens and present them to your squire."

"And present herself to my notice, as well?"

"Aye, well..." Joanna floundered for a moment, then recovered. "In any case, you had no business speaking to a tender virgin of... of oils and such."

"Virgin she may be," Ivo drawled, "but mayhap not as tender as you think. Nay, don't fly up into the boughs like an angry peahen. I but requested her to apply the oil to a part of me that aches."

Joanna gasped.

"The girl reacted as do you," Ivo admitted, shaking his head in bafflement. "Although why she should take such umbrage at a simple request to spread oil on a man's back is beyond my understanding."

"Oh, aye, your back!" Joanna sneered. "Well, you and your back may go straight to— Holy Mary!"

He had turned to take the shirt the squire held out, giving Joanna her first glimpse of the part of his anatomy under discussion. Her hand went to her mouth to stifle her strangled cry.

As a girl, she'd assisted her mother in tending the hurts of the manor folk. As chatelaine of Greystone, she'd stitched wounds, set bones, helped birth babes and smoothed ointments on bruises and cuts from accidents and punishments. But never had she seen a back as webbed with scars.

"The Saracens did this to you?" she whispered.

Ivo hesitated, then shrugged. "They left their mark."

"Sweet Mary, I would say so. I have potions that will ease the ache and loosen the drawn skin. Good, home-brewed potions—" she sniffed "—not some heathenish oils concocted by the inhabitants of a harem. You, squire, go and tell my woman to bring the chest of medicaments I keep in my chamber."

Snatching up a three-legged stool from its place beside the hearth, she plunked it down in front of the narrow slit that served as a window.

"And you, sir, sit you down and let me examine those scars."

They were old, Joanna soon saw, and for the most part well healed. Some were obviously made by the lash, others by instruments she couldn't begin to imagine. One particularly ugly gash, just below his right shoulder blade, had left the skin puckered and badly closed.

When her maid delivered her precious box of remedies, Joanna delved among the bottles and jars until she found the one she sought. Pulling out the stopper, she poured the greenish liquid into her palm and began to massage it into his back.

Ivo sucked in a quick breath as burning heat sank into his flesh, then let it out on a long, low hiss. Joanna felt his tense muscles relax, one by one, beneath her kneading fingers. He leaned forward, resting his elbows on his thighs to give her freer access.

Methodically she worked the potion into the white, ridged scars, so startling against his otherwise tanned skin. As she labored Joanna couldn't help but note the symmetry of the body beneath her hands. He possessed a raw male beauty, despite his wounds.

Broad, muscled shoulders.

A back that tapered to a narrow waist.

Lean hips.

Firm white buttocks showing where his braies gapped away from his back.

Of a sudden, the small chamber seemed unaccountably warm. Joanna lifted one arm and wiped her brow. Pouring more unguent into her palm, she worked it into his shoulders. The scars weren't so bad there. At the feel of hard sinew and warm skin, Joanna's stomach slowly knotted.

Almost of their own accord, her hands slid along his flesh until her thumbs met at the back of his neck. Applying a slight pressure, she gently massaged his spine.

"Ah . . ." Ivo murmured. "Do that higher, and lower."

Biting down on her lower lip, Joanna complied. When her hands slid up to rub his neck, her thumbs brushed the ends of his dark hair. It was still damp from his bath, and fine to her touch, although she knew it tended toward stiffness when dry. Joanna decided she liked the way its short length shaped his head. A swift, fierce urge to bury her hands in its thickness swept through her.

"Ouch!"

At Ivo's exclamation, Joanna jumped and dropped her hands. He swiveled on the stool, catching her between his outspread knees. She would have backed away, but the wall blocked her escape.

"I'll admit your unguent is more potent than the oil brewed by the harem women," he said with a crooked grin, "but I must teach you their skills with their fingers. Here, give me your hands."

Joanna tucked her hands behind her back. "As if I wished to learn such heathenish skills!"

"Truly," he teased, "'tis amazing how many ways a simple touch can bring pleasure."

Her brief enjoyment in their banter faded. The mere mention of pleasure was enough to send a shiver of guilt down her spine.

"Let me go, sir. There are tasks I must attend to."

"Joanna..."

"Let me go, sir!"

His eyes thoughtful, Ivo pushed back the stool.

She left the small chamber almost at a run. Lifting her skirts, she dashed down the stone stairs to the floor below. She was panting by the time she stumbled into the small, dark chapel. Giving a silent prayer of thanksgiving that the sparse sanctuary was empty, Joanna sank to her knees on the well-worn, unpadded prayer bench and buried her face in her hands.

She desired him! Holy Mother of God, she desired him with an ache so sweet and so painful that all other feelings paled beside it. She had but to look on his face, see his grin, and she forgot to breathe. Forgot to think. Forgot to have a care for her immortal soul.

In desperation, Joanna began the litany she'd learned by heart and said so often in the first weeks and months of her marriage.

When she left the chapel hours later, she was calm, clear-eyed, and more determined than ever to see Ivo wed and herself removed from all carnal temptation.

Lady Barbara was her next candidate.

The daughter of a landless knight, she was slender and russet haired, and so graceful in the dance that she caught everyone's admiring glance. The girl was yet unmarried, only because her father had so many petitions for her hand that he couldn't decide which was the most advantageous. She had of late been in the south, visiting a married sister. Joanna regarded Barbara's return to Greystone just the day after Lady Alice's debacle as an omen.

Ivo regarded it as a supreme test of his willpower. By all the saints, the girl was magnificent. At any other time in his life, he might have done his utmost to sweep her out of the great hall and into his bed.

But she was also as avaricious as any sharp-eyed merchant he'd ever haggled with in the bazaar. Within moments of leading the beauty out to take part in a stately circle dance, Ivo wanted only to restore her to her covey of admirers and return to Joanna's side.

Where Joanna's eyes tended to sparkle with suppressed laughter, Barbara's held a narrow, assessing gleam.

Where Joanna had been intrigued, despite herself, by his tales of the East, Barbara let him know immediately that she was interested in his past only insofar as it pertained to his ability to provide for a wife with expensive tastes.

"Aye," he drawled in answer to an unsubtle probe, "I'm well able to drape any woman I take to wife in jewels."

A small, feline smile traced her red lips.

"Of course, I would be the only one to see her so adorned," he added casually.

"How so, my lord?" Barbara arched her swan-like neck. "Would you not want others to admire her... your munificence?"

"Nay, I fear I've been too long in Outremer. I would expect any woman I take to wife to cover herself in veils, one atop the other."

Delicate, wine red brows drew together.

Across the hall, Joanna watched Ivo's dark head bent over the flame-haired maiden. They were well matched, she told herself resolutely. He was so tall and well proportioned, she so graceful and elegant. Joanna refused to admit that sight of them together didn't generate within her nearly the degree of satisfaction it should.

"He'll not stay at Greystone, you know."

A waft of breath redolent of boiled onions and garlic assaulted Joanna. Controlling an involuntary flinch, she turned to face Sir Arnould.

The man grinned, showing wide gaps where he'd lost teeth to rot or to blows in battle. "It has long been rumored that the spear Ivo took at Acre was meant for King Richard. When the Lionheart hears of this rogue's return from the dead, he'll grant him far greater honors and, I doubt not, leave Greystone as your widow's portion."

Joanna felt a familiar dread at the gleam in his bloodshot eyes when he raked her with a slow, possessive glance. Swallowing, she gave silent thanks for the bride-price Richard had set on her. The stiff fee was all that had saved her thus long from Sir Arnould and the other suitors who had descended on her within days of Fulk's death.

"Greystone is Sir Ivo's birthright," she countered coolly. "He'll claim it."

He must, she thought, turning once again to view the circle of dancers.

The next morning an irate Joanna caught Ivo just before he strode out of the great hall to join the hunt.

"What is this nonsense about veils and such?" she demanded.

His lips curved in the grin Joanna was beginning to recognize all too well.

"You've been querying Lady Barbara, I take it?"

Lifting her chin, she assumed her best chatelaine's demeanor. "You appeared most taken with her in the dance. 'Tis my responsibility, after all, to have a care to the maids in my charge."

Ivo ran a finger down the slope of her nose. "I think mayhap you take your responsibilities for those in your care too much to heart."

He turned to leave, but Joanna's natural curiosity made her call out. "Wait, sir. Tell me why Lady

Barbara says that you would swathe your wife all over in veils, like a corpse wrapped in linens?''

He swung back to face her. ''Because, my little goose, 'tis so much fun to pluck them off, one by one.''

''Oh.''

''Nay, Joanna, don't stiffen up and turn away.'' Planting one hand on the huge oak door, Ivo blocked her retreat. '' 'Tis no sin for a man to take pleasure of his wife, and she of him.''

''But it is.''

''If so, would God have given us the means to create such splendor?''

In Joanna's experience, limited as it was, what occurred between a man and his wife in the privacy of their curtained bed held little of splendor.

''The Lord also gave us the means to build pigsties,'' she retorted, her face flaming, ''but that doesn't mean we should wallow with the pigs.''

He threw back his head and gave a rich, delighted bellow of laughter. Joanna's heart thumped against her ribs at the way the hazy sunshine painted his lean, chiseled features. Sweet Mother, he was a handsome devil, with his tanned skin, and eyes the color of an April sky washed with rain. In deference to the midsummer heat, he'd left off his black surcoat and wore only a jerkin of boiled leather over his linen shirt.

The leather molded his chest and broad shoulders most faithfully. Joanna flattened her palms against the wood door, denying the need to run her hands up the leather.

"You know, lady, you would make a good candidate for a *nadim*. Such quick arguments are the kind that used to delight the caliph. As they delight me," Ivo finished softly.

He was gone before she could give any answer to that. Indeed, before she could think of one.

Chapter Four

Tired and sweating in the afternoon heat, Ivo reined in his mount on a stretch of path that ran along a high bluff overlooking the sea. Behind him he heard the distant baying of the hounds in the woods as they raised yet another quarry.

The hunt had gone well so far, with several hinds, a boar and a bear to be added to Greystone's provisions. It would continue until the hunters or the squires who ran alongside them with extra spears and lances gave out. Ivo had just sent his squire back to rest and refill the aleskin at the temporary camp the huntsmen had set up. He had a few moments yet before the lad returned.

Resting one arm across the high pommels, he breathed in the tang of salt air. His gaze swept the cove below and lingered on the tumble of thatched huts that had been one of his favorite haunts as a young boy. 'Twas there, in that small fishing village, that he'd "borrowed" the boats he took out whenever he could escape his training sessions with the master-at-arms, or Fulk's endless prayers and penances. 'Twas there he and his most constant companion, the armorer's son, had visited the accommodating fisherman's wife. He grinned, remembering how they'd strutted out of her hut like men, then scrambled like children along the rock-strewn shore.

His grin widened as he recalled the time they'd stumbled over the remains of a huge, many-armed sea monster that had washed ashore. They'd near pissed in their braies in fright, but had summoned up enough courage to poke at it with a stick from a safe distance. Assured that it was dead, they'd carried it back in triumph to Greystone, where everyone had exclaimed over it until the thing began to stink so badly it was at last added to the pile of rotting fish heads that the cats feasted on.

Strange, Ivo mused, how time and his years in Outremer had changed so many things. The sturdy, towheaded armorer's son was dead now, felled by a pestilence that had swept Sussex a few years after Ivo left. The monster that had so terrified and fascinated them he now knew was an octopus. 'Twas a favorite dish in the East, one he'd dined on many times.

And Greystone, which had seemed so huge and solid to him as a child, Ivo now saw for what it was—a small, dank keep with a hall blackened by the smoke of many winter fires. It wasn't even as large or as pleasing to the eye as the gatehouse of the palace he'd lived in these past few years.

He shifted in the saddle, accepting that he felt no more at home in Greystone than he had in the palace. He'd spoken the truth when he told Joanna he didn't wish to claim the keep. After he settled with Fulk, Ivo had planned to take his sword to the Continent. He didn't need to earn his living with it anymore, but 'twas all he knew. All he wanted.

Until Joanna.

Ivo's smile twisted as he pondered the slight female with the firm, determined chin and the generous heart who'd snared his interest as none of the caliph's willing, well-trained beauties had. What was he to do about Joanna?

He was still trying to settle the issue in his mind when hooves thudded on the path behind him. Ivo straightened, his hand moving with a warrior's instinct to the sword hanging from his leather belt. He relaxed only a little when he recognized the burly, red-faced Sir Arnould.

The knight drew rein a short distance away. "Have you quit the hunt?"

"Nay," Ivo replied, "I but await my squire. He's gone to fetch ale, and more spears."

Arnould nodded, wiping a forearm across his forehead to clean the sweat and traces of gore that clung there. He'd been the one to kill the bear, taking great pleasure in taunting it with spear and sword and frenzied dogs until the maddened beast fell. Ivo had seen the blood lust in the man's eyes as he stabbed the creature over and over and known that Arnould would be a dangerous man to have as either foe or ally.

"So, my lord," the knight asked after a moment, "is it true what they say? That you spent your days wielding a sword for some heathen prince, and your nights spearing his women?"

Ivo didn't bother to reply.

"'Tis no wonder you don't plan to claim Greystone and settle here." Arnould scratched under his beard, then idly flicked away the fleas that dotted his fingers. "Once a man has acquired a taste for the exotic, it's hard to be satisfied with plain English fare, eh?"

His lips stretched in a gap-toothed leer. "Although even the sturdy wenches 'round these parts can be taught a few tricks. It may take a fist or two, or a taste of the whip, but I manage to get what I want from them."

"Aye," Ivo said with a faint sneer, "I doubt not you do." He gathered his reins, and was turning his mount's head when Arnould's words stopped him.

"Take that bitch your uncle wed. She acts so cold, but 'tis my guess it won't take much to heat her up." He paused, his small eyes intent and gleaming. "There's something in her face that says she wants it. She doesn't belong in any nunnery, not that one."

Ivo swung back to regard the brawny knight. He knew now that this was no chance meeting. He knew, as well, that Arnould would not leave this small clearing alive.

"'Tis as well you don't want Greystone," the man continued, in a low, goading voice. "Thus it devolves on Joanna, and she is bound by her promise to Fulk to take another husband. 'Twill near break me to come up with the bride-price Richard's put on her, but one more tourney prize and I'll have it. And her."

"Nay," Ivo said softly. "I think not."

Arnould's lips curled in a feral grin at this answer to his unspoken challenge.

"Aye, I'll have her, and much enjoy wringing a response from the whey-faced wench." The grin became a sneer. "I've seen how you strip her with your eyes. Mayhap I'll share her with you afore you leave, so you can teach her a few of the tricks of the East to pleasure me with.''

''And mayhap 'tis you I must teach a few tricks,'' Ivo drawled. ''Draw your sword, man, and prepare to meet whatever devil spawned you.''

It was over almost before it began.

For all his bulk and brawn, Arnould was no match for a man who'd mastered the war-fighting skills of two worlds. Leaning low over the side of his saddle, in the manner of a desert warrior, Ivo charged in under his opponent's guard. Arnould's tough leather jerkin deflected the sword thrust, but the blade slid up and sliced through the fleshy underside of his arm.

Bellowing like the bear he'd so recently dispatched, the red-faced knight swung his huge broadsword. It whistled through the air inches from Ivo's head. While Arnould was still unbalanced from the wild swing, Ivo yanked hard on his reins. His mount reared, and the back of a leather-covered fist smashed into a gap-toothed, swearing mouth.

Ivo had the satisfaction of knowing that he'd knocked the man's few remaining teeth down his throat before he skewered him.

He reined in and dispassionately surveyed the body.

''Christ's toes!''

His squire's oath held reverent awe. The youth pushed through the underbrush that blocked his path and emerged into the clearing, a huge grin splitting his face.

"There isn't a knight on the coast who could best Sir Arnould at arms! And many have tried. The bastard spilled more blood than any pig-butcher ever did. Will you show me how you hung sideways in the saddle like that, yet managed to thrust upward with such force?"

Ivo returned to Greystone some time later, with Sir Arnould slung over a horse's withers in much the same manner as the bear. Summoning the cleric who served as scribe, he dictated a brief account of the fight and then sent it to the baron who acted as the king's sheriff at Eastbourne. He would be levied a stiff fine, no doubt, but that didn't trouble him.

What did trouble him was the swift, powerful, almost uncontrolled fury that had sliced through him at Arnould's taunting words. It had taken all his hard-won discipline to master his cold rage and concentrate on the battle at hand. Even now, the thought of Arnould, or anyone else, for that matter, laying hands on Joanna made his gut twist.

For her part, Joanna managed to hide her relief at her suitor's demise. She arranged burial for his mortal remains and sent his personal effects to a distant kinsman in the north. First, however, she deducted two silver coins from his secret hoard to give the timorous dairymaid. The poor girl could only now admit without fear of reprisal that 'twas Sir Arnould who had brutalized her so savagely some weeks ago.

Although Joanna questioned Ivo several times as to the cause of the fight, he would only shrug and say that the man had challenged him and paid the price of it.

The gleeful squire wasn't nearly as reticent, however. His highly embellished and much garbled account of what he'd overheard soon made its way to the women's bower. Joanna sat with her hands frozen over the wooden loom in her lap as the women eagerly dissected the few known facts in the story.

"'Tis clear they fought over Greystone," one lady concluded. "Arnould made no secret of how much he wanted it. Mayhap Sir Ivo is at last coming to accept his responsibilities."

Gray-haired, sober Lady Matilda, wife to Joanna's senior vassal, wrinkled her brow. "But will he make a good master for Greystone? He was such a wild lad, and appears to have grown even more dissolute in his ways. That business of the oils..."

A calm, mature voice interrupted. "Would that I had the chance to spread oil on a man like that."

Joanna threw a surprised look at the plain, matronly woman seated on a low stool. Widowed and recently dispossessed of her house, Dame Catherine had packed her few belongings in a cloth and set out on foot for a nunnery in the south. When she stopped at Greystone to beg shelter for the night, Joanna's kind heart had caused her to offer the woman a place at the keep. Dame Catherine had proven herself efficient and most skilled at weaving, but this was the first time Joanna had heard her voice an opinion on any matter.

"This Ivo is much a man," Dame Catherine continued, unperturbed by the stares of the other women.

Lady Matilda glanced at Joanna, then sent a warning frown at the older woman.

Catherine ignored it. "If I'd had one such as him in my bed instead of the limp-lanced, spindle-shanked shopkeeper I was wed to, mayhap I'd have a clutch of children and some warm memories to comfort me in my middle years."

"We don't speak publicly of what occurs in the privacy of the marriage bed, Dame Catherine." Joanna's reprimand was spoken gently. "Lord Fulk thought such matters should be between a man, his God and his wife."

"Lord Fulk is dead," Catherine replied with blunt candor, adding a belated "God rest his soul. Mayhap 'tis time someone did speak of such matters to you, my lady, and openly."

She hesitated, then folded her hands in her lap. "I mean no disrespect, not after your many kindnesses to me. But I much mislike to see you denied one of the few pleasures we women find on this earth."

One or two veiled heads nodded in emphatic agreement.

Joanna saw the movements, and sighed. She was no fool. She knew well that many women took joy in joining with a man. She'd assisted at too many birthings, where women cursed the few moments of mindless passion that led to such results. She'd arranged marriages for too many maids who'd tumbled willingly into the hay with this man or that. She'd felt, God help her, strange, unsatisfied longings herself over the years. Longings she'd struggled to repress. Longings that had grown more intense, more unsatisfied, since Ivo had returned to Greystone.

But the impact of Fulk and his persistent schooling on her spirit was too strong to deny. Other women might give in to their desires, but Joanna would not. Could not.

She drew upon one of her husband's oft-repeated quotes. "Such earthly pleasure is fleeting, Dame Catherine, and not to be compared with the joy of a pure soul."

Catherine snorted. "'Twould not be so fleeting, I suspect, if Sir Ivo supplied it."

The other women laughed in agreement. For some unknown reason, Joanna felt heat rising in her cheeks.

The older woman's face, as yet unlined by her years, softened. Setting aside her weaving, Catherine leaned forward and took Joanna's hand. "For all that he carries a troubled look in his eyes, he's the kind of man a woman could find much joy with."

"You've seen it, too?" Joanna asked, her voice low. "That distant, lost look?"

"Aye, I've seen it. It makes me want to cradle his head to my bosom and croon soft songs to him."

It made Joanna want to cradle his head to her bosom, as well, but until this moment she hadn't thought of singing songs to him. A familiar wave of shame coursed through her.

"Go to him," she whispered, squeezing Catherine's hand. "He needs someone like you to comfort him and soothe his hurts and...and make him sweetmeats."

The older woman blinked. "Make him sweet-meats?"

"Give him the love he never had as a child."

Catherine stared at Joanna for a long moment, then rose. Shaking her head, she left the sewing room.

Ivo sat at a makeshift table in the outer bailey with Joanna's senior vassal and the captain-at-arms. A rough charcoal sketch of Greystone's bulwarks lay between them, marked by dark arrows where Ivo had seen the need for improvements.

"Aye, my lord, that will work!" the captain exclaimed. "If we but move the forge closer to the outer wall, we can use its fires to heat the caldrons of pitch. I won't lose so many men to burns when they carry the stuff to the walls to pour over attackers. By all the saints, I wish I'd thought of it afore."

"And here." Ivo pointed to the single, elevated entry to the fortresslike keep. "Tear out these stone stairs and construct them of wood instead. When you're forced to retreat inside the keep, you may set fire to them, and thus deny an attacker access."

"I tried to tell Lord Fulk 'twas folly to lay the steps in stone," Sir Eustace muttered in disgust. "But he was ever more comfortable at prayer than at the business of war."

"Aye," Ivo commented dryly.

He skimmed a quick glance along the ramparts, noting the disrepair and outmoded defenses. The caliph's army could have taken Greystone in less than a day. Arnould, had he been driven to it, could have taken Joanna as easily by force of arms as by paying King Richard her bride-price.

No one, Ivo had decided, would take either Greystone or Joanna. Except him. He'd come to realize he could not have one without the other, and now would have both.

He'd half turned back to the captain-at-arms when the still, patient figure of a woman standing a few feet away caught his attention.

"Your pardon, my lord," she said in a calm voice. "I am Dame Catherine. Lady Joanna sent me."

Ivo eyed the woman in mingled amusement and exasperation. Was this yet another one of Joanna's candidates? Alice, Barbara, and now Catherine. Just how many unmarried women did Joanna house at Greystone? Was there a Dora? An Ermengarde? Mayhap an Yvette? Would he be able to come up with enough shocking tales of the harem to turn away an entire alphabet of eager women? This one, with her mature face and steady gaze, looked to be particularly unshockable.

As Ivo searched his mind for some suitably outrageous harem practice, he nodded a dismissal to the other two men and stood. Deciding 'twas best to attack the matter head-on, he folded his arms across his chest.

"And why did Lady Joanna bid you attend me, Dame Catherine?"

"She sent me to make you sweetmeats."

"Your pardon?"

"I'm to make you sweetmeats and soothe your hurts," she replied in a droll tone. "I believe she's decided you need a mother."

Ivo stared at her.

Catherine shook her head, smiling. "I know, I know. 'Tis passing foolish. You've no more need of mothering than I. But..."

"But?"

She searched his eyes. What she saw there evidently satisfied her. "But I thought you should know that my lady has a concern for you in her heart."

"As I do for her," he admitted.

Ivo felt a curious twist in his belly at the admission. The words were simple enough, yet seemed to fill some dark corners of his soul that had long been empty.

Dame Catherine heaved a satisfied sigh. "I thought as much from watching you and her together these past days. I must say I'm glad you've come. I've been fair troubled about her, my lord."

"You need trouble yourself no longer." Ivo tucked her hand into the crook of his arm to lead her back to the keep. "Were it not for Lady Joanna, however, I just might pursue you, Dame Catherine. You're much a woman."

"Were it not for Lady Joanna," she replied, laughing, "I just might let you catch me."

In the midst of the bustle of preparing for the evening meal, Joanna snatched a moment with Dame Catherine. "Did you talk with him?"

"Aye."

The older woman swiped the trestle table with a clean cloth and nodded to the waiting servants to lay the trenchers.

"Well?"

"Well what, my lady?"

"Did he . . . did you . . . find things of mutual interest to speak of?"

"Oh, aye." Catherine bent over the boards to lay out wooden spoons.

Joanna tapped a slippered foot against the rushes. Sweet Mary, the entire keep was gathering to sit down to dine. She should be checking the dishes that would be served and making sure the wine was appropriately watered, yet she dallied here, burning with a most unseemly curiosity.

"What sort of things?" she asked, a slight touch of impatience in her voice.

Catherine swallowed a smile and straightened. "We spoke of sweetmeats."

"In truth?"

Joanna's heart melted. At last she'd found the answer to Ivo's needs. Someone who would care tenderly for him and . . .

"Aye," Dame Catherine continued. "I must admit, I was quite astounded at the ways the women of the harem feed them to their lord. You'd be amazed, my lady, at what they use as table. Why, Sir Ivo said that . . ."

Joanna's face was flaming when she stomped up to take her seat at the high table some moments later. Refusing to so much as glance at Ivo, she gave the signal for the meal to begin.

Ivo met Dame Catherine's mischievous look far down the boards and smothered a grin. 'Twas all he could do not to laugh every time he glanced at Joanna's scarlet face.

His urge to laugh quickly died, however.

Just as the line of servants bearing the first course entered the great hall, the captain-at-arms came running in. Although Joanna was lady of Greystone, he instinctively turned to Ivo.

"One of the serfs just brought word that there's a great troop approaching, my lord. He wasn't able to identify the banners."

"Send the alarm to the farms and to the fishing village," Ivo ordered, swiftly taking command. "Have those folk who may do so safely come to the keep, the others disperse into the woods."

He turned to Joanna. "Set servants to stoking the fires in the kitchen sheds and the armory. We'll need extra caldrons for hot water and oil. I'll come back to discuss with you where to shelter the women and children after I see what siege engines, if any, we'll face."

Joanna nodded, not a little awed. She'd seen Ivo in many moods and manners since he'd come to Greystone. Grim faced when he'd first arrived, distant when he'd recounted being sold in the slave markets, smiling wickedly when he'd teased her about the harem she still harbored doubts about. But Joanna had never seen him quite like this.

This was not the rebellious youth she'd heard so many tales of. Not the rogue knight who hired out his sword to any and all. This was a man of authority and decision, used to commanding armies.

Within moments, the great hall had emptied. Squires and pages ran for armor and weapons while knights crowded onto the battlements to peer into the distance.

Joanna joined them on the ramparts some time later and moved to stand beside a now-armored Ivo. The sun hung low on the horizon, its fading rays illuminating the long, winding road that stretched from Greystone's gates to the distant woods. A damp sea breeze whipped her veil and tugged tendrils loose from her neat braids.

Putting up a hand to push her hair out of her eyes, Joanna searched the empty road. "Any sign of them yet?"

"Nay," Ivo replied. "But some of the peasants coming in to shelter say they've seen red banners."

"Red?"

"Aye, with a gold device, but they could not identify it."

Joanna frowned. "I know not any such—"

She broke off as a lone horseman emerged from the shelter of the distant woods. A hush settled over the keep as he galloped up the dusty road.

Unaware that she did so, Joanna clutched Ivo's hand. "Do you recognize the banner?"

"Aye."

"Whose is it? Tell me who comes. Is he a foe? A villain?"

"Some would say so," Ivo replied dryly. He reached out to tuck an errant strand of hair behind her ear. "Come, lady, you'd best descend to the bailey and prepare to greet your king."

Chapter Five

Richard, king of England, duke of Normandy and Aquitaine, count of Anjou, Maine and Poitou, and lord of countless other fiefdoms on the Continent, swung off his mount with the agility of a man who'd spent most of his forty-two years in the saddle. Disdaining all ceremony, he strode toward the waiting group.

Clad in a scarlet mantle worked all over with the rampant golden leopards of Anjou, his skin burned to umber by the fierce southern sun of his beloved Aquitaine, his fair head bare of its great coroneted helm, Richard was a magnificent sight. Joanna gulped in awe, and then in astonishment when the king buffeted Ivo on the shoulder with a force that rocked him back on his heels.

"Ivo! You damned rogue! So 'tis indeed true that you've returned from the dead. My ship had just landed when I had word of it from the sheriff of

Eastbourne, but I wouldn't believe it until I saw you with my own eyes."

Ivo smiled wryly. "You may believe it, my lord."

"Christ's bones, I saw you take the spear that was meant for me through your neck. You fell before my very eyes."

"It passed through my shoulder, not my neck."

Richard swept an arm around Ivo's shoulders. "Come, I would hear how you survived while the battle raged yet another four days—and where the devil you've been these many years!"

At that moment, he caught sight of Joanna, rooted to the spot.

"Oho. I see now why you didn't seek me out immediately on your return. Nor would any man who had such a delightful lady awaiting him."

For all the rumors that had circulated for years about Richard's lack of interest in his wife—or in any other woman—he was the son of the fabled Eleanor of Aquitaine. His charm flowed over Joanna like a shower of gilded raindrops.

Ivo drew her forward. "I would present Joanna, widow to Lord Fulk, and lady of Greystone Keep."

"Fulk's widow? Did I not have several offers for you, lady?"

Joanna swallowed. "Aye, my lord."

"Well, now that Ivo's returned to take charge of Greystone, we must settle your widow's portion and get you wed forthwith. I have a pressing need of your bride-price," he admitted with a beguiling smile. "Philip of France has made another grab for the Vexin. I've only come to England long enough to raise the moneys I need to pay my armies."

Lifting her chin, Joanna met the king's look with one decidedly less beguiling. "I appreciate your dilemma, my lord king, but I've decided to retire to—"

"Come, lady," Ivo interrupted. "We can discuss such matters later. I'm sure you wish to see that supper is held for the king while I help him divest his armor."

A flush warmed Joanna's cheeks at this gentle reminder of her duties as chatelaine. With a swish of her skirts, she turned and led the way inside the great hall. A brisk order sent servants scurrying to remove her chest from the tower bedchamber and make it ready for the king.

"Do you go upstairs and take your ease, sire," she said, still unsettled by his talk of marrying her off immediately. "I'll send wine and fruits and see to the comfort of your men. Supper will await your pleasure."

Joanna stood at the foot of the stone stairs while Ivo escorted the king to Greystone's best bedchamber. Her mind whirled with the implications of this unexpected visit. The days and weeks of scheming to get Ivo to accept his responsibilities were at an end. The king would resolve the issue, and her fate, as well.

Like one who has long prayed for something, only to feel the first tendrils of dismay when that wish is granted, Joanna tasted bitter gall.

Ivo would stay at Greystone, should Richard so command it. And he'd no doubt take Dame Catherine to wife, given her shocking complaisance at what he'd suggested could be done with sweetmeats!

Joanna, on the other had, would wed whatever knight would pay the reduced bride-price for one who now claimed only a widow's portion. Or, she thought in desperation, she could convince the king to keep her widow's portion and allow her to retire to Lessingham.

Swallowing the vile taste in her mouth, she turned to go about her duties.

It took some time to divest Richard of his weapons and heavy armor. One squire took charge of his sword and dagger, while two others stripped him of gauntlets, knee protectors and mail leggings. Ivo himself unbuckled the arm and shoulder guards that protected the king from slashing side blows, then detached the sleeves from his mailed shirt.

As soon as two squires had pulled off the shirt, Richard waved a hand in dismissal and sent all except Ivo from the chamber. Pouring the wine that Joanna had sent into silver goblets, he sprawled in a wooden chair and pointed to the other.

"Sit, sit, and tell me now what happened at Acre."

Wine goblet in hand, Ivo took the seat and related the bare facts of his fall and subsequent capture to the man whose side he'd guarded in battle for over a year.

"But why didn't we get an offer of ransom for you? The Saracens knew I would've paid well to get you back. Even Saladin himself had praised your skill in that earlier skirmish."

Ivo shrugged. "At first, no one, not even I, knew who I was. I was three days in the sun, without food or water, trapped under a dead horse with a spear through my shoulder. It was some months before I fully regained my senses."

"And then?"

"And then Acre fell."

Ivo swirled the wine in his goblet. It was red, dark red. As red as the blood of the almost three thousand men, women and children Richard had ordered massacred after Acre's surrender.

The king's face hardened. Brave and bold in battle, he was also pitiless when necessary.

"I couldn't wait any longer for Saladin to pay their ransoms. I had to march on to Jerusalem before we lost the advantage of Acre's fall. You know as well as I that we couldn't feed and guard so many prisoners on the march."

Across the expanse of the small table, the two men's eyes met. Richard was the first to look away, but his hand was steady as he raised his goblet and took a long swallow.

"I answer to no one but my God for what happened that day."

"After Acre," Ivo continued in a neutral voice, "no quarter was given to the Frankish prisoners, no ransoms offered. Those of us who'd been taken from the city before it fell were sent to the mines in the northern desert."

"I heard of them," Richard admitted after a moment. "'Tis said no one escaped or emerged alive."

Ivo's jaw hardened. "A few made it out. Not I, however. But my last escape attempt brought me to the attention of a traveling prince. The caliph took me to Rabat, and promised me freedom, did I serve him faithfully for four years."

"And did you?"

"Aye."

Once more Ivo swirled the wine in his goblet, his thoughts now not of a bloodstained plain of death outside Acre, but of a fantastic palace, a magical garden, a library filled with more volumes than he'd ever imagined.

"During those years, I became captain of the prince's household guard, numbering some four thousand men. He also made me one of his *nadim*. He wanted very much for me to stay there."

"Why did you not?"

Richard's voice held no censure, only curiosity. He'd seen for himself the rich palaces where East met West. His own brother-by-marriage, William of Sicily, had entertained him amid the Moorish arches and fountained gardens of his royal residence, Monreale. In Palermo, a capital city richer than all of England, Norman rulers kept harems and eunuchs and awed guests within their magnificent houses.

With his southern blood, Richard felt far more at home among these peoples and their sunny land than in the cold mists of England. He had spent less than six months on English soil in the nine years of his reign, and could well understand if Ivo had decided to reside elsewhere.

"Why did you return?" he repeated, when Ivo didn't respond.

Ivo glanced up, and the king was taken aback by the cold, hard glitter in his eyes.

"Because the caliph in his goodness sent word of my situation to Fulk with offers to ransom me. I learned later that my uncle refused all such offers."

Richard swore, viciously. He was no stranger to the intrigues of brother against brother, father against son. But for a man to refuse to send ransom, which was the accepted means of regaining those taken in battle, was a breach of all the codes knights lived by. Even his own brother John, who coveted his throne, had helped raise the ransom Leopold of Austria demanded for Richard's release.

"So the pious, sanctimonious uncle you told me of condemned you to years of solitude."

Ivo's mouth twisted. "He believed it God's punishment for my sins, I doubt not. Of a certainty, he had the moneys for the ransom. I'd sent my own purse to him for safekeeping when I left for the Crusade."

"The bastard. And you came home to settle with him?"

"Aye, and found him dead of a dish of boiled eels."

Ivo's profound disgust eased the dark tension in the air.

Richard laughed and set aside his goblet. "Well, now you are returned. You know I want your sword at my side when I battle Philip of France. Can you join me straightaway?"

"First I must settle the matter of Greystone."

"What is there to settle? You're Fulk's only kin. I'll take your oath of homage for it on the morrow."

Ivo set aside his goblet, as well, his eyes glinting. "Lady Joanna has a claim to the keep, as well, and is bound by an oath she pledged her lord."

Richard caught his look and settled back in his chair. "Tell me of this oath."

By the time the two men descended the stairs and entered the great hall, Joanna was struggling to regain a composure sorely beset by the frantic preparations for entertaining a king.

In the short time since Richard had arrived, a constant stream of servitors had scurried about the hall, whisking platters of meat back to the kitchen sheds to keep them warm, shooing dogs outside, lighting additional candles. A distraught head cook had demanded a quick trip to the cellar storeroom for more spices for the dishes to be set before the king. The chief falconer, whose clear, ringing tenor would entertain during the meal, appeared to have lost all power of speech.

Even calm, levelheaded Dame Catherine was flustered. She directed the pages to lay out fresh trenchers of white bread for the king's men instead of the coarse, dark loaves normally used, then changed her mind in midstep and sent for another basket of the dark. Muttering to herself, she decided once again on the white.

Joanna's other women had all hurriedly donned their finest robes. The scent of lavender and rosewater and musk competed with the acrid odor of tallow candles that drifted through the hall. The women clustered now in a colorful group, adjusting the drape of each other's veils and retying girdles.

Joanna herself had barely had time to throw on her best robe. It was a rare silk in the pale green color called alexandrine, its low, square neckline sporting a rich border of embroidered golden blossoms and vine leaves in a darker shade of green. The sleeves were so long she had to tie fashionable knots in the ends to keep them from sweeping the rushes. Her serving woman had attacked Joanna's disordered hair, scraping the loose tendrils back and covering the tawny braids with pearl-encrusted cauls. As Joanna dashed out, the much-tried woman slapped a veil atop her head and anchored it with a circlet of beaten gold.

Breathless, distracted, her stomach churning over her impending discussion with the king, Joanna tested the last of the sauces whipped up by the harried cook and arrived at the foot of the stairs just in time to greet her guest.

Richard took her hand to raise her from her somewhat shaky curtsy. "You look like the veriest breath of springtime, Lady Joanna, all gold and green and radiant as the sun."

She looked, Ivo thought in some amusement, as discomfited as he'd ever seen her. Her cheeks held a high color, her breasts rose and fell rapidly under the thin silk, and she had a smudge that looked suspiciously like mustard sauce on one cheek.

She was, he feared, about to become even more discomfited.

Richard wasted no time in getting down to the business at hand. He escorted Joanna to the high table, but declined to take the seat held out for him. She stared up at him in some confusion, knowing full well she should not sit before he did. Richard smiled at her, and held up a hand to still the excited murmurs that filled the great hall.

"Many of you were witness to my pleasure at greeting Sir Ivo, who was lost to us for many years. He's come home at last, only to find his kinsman dead and this keep without a lord. Lady Joanna has held it in her husband's name these many months, but 'tis time to enfeoff a new lord. Accordingly, I will take Sir Ivo's oath of homage for Greystone on the morrow.''

Joanna put her fingertips on the edge of the cloth-covered table to steady herself. 'Twas what she wanted, she told herself fiercely. 'Twas what was right.

A buzz of approval rose throughout the hall, then quickly died. Joanna heard her name whispered and caught the worried glances thrown her way. She smiled reassuringly at the knights seated at the boards below the high table, letting them know that she concurred in this development.

Once more Richard held up a hand. "You need not worry that your lady will not be cared for. Ivo has told me of her vow to her dead lord.''

In the midst of her sudden, wrenching dismay at having her fate so publicly pronounced, Joanna had time to wonder at the coldness in the king's voice when he spoke of Fulk.

"Since she pledged a sacred vow to provide an heir to Greystone, and she is not within the forbidden degree of kinship to Ivo, I decree that they shall wed. Thus she may keep her vow, and he will ensure she's cared for.''

The king's deep voice rang through the hall. "I've sent a herald to the bishop pleading dispensation of banns so the ceremony may take place in my presence on the morrow."

A hush fell over the hall, to be broken a few seconds later by an involuntary shout of approval from the captain-at-arms. Far down the boards, Dame Catherine began to clap, slowly at first, then with gathering enthusiasm. Within moments, the whole hall rang with cheers and wild applause.

Joanna heard none of it. Nor did she see the pages jumping up and down in the aisles. Nor feel the waves of excitement that shook the hall. She stood stunned and unmoving, as though carved from the same gray granite as the keep.

Richard cast her a curious glance, then stepped aside as Ivo moved to her side.

" 'Tis not much of a betrothal, I know," Ivo said, his voice low and calm, in contrast to the great din around them. "But we should observe the proprieties and seal it with a kiss."

With that, he slid an arm around Joanna's waist, pulled her up against his chest, and bent his head.

This was no formal kiss.

No ritual sealing of a promise.

No polite brush of his lips against her cheek.

He took her mouth with a raw male hunger held too long in check. She was bent backward over his arm with the force of it, and had to grasp at him with both hands to keep from toppling over.

The cheers in the hall grew deafening. Joanna's circlet fell off. Her veil floated to the floor. And still he kissed her.

Under his deliberate and most skilled assault, her frozen stupor shattered. A wild heat flooded her veins. A roar sounded in her ears, drowning out the hoots and calls. Shock, amazement, fierce longing, and an even fiercer shame, engulfed her.

When at last Ivo righted her, Joanna abandoned her dignity. She forgot that the king stood not three feet away. She lost sight of the fact that some two hundred interested observers were watching with varying expressions of glee on their faces. Fists clenched, cheeks flaming, she glared at Ivo.

"Are you mad? I'll not wed with you!"

Ivo's blue eyes gleamed. "Aye, lady, you will. The king has so decreed."

"Well, he can just so undecree."

Richard's golden brows shot up.

Joanna was too incensed to take heed. "'Twas understood that if you stayed at Greystone, I would retire to Lessingham!"

"By you, mayhap, but not by me."

"But Dame Catherine, or Lady Barbara, or—"

"Both admirable women." Ivo grinned. "You have an entire lexicon of admirable women in your care. But my conscience would not allow me to woo any of them. Not when 'twas Fulk's dying wish that you give Greystone its next heir."

"Conscience!" she hissed. "You have no conscience! And don't try to tell me you've ever given a care to Fulk's wishes, in this matter or any other!"

"But I must in this case, especially since they accord with my own."

Joanna lifted her chin. "I refuse to wed with any man who's spent his days in a harem."

Ivo laughed and brushed a knuckle down her cheek. "I spent only my nights, sweeting, only my nights."

Joanna filled the hours between darkness and dawn with prayer and painful reflection. After much inner turmoil, she at last accepted that she must wed with Ivo.

To all intents and purposes, 'twas a practical arrangement, and the best for Greystone itself. Although Joanna had brought with her only a modest dowry, Fulk had begged the use of it for the cathedral under construction in Norfolk. He'd meant to restore her moneys from the rents and revenues, but had never gotten around to doing so.

In the meantime, much-needed repairs to the keep and its farms and fisheries had gone undone. Joanna knew that stripping Greystone now of both her dowry and her widow's portion would severely drain its already depleted treasury. That would mean less seed bought for the fall planting, fewer milk cows to replace those taken by the sickness that had plagued the area this spring. Joanna could not bring herself to abandon the people she'd assumed responsibility for these past years to such dire straits.

True, Ivo had expressed little concern over moneys since his return. Except for attending to the defenses, he'd left Joanna to run the keep as she wished. But he had to have noted its sorry condition and decided that 'twould take much to restore it.

Aye, she could accept that Ivo, having at last acknowledged his responsibilities toward Greystone, would wed with her as a matter of practical expediency.

What she could not accept as readily was the fact that he appeared to have other, less fiscal reasons, as well.

Joanna was woman enough to recognize the desire in his eyes when they rested on her of late. To her constant shame, she'd felt a similar desire for him. She'd buried it deep within her, prayed over it most devoutly, and finally brought herself to confess it to the castle's doddering old priest.

She'd done the penances he prescribed, and many more she'd prescribed for herself. But she couldn't seem to tear the lust from her heart.

Now, as she lay in the airless, curtained bed, fear for her immortal soul battled with a fear that, did she give in to the lust she felt for Ivo, she would count her soul well lost.

And yet . . . she was to wed with him.

Bound by the laws of God and man, she would lie with him when he wished it, and make her body available to him.

The only solution, she decided in the dark hours before dawn, was to control her base desires and do her duty as his wife. No more, no less.

Chapter Six

'Twas a wedding and a bedding to daunt even the skilled Ivo.

His bride stood stiff and silent through the brief ceremony, which had been sanctioned by a hasty missive from the bishop. The castle priest, whose hearing had suffered much over the past years, had to ask three times for her response. After replying twice in a low voice, Joanna all but shouted in Father Dominic's ear the final time.

Ivo smothered a grin as he led her from the church. There could be no doubt among the twelve witnesses that she'd agreed to the match, even if she did show little enthusiasm for it.

Gowned in a robe of gold silk, her hair covered with a pearl-encrusted caul and sheer, transparent veil, she should have glowed with life. Instead, her face was pale and showed none of the animation that normally characterized it. Around her neck she wore an oval emerald the size of a pigeon's egg. Ivo had presented the stone to her as a bride gift, thinking it would match the glowing color of her eyes. On this occasion, at least, the gem held far more life and sparkle in its depths than Joanna did.

During the feast that followed, Ivo tempted her with the choicest morsels from each dish. She would take what he offered, answer readily enough when addressed, but otherwise appeared to derive little pleasure from the occasion.

Ivo had a good idea of what had caused Joanna's retreat from the warm, laughing creature she normally was. His own years under Fulk's repressive piety were enough for him to understand why she would not look forward to the night ahead. He was, however, most confident in his abilities to help his wife shed her fears and inhibitions—along with her clothes.

He sat back in his chair, his long legs stretched out under the table, and contemplated with tightly controlled anticipation the night to come.

Several hours later, Ivo was beginning to wonder if he'd overestimated his own abilities and underestimated his lady wife's strength of will.

Stripped of all clothing by the rowdy crowd who escorted him to his nuptial chamber, he'd submitted with good grace to their lewd jokes and highly impractical suggestions for extending his pleasure this night.

He'd found Joanna awaiting him in the keep's second-best bedchamber, already ensconced in the curtained bed that occupied most of the space in the small tower room. As Ivo was ushered to her side, he'd known a moment's relief that Richard's presence precluded use of the lord's chamber. He had no desire to take Joanna in the bed she'd shared with Fulk.

'Twas only after the boisterous crowd filed out that Ivo began to wonder if he would take her at all. He studied her pale face and tight-closed eyes for some time, then slipped into bed.

Leaning on one elbow, he smiled down at her still form. "Joanna, 'twould help matters greatly if you'd at least look at me."

Her lashes lifted. "As you will, my lord."

Ivo's smile twisted at the flat obedience in her voice.

"You've been lying still as a board since I entered the chamber," he remarked. "Now that the others have left and we're alone, you can relax."

"Nay, my lord," she replied with painful honesty. "I cannot."

Ivo felt a swift stab of fury, quickly quelled, at the man who had robbed this woman of her own desires. Then he pushed aside all thoughts of the past. As he'd learned to do to survive during the grueling years in the desert, he concentrated only on the present. And on the woman whose lips he longed—most painfully!—to kiss.

Dragging in a deep breath, he lay back on the bed and crooked one arm above his head.

"Mayhap you should take some wine," he suggested after a few moments of utter silence.

"Wine?"

"Aye, to give you the strength for what must come."

She stiffened even more. "If you wish it," she replied woodenly.

"I do."

She slid out of the bed and padded barefoot to the low table where a thoughtful Dame Catherine had left a pitcher of wine and a tray of foodstuffs.

Ivo's loins tightened at the sight of her golden hair cascading down a sweetly curved back. Although the beautifully embroidered shift she wore was modest enough, the linen was so fine it was nearly transparent. In the glowing candlelight, Ivo caught tantalizing glimpses of white, rounded buttocks and slender thighs. He glanced away before she turned back, a silver goblet in one hand. He didn't want to test even his own iron control with the sight of her high, proud breasts.

"Would...would you have some, my lord?"

"Nay. You drink it. Wine only makes it worse for me."

He heard rather than saw her pause.

"Worse?"

Ivo wouldn't look at her.

"How so, worse?" she asked again. A faint trace of the concern that was so characteristic of Joanna threaded her voice.

Turning his head, he met her gaze. And caught a quick glimpse of the breasts he'd tried to avoid. His jaw tightened until he felt his back teeth grind, one against the other.

"I tried to escape several times when I was first taken," he admitted at last. "With each attempt, the punishment grew ever more torturous. I was warned that on the next attempt I would lose my manhood completely."

It took some moments for Joanna to understand the import of his words. When she did, her mouth dropped, and her startled gaze fastened on that part of him in question.

To her inexperienced mind, it looked as though Ivo had lost little of his manhood. In fact, Joanna decided, her mouth suddenly dry, it looked as though

Ivo was considerably better endowed with manhood than most.

Although... She had to admit that after all the tales she'd heard of his youthful prowess, she'd expected him to be a bit more... eager. She put a hand to her throat as realization and compassion swept through her.

"Oh, my lord!" she whispered. "Are you unable to rise?"

Ivo's blue eyes took on the distant look that so pierced her heart. "I can rise," he growled out after a long, tense stillness. "But stimulation greatly aids the process."

Joanna drew back.

Ivo smiled grimly. "I know. 'Tis not what a woman wishes to hear of the man she's just taken to husband, that she must coax him to do his duty by her."

Of a sudden, Joanna remembered the vow she'd made to herself in the dark hours before dawn. She'd sworn she'd be a dutiful wife to him, no more, no less. It now appeared that such duty might include more, not less, than Joanna had anticipated.

Still, these past weeks in Ivo's company, and her own innate intelligence, made her hesitate. She wasn't suspicious, exactly, but this Ivo didn't accord with the man who took such apparent delight in describing the pleasures of the harem. She folded her arms across her chest.

"What about this business with the oils and the veils and . . . and sweetmeats?"

He gave a small shrug. "They all help."

Joanna bit down on her lower lip, torn by conflicting, confusing thoughts. Although she still harbored some reservations, everything that was female in her cried out to go to him, to stroke his flesh and bring that magnificent manhood to full glory. Her mind urged her to accept the logic that 'twas her duty, her obligation.

"Where is this flask of oil?" she asked at last, in a strangled voice.

Ivo felt a stab of fierce satisfaction at the light in her green eyes. They were no longer dull, no longer lifeless. Ignoring the fact that the gleam in their depths spoke more of determination to see this matter through than of passion, he shook his head.

"Nay, I would not have you resort to the heathen practices you so despise. You must find your own way, lady wife."

Ivo had been sure that his years under the lash had tested his control to its limits. He now realized that he'd never felt half the strain he felt at this moment.

Tiny beads of sweat broke on his brow.

His breathing became so shallow that it ceased altogether.

With every ounce of determination he possessed, he willed his rod not to stiffen under Joanna's narrow-eyed, assessing look.

After what seemed like half a lifetime, she expelled a slow breath, set the silver goblet on a chest beside the bed, and reached for the hem of her shift. In one swift movement, she drew it off and tossed it to the rushes.

Ivo's hands curled into fists at the sight of her gleaming body.

"If what you say is true, my lord," she got out through clenched teeth, "'tis my duty to bring you to fullness, and I will do so. If 'tis not, I swear I'll strangle you with my bare hands. And this time you'll not return from the dead!"

Ivo managed a weak grin as she straddled his hips.

Joanna's deepest, darkest fears were immediately realized.

As soon as she felt his flesh under hers, the ache at her core expanded painfully. Heat spiraled in her belly as she bent over to take his face in both hands and press her lips to his.

With the touch of his mouth on hers, Joanna put her fears aside. She would pay the price of her depravity later. She would try to reclaim her soul later.

Now, she would take what she would of this man. This husband she'd vowed to honor with her body and all her worldly possessions. This rogue who'd stolen her heart as he'd stolen a horse and a sword so long ago and ridden away from Greystone.

He was back. He was hers. And she wanted him with all the passion she'd denied herself these many years.

Slanting her head, Joanna deepened the kiss. Her back arched, causing the tips of her breasts to rub against his hair-roughened chest. Driven by an instinct she had never known she possessed, she ground her hips down on his loins.

Within moments, every one of Joanna's senses sang with sensual awareness. She heard the rasp of his breath when he reached up to cradle her head with his big hands. She tasted his essence with her lips and her tongue. She smelled his scent, warm and male and intoxicating.

And she felt his reaction against her inner thigh.

Dragging her mouth from his, Joanna sucked in a shaky breath. "'Twould appear I've found the proper...stimulation, my lord."

Ivo's eyes widened. "Aye, lady wife, 'twould appear so."

Before she quite knew how it happened, he grinned wickedly and rolled them both over in a tangle of legs and clutching hands. His mouth took hers this time, hard and demanding. One hand wrapped around her waist to arch her up against him as his tongue and teeth explored her mouth, her cheek, her ear.

Gasping, Joanna hunched a shoulder to deny the hot, wet invasion.

Willing to concede that particular pleasure for another, Ivo slid his arm from around her waist and mounded her breast in his hand. His dark head bent, and he suckled the tight, tingling bud until Joanna moaned and tugged at his hair with desperate fingers.

"Ivo!" she panted. "Holy Mother, what do you do to me?"

"Naught but my duty," he replied, his voice husky.

"But—"

"Here, see what miracle you've accomplished?"

He took her hand and wrapped her fingers around his shaft.

"Miracle!" she sputtered, red faced, although secretly she was forced to agree with him.

"Aye," he intoned in awe. "And without oils, too!"

Joanna dissolved into helpless laughter.

"'Tis no matter for levity," he admonished, shaking his head. "If we're to fulfill our conjugal responsibilities, I must ready you as you have me, else you'll not be able to receive me."

"Ivo..."

"Don't distract me, lady wife. Just lie back and let me work."

Retaining a firm hold on the miracle she'd wrought, Joanna lay back as directed. At Ivo's fierce scowl of concentration, her lips curved into a rueful smile.

Never in all her hours of dark despair over her body's weakness had she thought she could approach this business of coupling as lightly as Ivo apparently did. Never had she lain naked and felt not shame but a wild, leaping anticipation, as when his hand trailed down her stomach to tangle in the thatch of hair between her thighs. And never—never!—had she experienced such a flood of hot, sweet desire as when his finger slid inside her.

At that precise moment, Joanna gave up all attempt to understand what was happening. She wanted only to experience it. To experience him.

"Ivo!" she gasped after he had stroked her inner flesh to the point of dewy wetness.

"Aye?" he growled.

"I...I am sufficiently readied!"

"Nay, not yet."

His thumb pressed the aching nub at her center. Joanna arched in surprise.

"Ivo!"

"Not yet."

He bent to suckle once more at her breast, while his fingers continued their slow, deliberate, wonderful torture. Her hand tightened involuntarily around his shaft.

"Joanna..." he whispered hoarsely a few moments later. "Now, sweeting, now. Open for me."

She opened her legs and her arms and her most private being.

Ivo filled them all.

In a smooth, fluid motion, he fit himself between her thighs and drove into her. His strong arms gathered her against his chest, and his mouth claimed the small, helpless moans she couldn't control.

Joanna wrapped her arms around his neck and strained to match his every thrust, every devouring kiss.

Her peak, when she reached it, was a shattering collision of heat and light and pure sensation.

His came shortly after. He buried his face in her hair, groaned something in a language she didn't understand, and drove into her a final, shuddering time.

Some moments, or mayhap hours, later, Joanna discovered another aspect of marriage that had hitherto escaped her. Not all husbands, apparently, withdrew immediately after performing their duty. Not only had this one collapsed on top of her, near smothering her with his weight, he was yet lodged within her. Frowning a bit, Joanna tried to wriggle out from under his inert, heavy frame.

Ivo mumbled an apology and rolled over, taking her with him. He raised one knee to hold her, and himself, in place. Joanna found herself sprawled across his chest while he lay with eyes closed and breath gradually slowing. Deciding to take advantage of her superior position, she folded her arms on his breastbone, rested her chin on them, and studied his face.

The light from the flickering candle cast his features in stark relief. Dark hair spilled across his forehead, causing Joanna's fingers to itch with the need to brush it back. Thick black lashes lay against high cheekbones. A scar from some long-ago battle traced a faint white line along his right temple.

Or mayhap the scar was one of the ones he'd collected after his capture.

Joanna's gaze traveled down his face and explored the contours of his jaw, then the sinews and tendons of his neck. Here his skin was less smooth.

The tail end of what could only be lash marks curled along one side of his neck.

Her heart contracted, and she quivered with the need to wrap her arms around him.

"So soon, lady wife?" he murmured.

"What?"

He opened his eyes. "Do you wish me to rise to my duty again so soon?"

"Nay, nay. Of course not."

She squirmed, embarrassed by the sudden, unexpected, and completely wanton realization that she wished exactly that.

His breath rushed out. "Joanna, sweet heaven..."

"I know, I know," she whispered after a breathless moment. " 'Tis another miracle!"

Only later, after the sweat had cooled on their skin and Ivo had swaddled them both in a rough sheet and drifted into a doze, did the familiar demons creep back to haunt Joanna.

She lay still, tucked against her husband's big body, his breath tickling her ear. Despite her sleeplessness of the night before, despite her exhaustion from Ivo's vigorous use of her body and her equally vigorous use of his, she couldn't sleep.

Beside her, Ivo's breathing deepened to a low, steady rhythm.

An hour passed, then another. The candle guttered out, extinguished by an errant draft. Heavy, still darkness hung over the bedchamber and the keep beyond.

With a silent, despairing sigh, Joanna eased herself from the circle of Ivo's arms, pulled a robe from the chest she'd ordered hastily removed from the bedchamber given over to the king's use, and slipped out into the deserted hall.

Chapter Seven

The taper Father Dominic kept lit at all times sent shadows dancing over the chapel's small altar. Joanna's bare feet made no sound on the stone floor as she approached the unpadded prayer bench. She stood beside it, running her fingertips along the smooth, dark-grained wood where her arms had rested so many times, her hands clasped together in supplication.

To her dismay, she found herself unable sink to her knees. Try as she might, she couldn't bring herself to beg forgiveness for what had just occurred.

She stood, unmoving, while the tiny candle flame leapt and twisted in the night.

"Your pardon, lady."

The deep voice came out of the darkness. Joanna spun around, gasping. When she peered into the shadows of the far corner, she saw the unmistakable golden hair and tall form of the king.

"I'm sorry if I startled you," Richard said, rising from a bench far back in a corner. "I should have made my presence known when you first came in."

"Nay, 'tis—'tis I who owe you pardon," she stammered. "I didn't realize you were here, else I wouldn't have intruded on your privacy."

He came forward into the small circle of light, and Joanna swallowed a quick exclamation at his appearance. Gone were the deliberate charm and the brave, careless smile the troubadours sang of. Joanna saw instead a man haunted by demons far fiercer than the ones that rode her.

He must have seen the quick concern in her eyes, for he twitched his shoulders, as if throwing off a weight, and managed a grin.

"What, do you come to pray? On your wedding night? Given the rogue you're wed to, I'm not surprised."

Following his lead, Joanna folded her arms across her chest and arched one brow. "Oh, so? And this from the man who gave me to him."

She felt most strange to be standing barefoot before the king, without even a shift on under her robe, in the middle of the night. But she sensed his need to keep the darkness at bay, and was willing to exchange banter with him, if he wished it.

Tilting her head, she fixed him with a polite, inquiring look. "Do you think that having just come from Ivo's bed I should be offering a prayer of thanksgiving, or one of deliverance?"

Richard's white teeth gleamed. "From all reports, his own included, most women would be giving fervent thanks."

"Aye, well, I'm not sure one should believe all Ivo's reports. He brought back some rather fantastical tales of the harem, you know."

The king's grin was more genuine now, the shadows fading from his eyes. "No, I didn't know."

"Aye," she sniffed. "Ridiculous stories that I take leave to doubt."

"You must keep an open mind, lady."

"Ha!"

"Truly. I've seen some fantastical sights myself in Outremer."

"If 'tis so wonderful, why would any man return?"

Richard shrugged. "Many don't. A good number have made their homes permanently in the East. But most are brought back by their responsibilities, as was I."

"Not Ivo," Joanna pointed out tartly.

"Nay," the king replied, "'twas revenge that brought Ivo back. Not that I blame him. I, too, would want to challenge a kinsman who refused my ransom and left me to face what Ivo did.''

Joanna's brows drew together. "What ransom? What do you speak of?''

"Did you not know?"

She shook her head.

"Ah, well, it happened long before you were wed to Fulk. Of a certainty, he wouldn't want a new, young wife to know that he refused ransom for his kinsman.''

"Do you…do you mean Fulk knew that Ivo lived? Nay, he did not. He could not!''

Richard merely raised one brow.

Joanna refused to believe it. She couldn't believe it. If she did, her whole life since coming to Greystone would be a lie.

All those masses Fulk had ordered sung for Ivo's soul! His reluctance to take a wife, overcome only because he believed his kinsman lost to the Infidels!

Sweet Mother, his gentle shaping of his young wife's spirit to deny her own flesh!

Joanna groaned, thinking of the endless hours she'd spent on her knees, mortified by her woman's longings. Of the guilt she'd carried for so long. She couldn't believe Fulk would do that to her in all piety, yet condemn one of his own blood to the Saracens' hands.

"Nay," she whispered, backing away. "I believe it not."

She whirled and ran from the chapel.

Ivo found her just after dawn, in the small garden where she'd first proposed that he marry Lady Alice. He padded forward, his feet and chest bare, his dark hair dampened by the morning mists.

"Joanna, what in the name of—"

She rose, her eyes wide and hard. "Did Fulk know that you lived? Did he refuse to ransom you?"

Ivo stopped in midstride. "Who told you of this?"

"It matters not. Is it true?"

"Aye."

"Why didn't you tell me? What game have you been playing with me?"

Not two hours ago, this woman had flamed in his arms. Now she regarded him with a glittering anger that didn't mask her hurt or bitter disillusionment.

"What happened was between Fulk and me," Ivo said quietly. "I knew the moment I first met you that you had no part in it."

"How did you know?" she snapped. "How could you know?"

"No one so strong and pure of heart could be party to what Fulk did."

He reached out to take her in his arms. Joanna batted away his hands, stepping backward.

"Oh, aye...pure of heart."

"Joanna, listen to me—"

She interrupted him, her eyes flashing. "Did you wed with me because you couldn't avenge yourself on Fulk? 'Twas a neat revenge, I'll admit. Take the wife your uncle worked so hard to strip of all base desires, and turn her into a wanton in one night."

He regarded her gravely. "Hardly a wanton. You wouldn't even let me eat sweetmeats from your—"

"Ivo!" Her voice was low and furious. "Do not dare, do not *dare* speak to me of sweetmeats! And if you mention harems or oils or dancing girls, I swear I will...I will..."

Laughing, he pulled her into his arms. "I know. You'll strangle me with your bare hands, and make sure that this time I don't return from the dead. Cease your struggles, Joanna, and listen to me."

It was some moments before she was calm enough for Ivo to curl a hand under her chin and tilt her face to his.

"I learned many things in the East. Things that didn't always accord with what I'd been taught. In the process, I lost more than just the flesh on my back. I lost myself."

Joanna's lower lip jutted out mutinously. She was either not able or not yet willing to grasp his meaning, Ivo decided.

His hand left her chin to smooth the tangled hair away from her cheek.

"Do you know the device I wear on my surcoat and shield? The two-headed monster?"

"Aye."

"That's how I saw myself. After Acre and the slaughter of so many innocents, I began to question all I held dear, to question even the purpose of the Crusade. And after I learned of Fulk's betrayal, I lost most of my belief in the bonds of blood. Yet I couldn't bring myself to accept the beliefs of the Saracens. So I had none. I looked east, and west, and found no answers, only questions."

He looked over her head for a moment, his eyes unseeing. Joanna held her breath until he fastened his gaze on her face once more.

"By the time I won my freedom from the caliph, my only goal was to avenge myself on the man who had cost me so much."

"So you came home."

"So I came home."

"And when you found him gone beyond your vengeance?"

He smiled. "Then I found you."

"Am I the substitute?" she whispered. "The instrument of your revenge?"

"Nay, my sweet. Vengeance doesn't seem to matter anymore."

She searched his face. "Do you truly mean that? How can you forgive him what he did to you? How can I, for what he did to me?"

"I can't answer for you, Joanna, only for myself."

He framed her face with both hands and brushed his lips over hers.

"You're worth the price I paid all those years, and more. If I was once lost between two worlds, now I know I need no other world but you. But you must decide for yourself if what we have together is sufficient for you, as well."

He caressed her face one last time, then stepped back. "I won't hold you to a marriage you despise. I lived too long in prison myself to keep you in one, also. If you distrust me after what you've learned, if you still find shame in my arms, then I'll give you release."

"Ivo..."

" 'Twill be difficult, after the bishop's dispensation and the night just past, but I'll find a way to annul our vows, do you wish it."

For a moment, Joanna thought she saw in his eyes a hint of the bleakness that so wrung her heart, but 'twas so quickly gone, she wasn't sure.

"Think on it," he said quietly. "I won't force you to a decision with my touch or my arguments. 'Twill be the hardest test of will I've ever endured, but I won't force you."

He turned away.

"Ivo, wait!"

Joanna ran her tongue over dry lips. "Did . . . did you truly keep four wives? And many concubines? In a harem?"

The slow, wicked grin that was Ivo's alone lifted one corner of his mouth.

"I kept no wives, Joanna."

Only after his broad shoulders and scarred back had disappeared in the morning mists did she realize that he'd neatly avoided the second part of her question.

"Rogue," she whispered, sinking down onto the stone bench. With a shaky hand, she pushed her tangled hair out of her eyes.

Mother of God, she felt as though her entire world had turned upside down in the past few hours.

Fulk, whose piety she'd always revered.

Ivo, whose youthful misdeeds were still talked of in the villages and farms.

Fulk, who had never raised his voice in anger or ordered a flogging without sadness in his eyes.

Ivo, who had skewered Sir Arnould with nary a qualm.

Yet the one was not as good as she'd always thought him, and the other, Sweet Mother, the other was so much better. For all his faults, for all his seemingly conscienceless ways, Joanna knew Ivo would never force her to be other than what she was. But Fulk had wanted only to save her immortal soul . . . or so she'd always thought.

She wrapped her arms about her waist and rocked back and forth on the bench. A thousand hurts chased themselves through her mind, a hundred emotions warred within her breast. Yet through all the anger, all the hurt, all the wrenching disbelief, one thought kept surfacing.

Ivo had said she was worth all he had suffered those many years.

In her heart, she knew he was worth the agony she now felt. And more. So much more.

The sun had burned through the last of the mists when Joanna made her way back to the keep. Ignoring the wide-eyed stares her half-robed appearance garnered, she gathered her skirts. Slowly at first, and then more swiftly, she began to run the length of the long hall.

She dashed up the stairs, calling breathlessly for her maid. When the tiring woman came running, Joanna grabbed her hand.

"I wish a bath at once, with perfumed oils. While I'm bathing, I want you to gather every veil I own and bring them to me."

The maid's eyes widened. "All your veils?"

"And send a page for a tray of sweetmeats."

"Sweetmeats, my lady?"

"Aye," she replied with a grin. "Sweetmeats."

*　*　*　*　*

Harlequin® Historical

WOMEN OF THE WEST

Exciting stories of the old West and the women whose dreams
and passions shaped a new land!

Join Harlequin Historicals every month as we bring you
these unforgettable tales.

Don't miss any of our **Women of the West!**

Take 4 bestselling love stories FREE

Plus get a FREE surprise gift!

Special Limited-time Offer

Mail to Harlequin Reader Service®

3010 Walden Avenue
P.O. Box 1867
Buffalo, N.Y. 14269-1867

YES! Please send me 4 free Harlequin Historical™ novels and my free surprise gift. Then send me 4 brand-new novels every month, which I will receive before they appear in bookstores. Bill me at the low price of $3.19 each plus 25¢ delivery and applicable sales tax, if any.* That's the complete price and a savings of over 10% off the cover prices—quite a bargain! I understand that accepting the books and gift places me under no obligation ever to buy any books. I can always return a shipment and cancel at any time. Even if I never buy another book from Harlequin, the 4 free books and the surprise gift are mine to keep forever.

247 BPA ANRM

Name _____ (PLEASE PRINT)

Address _____ Apt. No. _____

City _____ State _____ Zip _____

This offer is limited to one order per household and not valid to present Harlequin Historical™ subscribers. *Terms and prices are subject to change without notice. Sales tax applicable in N.Y.

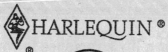

HARLEQUIN ®

Coming in August!
Award-winning author

Jasmine Cresswell's

Rakes and Rascals

Harlequin Regency Romance presents
The Abducted Heiress and *The Blackwood Bride*—
together in one exciting volume!

The Abducted Heiress is Georgiana Thayne, who has
for years disguised her wit and beauty in order to avoid
marriage to her odious cousin. But life takes a turn for the
adventurous when Viscount Benham comes to Town....

The Blackwood Bride is a supposedly dying woman from a
London workhouse. But Viscount Blackwood's bride is
made of sturdier stuff than he imagines, and what had
been intended as a very brief marriage of convenience
soon becomes inconvenient in the extreme!

Rakes and Rascals. Available in bookstores in August.

REG6

Want a little romance in your life, without having to leave the house or car?

Well, we have the answer.
For your listening pleasure we are
proud to introduce

Best of the Best™ AUDIO

In September listen for:

FIRE AND ICE
written by Janet Dailey
read by Erin Gray

THE ARISTOCRAT
written by Catherine Coulter
read by Emma Samms

In October

THE MAIN ATTRACTION
written by Jayne Ann Krentz
read by Emma Samms

RAGGED RAINBOWS
written by Linda Lael Miller
read by Erin Gray

Available wherever audio books
are sold.

Best of the Best™ Audio

AUDT

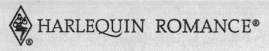

HARLEQUIN ROMANCE®

brings you

Romances that take the family to heart!

#3377 FOREVER ISN'T LONG ENOUGH
by Val Daniels

In one rash moment Mark Barrington had told his sick father that he was engaged to a truly wonderful girl. A white lie designed to make his father's dreams come true— after all, all his Pop wanted in life was to see his son safely settled down and, of course, meet the woman in question! And that was the problem—Mark need a fiancée and he needed one fast!

Sarah Fields could have been made to order! She had just lost her job, and Mark had appeared on the horizon like the proverbial white knight in a fairy tale, offering her a rather unusual post as his prospective bride. But for Sarah there was just one difficulty with this make-believe romance—the magic couldn't last forever!

Coming next month, from the bestselling author of *Silver Bells!*

HARLEQUIN PRESENTS®

Don't be late for the wedding!

Be sure to make a date in your diary for the happy event—

The third in our tantalizing new selection of stories...

Wedlocked!

Bonded in matrimony, torn by desire...
Look out next month for:

Dark Fate

by internationally bestselling author

Charlotte Lamb

Harlequin Presents #1763

"It's fate—even when we're miles apart, the link between us holds!" After two years, Saskia was convinced she'd never be reunited with her estranged husband, Domenico. But there seemed to be no escape from the physical and mental ties between them—especially now that Domenico had decided no marriage was complete without children....

Available in September wherever Harlequin books are sold.

LOCK3

As a *Privileged Woman*, you'll be entitled to all these *Free Benefits*. And *Free Gifts*, too.

To thank you for buying our books, we've designed an exclusive FREE program called *PAGES & PRIVILEGES*™. You can enroll with just one Proof of Purchase, and get the kind of luxuries that, until now, you could only read about.

*B*IG HOTEL DISCOUNTS

A privileged woman stays in the finest hotels. And so can you—at up to 60% off! Imagine standing in a hotel check-in line and watching as the guest in front of you pays $150 for the same room that's only costing you $60. Your *Pages & Privileges* discounts are good at Sheraton, Marriott, Best Western, Hyatt and thousands of other fine hotels all over the U.S., Canada and Europe.

*F*REE DISCOUNT TRAVEL SERVICE

A privileged woman is always jetting to romantic places. When you fly, just make one phone call for the lowest published airfare at time of booking—or double the difference back! PLUS—

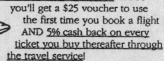

you'll get a $25 voucher to use the first time you book a flight AND 5% cash back on every ticket you buy thereafter through the travel service!

HPT-PP4A

ℱREE GIFTS!

A privileged woman is always getting wonderful gifts.
Luxuriate in rich fragrances that will stir your senses (and his). This gift-boxed assortment of fine perfumes includes three popular scents, each in a beautiful designer bottle. <u>Truly Lace</u>...This luxurious fragrance unveils your sensuous side. <u>L'Effleur</u>...discover the romance of the Victorian era with this soft floral. <u>Muguet des bois</u>...a single note floral of singular beauty.

YOURS FREE!

$50 VALUE

ℱREE INSIDER TIPS LETTER

A privileged woman is always informed. And you'll be, too, with our free letter full of fascinating information and sneak previews of upcoming books.

ℳORE GREAT GIFTS & BENEFITS TO COME

A privileged woman always has a lot to look forward to. And so will you. You get all these wonderful FREE gifts and benefits now with only one purchase...and there are no additional purchases required. However, each additional retail purchase of Harlequin and Silhouette books brings you a step closer to even more great FREE benefits like half-price movie tickets... and even more FREE gifts.

L'Effleur...This basketful of romance lets you discover L'Effleur from head to toe, heart to home.

Truly Lace...
A basket spun with the sensuous luxuries of Truly Lace, including Dusting Powder in a reusable satin and lace covered box.

Complete the Enrollment Form in the front of this book and mail it with this Proof of Purchase.

PROOF OF PURCHASE
Offer expires October 31, 1996

HPT-PP4